A Witch's Kitchen

Dianna Sanchez

Dreaming Robot Press
quality middle grade and young adult science fiction and fantasy
• **Las Vegas, New Mexico** •

Dreaming Robot Press
Las Vegas, New Mexico

1 3 5 7 9 10 8 6 4 2

First published in the United States by Dreaming Robot Press. 2016
Copyright © 2016 by Dianna Sanchez. All rights reserved.

Publisher's Cataloging-in-Publication data

Names: Sanchez, Dianna, author.

Title: A Witch's Kitchen / Dianna Sanchez.

Description: Las Vegas, New Mexico: Dreaming Robot Press, 2016.

Summary: Millie is a fabulous cook, but at the Enchanted Forest School, Millie struggles in the unfamiliar social environment, while encountering fellow students of magical races, making new friends, and discovering that her mother's style of magic isn't the only one available.

Identifiers: ISBN 978-1-940924-18-2 | LCCN 2016939891

Subjects: LCSH Witches--Juvenile fiction. | Magic—Fiction. | Cooks–Juvenile fiction. | Cooking—Juvenile fiction. | Mothers and daughters—Juvenile fiction. | Schools—Juvenile fiction. | Fantasy fiction. | BISAC JUVENILE FICTION / Fantasy & Magic

Classification: PZ7.S1947675 Wi 2016 | [Fic]—dc23

Cover Illustration by Nataliia Letiahina
Cover Design by Pixel Dizajn

To Nora, who set me on the Path.
and
To Annie, who has always wanted to fly.

Chapter 1
The Trouble with Chocolate

Cooking always got Millie into trouble. Once she'd been thinking about pumpkin tarts and turned her mother's cauldron into a pumpkin. Which exploded. Another time she'd turned their entire supply of elephant eggs into quiche. But chocolate — chocolate was the worst.

"Ludmilla!" her mother snapped. "Are you paying attention?"

Millie blinked and looked up at her mother across the bubbling cauldron. Millie's mother, Bogdana, had horrible, tangled black hair, warty greenish skin, and long, bony fingers. A tall, velvety black witch's hat crowned her head. "Yes, M-mother," Millie said.

"Very well," Bogdana continued. "The eye of newt. Just a pinch, delicately, as I showed you."

Maybe this time, Millie thought, trying not to get her hopes up. *Maybe, maybe this time it will work.* Carefully, she took some newts' eyes from a bowl. They were dried and crunchy, crumbling under her fingertips.

Her mother spotted this. "No, no! Delicately! The eyes must be whole when you put them in the brew!" Bogdana frowned, glaring down her crooked nose at Millie. "Throw those away and try again."

Millie tossed the eyes in the wastebasket. *Like a pinch of salt to season chocolate sauce*, she thought to herself. Millie tried again, and this time she managed to pick up the eyes without crushing them.

Bogdana nodded. "Good, good! Now, into the brew! Carefully! And remember the incantation!"

Millie concentrated, her stomach clenching. She couldn't stutter, not now. "*Muutu sammakoksi*," Millie chanted out the phrase of High Mystery. *Please*, she thought. *Please let it work this time. Just this once.* She took a deep breath and sprinkled the eyes gently into the bubbling pot. The potion hissed, steamed, and turned a thick, muddy brown. The scent of chocolate filled the room.

"Chocolate! Chocolate!" screeched Bogdana, her cheeks flushing a darker shade of green. "This is supposed to be a transformation potion! How can you expect to properly curse your enemies if you can't turn them into frogs?"

Millie stared at her shoes. "I'm sorry, M-m-mother." But she was thinking, *If only I had some nice orange peel to go in that chocolate.*

"I should think you're sorry," Bogdana said. "You are the most pathetic excuse for a witch I have ever known. You are eleven years old, and you cannot master even the most basic spells and potions." Her mother began to pace the room. "Why, when I was your age, I could not only ride a broom but enchant one myself. I enchanted my hat at seven years old, and I'd started brewing my own potions at six..."

Here we go again, Millie thought, huddling into herself. She'd heard the When-I-Was-Your-Age speech so many times now, she had it memorized. In about five seconds, Bogdana would switch to the You're-a-Disgrace-to-the-Coven speech.

"Look at your cousin Cretacia! She can induce warts on

an unwary subject from fifty paces away! You're a disgrace to the Coven."

"Y-yes, M-mother," Millie mumbled. "S-s-sorry, M-mother. I'll t-try to do better."

"Oh, get out of my sight," Bogdana spat. "Go and make dinner, since that seems to be all you're good at. And when the cauldron has cooled, you can scrub it out."

Gratefully, Millie scurried out of her mother's basement workshop and headed up the stairs. *She's right*, Millie thought. *Cooking is the one thing I'm good at. Why can't I just do that?*

The worn wooden stairs creaked under Millie's feet. The entire staircase tilted slightly to the left, so Millie ran her fingers along the wall to help keep her balance, skipping over the curled edges of the dark gray wallpaper, avoiding the occasional mold stain.

Millie hopped over a broken step to the first floor landing and stepped into her warm, tidy kitchen with its enormous cast iron stove and bundled herbs hanging from the ceiling beams. Of all the rooms in the house, this one Millie kept neat and tidy. When she'd taken over all cooking duty at the age of eight, Millie had whitewashed the walls until they gleamed.

Sunlight streamed through the window over the sink. On one wall, a cupboard held jars and pots labeled "Ginger" and "Star Anise" and "Cardamom," so different from her mother's collection of eye of newt, dried salamander sweat, dragon's toenails, and crushed wyvern bone. On the opposite wall, a rack held all of Millie's pots and pans and mixing bowls.

A sudden chill made Millie shiver as Horace, their house ghost, glided into the kitchen through the pantry door. "I smell chocolate, Millie," he said in his hollow voice. "Are you baking a cake? Can I have a slice?" His misty form passed easily through the kitchen table, ghostly chains clanking as he moved.

Millie sniffed. The scent of chocolate had wafted up from the basement. "No, that's my f-frog potion."

Horace rattled a chain mournfully. "Oh, dear. I'm sure your mother wasn't happy with that."

"No." Millie shoved her hands deep into her apron pockets. "What's wr-r-rong with me, Horace? Why can't I use magic?"

The ghost's cloudy face turned dark with sadness. "I wish I knew, Millie. I'd teach you if I could, but I was never a magician, even when I was alive," Horace told her. "Now, hadn't you better get dinner started before your mother comes up from the workroom?"

"Oh, darkness!" Millie exclaimed. "I'll roast some t-toads. They always put M-mother in a better mood."

Horace sidled up to her, giving her goosebumps. "And could you make something chocolate? Cookies, perhaps? Please?"

"I think I've had about enough of chocolate today," Millie replied.

Horace moaned, rattling her pans. "Come on, Millie. Please?"

"Chocolate always gets me in t-t-trouble," Millie told him. "How about oatmeal raisin?" Those were her half-brother Max's favorites. Or at least they used to be. Millie hadn't seen him in about five years, ever since Bogdana had a big fight with Max's father. She wondered whether she could send him a batch somehow.

Horace rolled himself into a seething ball of grey mist. "I want *chocolate*." He pinged around the room, banging into pots and jars, raining dried herbs on Millie's head.

"Oatmeal raisin or nothing at all," Millie said firmly.

Horace came over and hovered just inches from Millie's nose. "Fine, whatever," he said, then soared off and, with an extra loud rattling of chains, swooped back through the pantry door.

Millie sighed and opened the firebox on the stove. She stirred the embers left from lunchtime and tossed in two more split logs, then pulled down a shiny copper pan and two mixing bowls from her rack. She rummaged through the root bin and selected some nice plump rutabagas, carrots, onions, beets, potatoes, and parsnips. She washed the vegetables in the sink, peeled them, and chopped them up, her knife beating a steady rhythm on the cutting board. Then she tossed them clattering into a bowl with some sunflower oil, salt, a touch of honey, and some chopped sage and thyme.

Millie relaxed. She loved blending the ingredients just so, finding the right balance between savory and sweet. Each vegetable had its own unique flavor — the hearty starch of the potato, the sharp bite of the rutabaga, the hidden sweetness of the beet. Together, they made something more, something better. Something delicious.

Millie turned to the pan and made the mistake of looking at her reflection. Suddenly, all her delight in cooking vanished.

I look nothing like Mother, Millie thought. She had long, straight yellow hair, unappealing as straw and almost impossible to tangle. Her eyes were the same shade of brown as the chocolate potion she'd just ruined. Her skin was pinkish, not even slightly olive, and depressingly free of blemishes. Despite her best efforts, she had yet to grow a single wart anywhere. Worst of all, she had dimples when she smiled, so Millie tried her best not to smile, ever. She sighed. *I look terrible. I should go put mud in my hair again to please Mother.*

Instead, Millie spread her vegetables evenly in the pan and added two fat toads basted with melted butter and rosemary. She put the pan on a high rack in the oven to roast. Then she pulled out one of her favorite cookbooks. *Simple Pleasures* had been a birthday gift from her mother last year. It was a neatly bound yellow volume, its title in large red letters rimmed with gold. It was written in English, rather than Canto, the most common language used in the Enchanted Forest, but Millie understood it pretty well, though she still wasn't sure what a microwave was.

The publishers had thoughtfully attached two red ribbons to the binding as bookmarks, to which Millie had tied half-a-dozen additional ribbons of different colors. She opened the book at the light blue ribbon, which marked the cookie recipes, and quickly found the oatmeal cookies. She took down the jars of raisins and oatmeal from their shelves. She measured and sifted and poured and stirred up the cookies, spooned them onto their pan, and set it in the oven on the lowest rack, below the sizzling vegetables.

Delicious smells wafted through the house. After a few minutes, Millie heard footsteps on the staircase. Bogdana came in, setting the cooled cauldron and its too-sweet contents beside the sink. "You can scrub this out after dinner." Bogdana sniffed the air. "Well," she said slowly, "that does smell good. Fresh toads?"

"Yes, M-mother," Millie said.

"Did you rub them on your hands first?"

"Yes, M-mother."

"And cookies?" her mother asked.

"O-o-oatmeal raisin. For H-horace."

"That ghost likes his sweets too much. He's getting fat," Bogdana snorted. "Well, I'll be in the dining room. Make sure the dishes are dirty."

"Yes, M-mother," Millie said.

As Millie smudged the dishes with a prune paste she'd made for this purpose, a knock sounded at the front door. Millie rushed over to open it. A young pixie girl stood at the door, no more than six inches tall, with blue skin and green hair, dressed in day lily petals. Powerful wards, shields of magic that surrounded Millie's house, kept the pixie from entering, and they also kept Millie from leaving. Millie could feel the faint tingle of them in the doorway as she smiled down at the pixie.

"Oh, hi, Petunia," Millie said. "Is your father's gout acting up again?"

"Yup, his foot's swollen up near as big as me," Petunia reported.

"Darkness, that sounds bad," Millie told her. "I'll go get M-mother."

But Bogdana had come into the parlor behind Millie. "Gout again?" she said. "Your father needs to lay off the bacon and the tipple." Bogdana rummaged in the potions cabinet and brought out a large bottle and a tiny vial. Cautiously, she poured a tiny amount of the potion into the vial, then put stoppers in both.

"This will do the trick," Bogdana told the pixie girl. "It may cause a little stomach upset, so have your father take it with food, just a drop, twice per day. He should also drink lots of water and eat plenty of fruit, especially cherries. If his gout hasn't cleared up by Foursday, come back here for another dose." She handed the vial to the pixie girl, who took it awkwardly, since it was half her height. Petunia nearly dropped the vial as she made a curtsy. "Thank you!" she said. "See you later, Millie." Petunia dashed away.

Bogdana swept into the dining room. "Irritating pixies. As if I don't have better things to do than cure every little ache and pain of theirs. Really." Hastily, Millie served dinner.

They ate in silence, except for an occasional contented *Mmmmm...* from Bogdana as she munched on her roasted toad and vegetables. Millie pretended not to notice. Finally, her mother sat back, wiped her hands carefully on her dress, and said, "Well, are you ready for the Coven meeting this evening?"

Millie's stomach flipped. "I... I forgot. Is it r-r-really C-coven tonight?"

Bogdana rolled her eyes. "Full moon, you useless child. Of course it's Coven night."

"D-d-do I have enough time to make another batch of cookies?"

"Oh, must you?" Bogdana said. "It's bad enough that you're so far behind on spellcraft. Do you have to flaunt your obsession with food, too?"

"Everyone w-will expect them," Millie pointed out. "I'll put pecans in them for Baba Luci. You know how she loves pecans."

Bogdana sighed. "Oh, very well. You have half an hour."

Millie started toward the kitchen, then stopped short when a loud croak erupted from the kitchen floor. "Breckkk! Millie! What have you done to me?" said the apparition.

"D-d-darkness!" she cried. "It's the g-g-ghost of those t-toads we just ate!"

Bogdana hurried into the kitchen after her. "That's a frog, not a toad," she said.

"It's me, Horace," said the ghost miserably. "Breeek! The chocolate sauce in the cauldron smelled so good, I couldn't resist just a taste. And then... then I turned into this! Breeek! Breckkk!"

Bogdana threw her hands into the air. "Ludmilla Octavia Noctmartis! See what you've done now."

"I'm s-sorry," Millie said, cringing. "I should have filled the c-c-cauldron with water to soak. I d-didn't think he'd eat any."

Bogdana turned to the ghost. "Horace, you idiot," she yelled. "You should know better than to go tasting Ludmilla's potions."

"Potions aren't supposed to work on ghosts," Horace croaked. "How was I to know?"

Bogdana turned to Millie. "All right, this is your disaster. You fix him."

"H-how?" Millie stammered. "We d-didn't even finish the p-p-potion."

"Well, you can try the traditional method. Give him a kiss."

"What?" cried Millie and Horace together.

Bogdana folded her arms. "True, you're no princess. But as you said, the potion was unfinished, so it may not matter. Go on then, kiss him."

Millie knelt on the floor. She leaned forward, lips puckered, and tried to kiss Horace. Her lips went right through him and bumped gently on the floor. Nothing happened. "I'm s-s-sorry, Horace," she said, feeling humiliated.

"Oh, what will I do?" Horace wailed. "How can I rattle my chains or scare off intruders like this? You've got to change me back!"

"Darkness, what a mess," Bogdana swore. "Horace, you're going to have to wait until tomorrow. I have to prepare for the Coven meeting, and Millie has baking to do."

Horace glared at Millie. "This is all your fault." And he sank through the floor to sulk in the basement.

.

Chapter 2
Cookies for the Baba

Bogdana swooped between the treetops, cackling gleefully at the stars and startling the occasional owl or wight. Behind her, Millie clutched the handle of the broom, sure that the roasted toads were fighting their way out of her stomach. Millie was forbidden to hold onto her mother as she had when she was smaller because Bogdana wanted her to learn to balance on the broomstick by herself. Her best dress of crushed black velvet and tattered lace flapped and swished wildly, threatening to upset the basket of cookies that hung on Millie's left arm. Millie clutched it to her chest with her left hand, leaving only her right hand and tightly clamped knees to keep her on the twisting, zooming broom. She wished she could bury her face in her mother's back and not look down.

Bogdana refused to glide sedately above the forest. She loved zipping between the branches of the trees, annoying the night creatures and terrifying the sleeping daylovers out of their slumber. Millie cringed every time the broom whipped past a tree branch. She could feel her face turning green.

At last they approached a bare hilltop crowned with a double ring of standing stones, a bonfire crackling in the center. Millie saw several witches there, including her Aunts

Hepsibat, Ospecia, Ingratia, and Suspicia, along with their many, many daughters. Two other brooms circled in to land, but Bogdana blew right past them to loud, admiring curses, and set down a hair's breadth from the altar stone. Millie scrambled off and backed away, taking care not to tip her basket of cookies and working hard to keep down her dinner.

"Well, if it isn't Ludmilla."

Millie knew that voice too well. Aunt Hepsibat's daughter Cretacia was a witch through and through. She had plaited her hair into stiff braids that stuck out all around her face like hissing snakes. Her dress was so black it seemed to melt into the night, and she had an enormous wart on the end of her nose, gleaming in the firelight like a ripening mushroom. Atop her head she wore a magnificent witch's hat of brushed black satin, artistically draped with cobwebs. She was flanked by the Hanterslash twins, who were Millie's third cousins, twice removed, and who also wore black witches' hats.

"Admiring my hat?" Cretacia asked, her voice oozing satisfaction. "Yes, it is a beautiful specimen, fully enchanted with some *very* special protections I devised myself. But still no hat for you, I see."

Millie shook her head. "N-no, not yet."

Cretacia smirked. "You have no talent at all, do you? You should be called *Dud*milla."

The Hanterslash twins giggled.

"How about Lud-zilcha?" asked Greely.

"Better yet," said Grooly, "Mudzilla."

Millie sighed, having heard this dozens of times before. "P-please call me Millie," she said.

"Oh, no, that will never do," Cretacia said. "Duddy is much better, I think."

"Duddy! Duddy!" shrieked the twins.

Millie rolled her eyes. "Well, then," she said, turning

away, "I guess you don't want any of my cookies."

Greely and Grooly instantly stopped their shrieking. "Cookies?" asked Grooly.

"What kind of cookies?" asked Greely.

Millie suppressed a smile. "Oh, nothing special. Just oatmeal raisin with pecans. But you wouldn't want any of those, I'm sure."

"Um," said Greely, glancing at Cretacia. "Well, maybe, just one."

"Yes, one," Grooly chimed in. "To see how terrible they are," she added.

Millie opened her basket, and the scent of raisins and nuts filled the night air. All around them, heads turned. The Hanterslash twins dived at the basket, but Millie snatched it away and deftly handed them each a cookie. They stuffed the cookies into their mouths, crumbs cascading down their black dresses.

"Cretacia, would you like one?" Millie asked sweetly.

Cretacia turned up her nose. "What witch would make cookies that aren't enchanted or poisoned?" She stomped off.

Millie made the rounds, offering her cookies to the other witches, who thanked her and patted her on her hatless head and clucked behind her back as she passed. "What a pity," they said. "All that cooking talent and not a whit of magic." Millie did her best to ignore them.

A low humming filled the air, like the sound of air blown over the mouth of a bottle, but much deeper. Millie turned just in time to spy an enormous mortar and pestle fly out of the forest with a woman seated neatly inside it.

"The Baba's here! Look, the Baba!" the other witches called out. You never knew when Baba Luci would decide to join a Coven meeting. She came or not, whenever she chose. Tonight she steered the mortar in and set it down gracefully

between the inner and outer circles, then clambered out.
Alone of the adult witches present, Baba Luci wore no
hat. Instead she tied back her steel grey hair in a long,
flowery scarf. Tradition stated that the same scarf had been
worn by the Baba, generation to generation, all the way
back to the first, Baba Yaga, more than a thousand years
ago. Gossip claimed that no mere hat could contain all the
enchantments laid on that simple square of cloth. Nor did
she bother wearing a black gown, as most of the other witches
did. Baba Luci wore a wide, red skirt with deep pockets, a
white linen blouse embroidered with roses, and a knit shawl
over her shoulders. In one hand, she carried a knobby cane,
its handle worn smooth with use.

Bogdana crossed her arms. "Mother, really. You're fifteen
minutes late."

"No good witch ever arrives on time," Baba Luci replied.

"Ha," said Bogdana. "And I suppose you'll want to
officiate tonight."

"Oh, shut up, Boggy," Aunt Hepsibat snapped. "Of
course Mother will officiate. She's the Baba." She turned and
gave the Baba a little curtsy.

Baba Luci stepped past Aunt Hepsibat, pointedly ignoring
her. "Yes, I'll run the meeting, but first I want to see my
granddaughters."

In a rush, half the apprentice witches ran up and flung
their arms about her, but Millie hung back.

Baba Luci hugged them all tenderly. "Cretacia, your
braids are frightful — nicely done," the Baba said. "Egberta,
stop pushing. Where are your manners? Hmm, and where's
Millie?" Her small dark eyes squinted, searching through the
crowd. Millie considered hiding behind a stone, but... "Ahh,
Millie, my dear. What did you bring us tonight?"

"O-oatmeal raisin pecan cookies," Millie said quietly,

knowing they were no substitute for a hat. She came forward timidly and handed a cookie to her grandmother.

Baba Luci took a bite and closed her eyes to savor it. "Delicious, my dear. As usual." She gathered Millie in for a great, bone-cracking hug.

Someone sniggered and said in a not-hushed-enough voice, "At least she's good at something."

Millie felt her grandmother stiffen, then the Baba patted her on the back. "Time to get to business," she announced. "Go on with the other girls, Millie, m'dear." She gave her granddaughter a little push, and Millie backed away to the outer circle of stones.

"What, business before the opening ceremony?" asked Aunt Ospecia.

"It's a minor matter," Baba Luci replied. "The Enchanted Forest Council has once again sent me a request that we enroll our girls in the Enchanted Forest School in the interests of Forest unity."

The Coven erupted with snorts and cackles and clucking tongues as all eyes turned toward Bogdana, their representative on the Council.

"Don't look at me," Bogdana said. "I told them it was pointless to ask. Witches learn from witches, that's how we've always done it. But they insisted on sending letters to the leaders of all Forest peoples who have no students enrolled, including the League of Infamy, wizards, gaunts, niplings, and mountain trolls."

"And elves?" someone asked.

"No, they've actually got an elf student — odd bird apparently — and though they'd like more elves in school, they're not pushing it."

Baba Luci thumped her cane on the ground for attention. "I have considered the matter," she said firmly. "And I think that we should send a representative witch to school. This could be a valuable opportunity to gather information about the other folk of the Forest, not to mention recruiting minions."

Several of the witches looked thoughtful, but most looked stubborn, and a few seemed shocked and angry.

"That's ridiculous. Who's going to send their daughter and interrupt her training?" Aunt Hepsibat demanded. "Who knows what drivel they teach at that school!"

A murmur of assent arose, but Baba Luci ignored it, looking pointedly at Bogdana. Bogdana's eyes grew round, and her mouth fell open a bit. "You can't mean..."

"Perhaps," said the Baba. "We have an opportunity, a new path available to us. What we need is someone brave, someone bold, to try this new thing, this school, and then report back to us. But who among us is brave enough?" She paused, waiting for someone to speak up. When no one did, Baba Luci turned to Millie.

"Millie, I offer you this path. Search your heart." Baba Luci's eyes seemed to pierce Millie through. "Is this a path you wish to take? Do you accept the challenge and the risks it might bring?"

Millie's head spun. School? But she couldn't go to school! She'd be the laughing stock of the Coven! Already she could feel Cretacia's malicious grin spreading. All eyes turned to her, and Millie began to panic. But then she saw Baba Luci give her a slow wink.

If I go to school, Millie realized, *I won't have to study with Mother anymore. That would be wonderful. And maybe, just maybe, I might learn to use magic. If I don't, at least I'll have learned something useful for the Coven. And I'll get to meet other people and go to new places.*

A Baba's gift, Millie knew, was never simple. There would be consequences if she accepted, not least of which would be her mother's disapproval. And she had to choose truly, to follow her heart, or the Baba would know. If she wasn't completely honest, she would at least disappoint Baba Luci and at worst make her angry. And you never, ever wanted the Baba angry with you.

So Millie thought hard and listened to her heart. And her heart said, *At school, you won't be Bogdana's daughter. You'll just be Millie.*

Millie looked her grandmother squarely in the eye and said, "Yes. I accept."

All the witches began talking at once, Bogdana arguing — actually arguing! — with the Baba. A laugh rang out, high and clear, drowning everyone out. "Perfect!" Aunt Hepsibat crowed. "Send our most useless member. It's no loss to us, and Ludmilla might actually do some good as a spy, for once. Unless she turns out to be useless at that, too."

"I seem to recall a certain girl of mine," Baba Luci said quietly, "who always got her invisibility spells tangled, making her clothes invisible instead of her person."

Aunt Hepsibat blushed. "Not my bloomers, though."

"Thank darkness for that," Aunt Ingratia quipped.

The Baba cleared her throat. "It's late. Time we began. Gather round, all." The Baba took her place before the altar. Still grumbling, the other adult witches formed a ring within the inner circle. The Baba raised her hands and began the opening incantation in the rolling tones of High Mystery.

With the other apprentice witches, Millie stood back and watched the ritual from the outer circle of stones. She was too shocked and confused to pay attention. *School! Does Baba Luci think I'm a lost cause, too?* But Millie had seen the Baba's wink. She was certain her grandmother approved of her decision.

Maybe school would be a good change.

Cretacia sauntered up to her. "Well, well, lucky you."

"R-really?" Millie stammered.

"Oh, yes!" said Cretacia brightly. "Now you'll have a whole new crowd of people to laugh at your utter lack of talent." She danced away, giggling.

"Oh, darkness," Millie moaned.

Chapter 3
First Taste of School

After five days of unbearable anticipation, Onesday finally arrived, and Millie rolled out of bed early with one thought on her mind: School! The last few days had been a whirlwind. Bogdana had dashed out shopping and come back with a selection of new gowns to wear instead of her simple dresses and aprons, and then she set Millie to tattering the sleeves and tearing the lace. She also bought Millie a new lunch cauldron.

Millie was in the kitchen making breakfast when, to her astonishment, her mother came downstairs, groaning and creaking, just as Millie pulled the finished scones out of the oven.

"I've come to help you get ready," Bogdana told her. "You will represent all witches to your schoolmates, so you need to make a good impression."

Bogdana slathered Millie's hair in mud and slime mold, which gave it a nice tinge of green, then teased it into a truly impressive cloud of tangles. She rubbed slime mold into Millie's face, arms, and hands and forbade her to wash up all day.

Her mother picked out Millie's most artfully ragged black dress. Millie chose red-and-black striped stockings to go with it. Bogdana raised an eyebrow at that.

"I suppose that will do," she said, "but I wish you would grow your fingernails instead of trimming them all the time. And couldn't you sprout a few proper warts?"

Millie stared at her shoes, black with pointy toes and tarnished silver buckles. "I'm s-s-sorry, M-mother."

"Well, they'll come with spellcrafting, I expect," Bogdana told her. "Now, come down to the dining room. I have a surprise for you."

The announcement terrified Millie. *Not another broom?* She had already broken three of them attempting to fly, along with her left arm the last time, which her mother had grumpily healed.

She followed her mother down the stairs. On the dining table there was a large, square box, tied with tattered black lace. Not a broom, then.

"Well, go on," Bogdana said impatiently. "Open it."

Millie untied the lace and lifted the lid. "Oh, M-m-mother!" she cried. "My first hat!"

It was indeed a witch's hat: black, of course, with a broad brim and a pointy peak. It looked a trifle big, but when Millie put it on, she found that the tangled mess of her hair filled it out.

Bogdana gasped and clapped her hands. "You look marvelous! Perfectly frightful! A credit to your line." She sniffed a little. "Of course, the hat is not yet enchanted. It is traditional for a witch in training to enchant her own hat, and properly you should not even wear it until you have enchanted it. So take good care of it."

Millie hugged her. Bogdana hesitated, then hugged her back gently. Hugging was not a witchy thing to do, but it was a motherly thing to do, and occasionally Bogdana remembered this.

"Now," she said, pulling away, "remember, you are a witch and worth any ten of your classmates. You should dominate your peers and strike terror into your foes. Never let them get the upper hand. Cow them, demean them, and they will fear and respect you. Do you understand?"

Millie wondered how she was supposed to accomplish all that, but she said, "Yes, M-mother. I understand."

"Good. Have you packed your lunch for school?"

Millie nodded. "Yes, M-mother. I packed it while I made breakfast."

"Good," Bogdana said. "I'll get the broom and take you to school."

Millie tried not to look worried. Or panicked. Or even slightly terrified. "Oh, th-th-that's all right, M-mother," she said in what she hoped was a calm voice. "All the children from P-p-pixamitchie walk right past us on their way to school. I'll just w-w-walk with them."

Bogdana considered. "I suppose if you are to be schoolmates, you may as well walk to school together. I certainly have enough to do this morning preparing for the next Council meeting. Council meeting, Coven meeting, it seems I spend all my time in meetings." She tapped her foot. "Well, then, I had better change the house wards to let you out and back in again."

Millie's mother crossed her arms and stared down at her shoes, mumbling to herself. Then she raised her arms and said, "*Ludmilla saa kulkea.*" Millie felt a pressure she'd never noticed before vanish.

"Now remember," Bogdana said, "Never stray from the Path. The Council has placed great enchantments on the Path so that no one may be attacked or harmed in any way so long as they stay on it."

Just then, Millie heard the happy sound of laughter from

outside. "That's them!" she cried. "G-g-goodbye, M-mother. I'll come home r-r-right after school and tell you everything."

"Naturally," her mother said, looking a bit disgusted. "Now get your lunch and get moving. But dawdle a bit, won't you? You don't want to be early on your first day."

"No, of c-c-course not!" Millie cried, though this was precisely what she intended to do. She dashed into the kitchen, snatched up her lunch cauldron, shoved several extra scones into it, and raced to the back door, pausing only to cry out, "Leftovers in the icebox!" For just one moment, she hesitated. She'd hoped Horace would be there to say goodbye, but he was nowhere to be seen. *Still sulking*, Millie thought, feeling guilty. She'd tried several disenchantments on Horace in the last two weeks, but none of them had worked. *Maybe I'll learn how at school today*, she thought.

Millie went out the kitchen door to the rear gate and hesitated. The Path stretched away on either side of her, west to the village of Pixamitchie, the Sleeping Castle, and the far cliffs of Westmarch that bordered the sea, and east to the deep forest and school, all the way to the Dwarf Countries under the Endel Mountains. For a moment, the possibilities made her head spin. *I could go anywhere*, she thought. *Anywhere at all.*

Millie dashed across the Path and curtsied to the graceful elm tree that stood opposite the kitchen gate. "Good morning!" she cried. "I just wanted to say hello and to thank you for shading me on hot summer days. I'm going to school now, so I can come and visit you every day."

The elm rustled and whispered to her in the language of trees. A branch brushed her shoulder, and reassurance flooded through Millie. "Goodbye," she told the tree. "See you this afternoon!"

A group of pixie children dashed around the bend, the

tallest of them no higher than Millie's ankle bone. Millie hesitated, then stepped up to them and said, "H-hi. Are you going to school?"

"Nah," said a green pixie boy. "I'm gonna wrestle alligators in the Salivary Swamp."

"I'm going to the Dragon Vale to steal a velociraptor!" cried a pale violet girl.

"I'm off to find my one true love!" declared an orange pixie boy, looking her over. "It sure ain't you." He stuck out his tongue and blew a loud, wet raspberry at her.

Petunia, dressed in rose petals today, yelled back at him, "Your one true love is a bogey, Hawthorne. Can't you see she's a witch? She's gonna hex you good."

Hawthorne bounced up and grinned at Millie. "Gotta catch me first!" He took off running down the Path, chased by the other pixies.

The blue pixie girl sighed. "Slugs and bugs. Don't mind him, Millie, he's got as much sense as a moth by a lantern." She peered up at Millie. "Now, why're you asking about school?"

"Um, actually," Millie told her, "I'm starting school today. I was w-wondering if I could walk with you."

Petunia frowned, scrunching up her small pointy nose and scratching the green curly hair under her brown acorn cap. "I thought witches didn't go to school. They stay home and learn from their mums."

"Well, the Baba decided I should go to school," Millie said.

Petunia cocked her head and squinted at her. "That should be interesting. Come on, it's this way." And they set off down the Path, Petunia sprinting along with Millie's longer strides.

"You know, you should wear a name tag," Petunia told Millie seriously.

Millie got worried. "I sh-should? Is it a rule?"

"Naw. That way, if any other witches come, people will

know which witch is witch!"

Millie chuckled nervously. "That's pretty good. Did you make that up?"

Petunia grinned and nodded. "I've got lots more. What's green and black and red all over?"

Millie rolled her eyes. "I have no idea."

"A witch with a sunburn!" Petunia burst into giggles, and Millie joined her.

"Tell me another!" Millie urged.

"Hmm. What do you call a witch with poison ivy?"

Millie grimaced. "Uncomfortable?"

"An itchy witchy!" Petunia chortled.

Millie imagined her mother with poison ivy, scratching furiously, and nearly fell over laughing.

"You're really good at jokes," she told Petunia when she could breathe again.

Petunia shrugged. "It's nice to have someone to tell them to. My family is so sick of my jokes, I'm forbidden to tell them anymore."

"Do you tell your jokes at school?"

"Sometimes," Petunia said. "Not in class, though. I get in trouble."

Millie grinned. "I can imagine. I wonder which class I'll be in."

"Depends. How's your spellcraft?"

Millie blushed. "N-n-not very good. Awful, actually."

"Well, then maybe school's a good idea," Petunia told her. "The teachers are mostly nice and helpful. They'll give you a test to figure out which class you should be in."

A little shiver of fear went down Millie's back. "What's the t-t-test like?"

"Oh, don't worry, it's easy-peasy. Or at least it was when I started school. It might be different for latecomers like you."

Which did nothing to reassure Millie at all. "Come on, we'd better get moving."

Millie didn't mean to dawdle. She'd intended to go straight to school as quickly as possible. But for the first time, she could stop and look at things that she'd only seen in a brief blur as her mother's broom zipped by.

Close to the Path, the trees were young and slender, singing each other their morning gossip, and the sun broke through their branches to dapple the Path with light and shadow, nourishing the ferns and holly, wild roses and blackberries, long nodding lilies, tiny bright pansies, and many other wildflowers that grew among their roots. Farther in, the trees grew larger and the Forest more dim. If she squinted, Millie could just make out the trunks of huge trees, wider than the Path. Shadows moved under those branches, large and strange, and Millie realized that her mother hadn't been exaggerating when she'd said it wasn't safe to leave the Path.

So Millie turned her focus back to the Path. She kept stopping to examine mushrooms and flowers or to greet fairies zipping about on iridescent wings, harvesting the morning dew and competing with brightly colored hummingbirds and buzzing bees for flower nectar. An elderly salamander ambled past them along the Path and wished them a very good morning. He wore a bright yellow waistcoat and a jaunty red beret.

"Well," Petunia announced. "Here we are!"

The Path branched off into a wide, shady glade carpeted in short, brilliant green grass. In the precise center of the glade stood the largest oak tree Millie had ever seen. It was at least as wide as her house. Its crown of glossy green leaves climbed high above the forest canopy and shaded a patch of the glade at least fifty strides from trunk to path.

Nestled amongst its roots was the base of a spiral staircase that circled the trunk, disappearing among the leaves. Beneath its branches, leprechauns, unicorns, dryads, fauns, pixies and many, many more people gathered in the glade. Fairies zipped about on their buzzing, fragile wings, then popped directly up into the branches. High above, Millie spotted winged students arriving: two dragons, several pegasuses, a few gryphons. A flying carpet circled, its pilot looking for a clear space to land. Millie noticed, though, that the pixies and fairies stayed apart from the others, as did the imps and goblins, the gnomes, the dwarves, the fauns, the centaurs... all of them kept to their own races.

Abruptly, Millie stumbled, nearly falling on her face.

"Grumpkin, you no-good, stinky, miserable brat of a goblin!" Petunia scolded ferociously.

Grumpkin, a fat, sickly green goblin dressed only in ragged leather pants, stood as tall as Millie's waist, which made him tall for a goblin. He stuck out his tongue, broad and purple under an even broader, impressively ugly nose. He was bald, but black hair sprouted out of his enormous ears. "Witches should watch where they're going when they walk. She nearly stepped on me."

"Oh," Millie said, regaining her balance. "I'm terribly sorry."

"No, you're not!" Petunia screeched. "He did it on purpose!"

"Did not." Grumpkin crossed his arms. "What's a witch doing at school anyways? I thought witches kept to witches."

"It's my first day," Millie told him. She felt a silly grin spread across her face and quickly covered her mouth with her hand to hide her dimples.

"Oh, ho ho ho! A witch at school!" Grumpkin crowed. "You must be a really terrible witch to get sent to school like this."

Millie flushed. "N-nonsense. My m-mother is a

Councilor. She's just setting an example for all the witches of the Enchanted Forest."

"Uh huh," Grumpkin said. "Sure, your mum's a Councilor. My mum is, too. And so's Titchy's, ain't she?"

A small, ghastly gray imp about twice the size of Petunia flew up and landed on Grumpkin's shoulder. With his left horn, he scratched idly at one leathery wing, smiling at them with his needle-sharp teeth. "Nah," the imp said. "She went to a Council meeting and ate all the other Councilors. Ha!"

"Your mum couldn't eat a slug without choking on a bone!" Petunia screeched back.

Grumpkin sniffed. "You look like a witch, but you sure don't smell like a witch. You smell like... fried bacon and cookies."

"Scones," Millie said, then blushed and tried to hide her lunch cauldron behind her. She hoped the blush wouldn't show through the slime mold.

"You don't even have real green skin. Look!" Grumpkin pointed to a spot on Millie's arm, where she'd scratched at the itchy coating of slime mold, and it had flaked off, revealing her pink skin beneath. Sneering, Grumpkin announced, "I don't think you're a real witch at all."

"I am so a r-r-real witch!" Millie cried indignantly, and Petunia shouted, "Yes, she is! She has a hat and everything!"

Grumpkin studied Millie's hat, a wicked glint in his tiny black eyes. "How do we know that's a *real* witch's hat?"

"Yeah," echoed Titchy. "How do we know? I think we should examine it."

Millie took a step back. "You wouldn't d-d-dare."

"I heard all witches' hats're enchanted," Grumpkin said, "so they don't fall off when they're flying. If that's a real witch's hat..."

Titchy launched himself into the air and snatched Millie's hat off her head.

"Give that b-back!" Millie cried. "It's my hat! My m-mother gave it to me this morning! I haven't had a ch-ch-chance to enchant it yet."

Petunia ran up Grumpkin's back to his shoulder and shouted in his ear, "Give Millie her hat back!"

"Ow!" Grumpkin cried. He made a swipe at her, but Petunia just jumped to the ground so that Grumpkin boxed his own ear and howled. "I'll get you for that."

Millie chased Titchy across the glade, trying in vain to get her hat back. Just as she had nearly caught him, he tossed it to a nearby goblin. "New game!" he cried. "Pass the hat!" All the goblins, imps, and a few young bogeys with their long, hairy arms joined in the game, gleefully throwing Millie's hat back and forth while Millie chased it helplessly.

Petunia whistled shrilly. Instantly she was surrounded by pixies and fairies. A moment later, the crowd scattered, the pixies swarming the goblins and the fairies chasing the imps. Several of the bystanders began taking sides and cheering them on. Millie kept trying to keep up with her hat, but she was also trying not to trample all the pixies underfoot, and she was getting more and more frustrated and angry.

Mother said I should dominate them, strike terror into their hearts, Millie thought frantically. *How do I do that?* And then she thought, *What would Mother do?*

"Stop it!" she screamed. "Stop it or, or I'll, I'll turn you all into frogs!" *Oh, darkness*, she thought. *How will I ever do that?*

Chapter 4
The Dragon, the Tree, and the Test

"That's a bit excessive, don't you think?"

Millie glanced behind her. A young wizard came up to her, still rolling up his flying carpet. He was human, like her, a couple of years younger, wearing rumpled purple robes, which looked good against his tan skin. Short, unruly brown hair stuck out every which way from under his pointy wizard's cap, and his green eyes glinted at her. He was trying hard not to smile, but even so, Millie could see his dimples. There was something terribly familiar about him...

"M-max?" Millie asked. "Max, is that really you?"

The wizard broke into a wide grin. "Indubitably!" He dropped his carpet on the ground and flung his arms around her.

Millie could hardly believe it. "Max!" she cried, hugging him back. Even though Max was two years younger than Millie, he wasn't much shorter. "You've grown so much! What are you doing here?"

"Same as you, my errant sibling," Max said. "I'm going to school."

Millie pushed back to look at him. "Really? How did you get your father to agree to that?"

Max gave her a wink. "I'll tell you about that later. Right

now, let's retrieve your purloined hat."

Millie had completely forgotten about her hat. With a final hug, Max let her go, drew his wand, and pointed it at the hat. "*Palaa omistajallesi.*"

The hat wrenched itself from the grasp of two imps, a goblin, and half-a-dozen pixies and sailed through the air to land neatly back on Millie's head. Petunia cheered, and several of the fairies and pixies applauded.

"Oh!" Millie said. "Th-th-thank you. How did you learn to do that?"

Max gave her a puzzled look. "Lots of practice. When did you start stuttering?"

Grumpkin was advancing on them, but now he stopped and howled with laughter. "Witchy's got a BOYFRIEND!"

Max frowned. "Stop that, you mannerless oaf."

Several goblins and imps gathered around them, pointing and laughing. Grumpkin began to dance in circles around Max and Millie, singing:

Witches and wizards, sitting in a tree,
K-I-S-S-I-N-G!

The other goblins took up the chant, dancing a ring around them.

Max turned a peculiar shade of red. His hair stood on end, and smoke began to trickle out his ears. He pointed his wand at Grumpkin, but before he could do anything with it, a gong sounded, and a voice boomed out across the glade.

"THAT IS QUITE ENOUGH. SCHOOL IS NOW IN SESSION."

Immediately, everyone in the glade fell silent, and the goblins ceased their capering. Max turned pale as a ghost.

"GRUMPKIN, THAT IS NO FIT GREETING FOR NEW SCHOOLMATES. APOLOGIZE. IMMEDIATELY." Grumpkin twisted a toe in the dirt, bowed his head, and muttered, "Sorry."

"MAXIMILLIAN SALAZAR," boomed the voice. "KINDLY PUT YOUR WAND AWAY. SPELLCRAFT ON YOUR FELLOW STUDENTS IS NOT PERMITTED." Max swallowed hard, put his wand back up his sleeve, and said, "I do beg your pardon." But he was definitely not looking at Grumpkin when he said it.

"TITCHY, YOU WILL APOLOGIZE TO LUDMILLA AND PROCEED TO THE HEADMISTRESS'S OFFICE TO RECEIVE YOUR PUNISHMENT FOR THEFT OF LUDMILLA'S HAT." Titchy approached Millie with a grimace, gave her a graceless and grudging, "Sorry," then flew toward the staircase.

"ALL STUDENTS, TO YOUR CLASSROOMS, PLEASE." A gong sounded, and the students formed lines and began climbing the spiral staircase.

"Excuse m-m-me," Millie said in a small voice. "I d-don't know which classroom to go to."

"WELCOME, LUDMILLA NOCTMARTIS," said the voice. "LOOK UP. DO YOU SEE ME?"

Millie peered up into the branches, looking for the source of the voice. Petunia poked her foot, then pointed at the trunk. Millie saw only a couple of knots and a wisp of moss, then she looked again. The knots were spaced just like eyes, a knob formed a nose above a wide slash in the bark, the moss a beard beneath it. The knots blinked, the slash spread into a kind smile. The great oak tree spoke to her.

"I AM QUERCIUS, CARETAKER OF THE ENCHANTED FOREST SCHOOL. YOU AND YOUR

BROTHER ARE EXPECTED. PETUNIA, WILL YOU PLEASE BRING OUR NEW STUDENTS TO HEADMISTRESS PTERIA'S OFFICE?"

Petunia made a tiny curtsy. "Certainly, Master Quercius. I'll take them right up."

"THANK YOU, PETUNIA." The face smiled again and then faded back into the bark. Now Millie couldn't find it at all.

Max looked unhappy. "My first day, and I'm already going to the Headmistress's office."

"Don't worry," Petunia said. "All new students have to go to the Headmistress's office. Oh, hold on a second. Here comes Wee Willie." She giggled.

A young giant approached the school, taking care to wade between the trees and not trample anyone, the ground shaking slightly with each cautious step. He crouched down, reached out a hand, and placed one finger upon the school's spiral staircase. In an instant, he shrank down to about Millie's size. With a shrug, he proceeded up the steps to class.

Petunia dashed after him. As she set foot on the first step, the pixie began to grow. By the time Millie and Max had caught up with her, she was nearly as tall as Millie. As Millie stepped up, she felt herself shrink ever so slightly. Max grew a bit, until they were all exactly the same height.

"See?" Petunia told her. "In the Enchanted Forest School, everyone is the same size, even the teachers."

Max whistled. "That is a highly complicated spell. Only a very talented enchanter could have created it."

"THANK YOU."

Millie and Max looked up at the tree trunk, but they saw no sign of Master Quercius's face. Petunia grimaced. "It's tricky when your school is also a person. You never know when he's listening in. Come on, I don't want to be late for class."

Petunia led them up the winding staircase. Before they had gone even a quarter-turn around, they reached the first branch, so broad it was at least four feet wide. Glancing along it, Millie saw that it led into a wide room formed of interwoven branches. Rugs covered and evened out the floor. Very young students sat cross-legged on the rugs, surrounding a cheerful leprechaun in a jaunty green cap.

They passed half a dozen large classrooms, climbing all the way around the trunk twice, before they came to a small side room with a moss curtain covering its entrance. A sign above the doorway read, "Headmistress."

"Here you are," Petunia told them. "Don't worry, Headmistress Pteria is a lovely person. I'm sure you'll do just fine on your test."

"Thanks, Petunia," Millie told her friend. "You'd better get to class."

Petunia nodded and went back down the stairs.

Millie glanced at Max. "D-do we just go in?"

"That seems rude," he replied and knocked on a large branch that framed the doorway.

"Enter!"

Max pulled aside the curtain for Millie. She stepped into a cozy room that reminded her of her well-ordered kitchen, though it was much smaller. The branch floor was covered with a beautiful red woven rug. Bookshelves and cabinets hung on the walls. In the center of the room stood a large desk made of dark, burnished wood.

Two wooden chairs sat before the desk, one of which was occupied by a much larger Titchy, and behind it, in a large stuffed armchair, sat a dragon, her scales shading from lavender to deep purple, her eyes gleaming and golden. The Headmistress dressed in deep green robes, and between her curving horns, she wore an elegant green cap with an

emblem of a tree, bordered in red and gold, just like the caps
Millie had seen teachers wearing in the classrooms. Her tail
curled neatly around her feet, and her folded wings rose just
slightly above her head. Millie found herself wondering how
large she'd be outside the school.

"That will be all, Titchy. You may leave," she told the imp,
who slunk out with a glare at Millie. "Welcome, Ludmilla
and Maximillian," said the dragon. "I am Headmistress
Pteria." She held out her hand.

Surprised, Millie reached out and took it. The Headmistress
shook her hand solemnly but gently, her claws neatly turned
to avoid causing injury. She shook Max's hand in turn.

"I am delighted to meet you both," Pteria said. "At last,
we have a witch and a wizard enrolled in our school. What
tremendous progress! Now, please be seated."

Max and Millie took their seats, Millie setting her
cauldron carefully at her feet.

"Before we begin," said the Headmistress, "let me explain a
few things about our school. It was founded sixteen years ago.
As you may know, the Enchanted Forest has seen frequent
outbursts of conflict between some of our peoples. Many
of these conflicts arose from simple misunderstandings, and
from the difficulty of seeing things from another person's
point of view. You just witnessed an example of that, the
age-old enmity between goblins and pixies.

"To foster greater understanding, the Enchanted Forest
Council decided that it would be best to educate the children
of the Forest about the history and culture of all the other
species with whom we share this Realm. What better way to
do this than to invite them to attend school together?

"Here, goblins sit side by side with gryphons, dryads with
dragons, brownies with bogeys. We learn to see each other
as people, not all that different from the people you see at

home every day. Unfortunately, we have had some difficulty convincing a few of the peoples to send in their children." Pteria laughed. "To be honest, we're still having some trouble with the more conservative dragon clans.

"But now, your parents have agreed to send you to school, in accordance with the Enchanted Forest Common Education Act of 7,843, also known as year 508 of the Sundered Age. And I am simply delighted to have you here. It is our hope that you will become shining examples to other witches and wizards of the Enchanted Forest."

Oh, darkness, Millie thought. *Does she want me to try to convince the other apprentice witches to come, too? I don't know if I could handle both Grumpkin and Cretacia at the same school with me.*

"Now," the Headmistress continued, "there are several rules at this school which absolutely must be obeyed. First, you may not harm any other student, either physically or with magic, nor may you steal from them or trick them in any way. Second, you may not perform magic on other students without their express permission and the permission of a teacher. Third, until you have been qualified, you may not use magic at all without the supervision of a teacher.

"Finally, you may not cheat. This is not so much a rule as a statement of fact. All examinations are enchanted to be entirely cheat-proof, so don't even bother trying. Do you understand?"

Millie nodded. Max said solemnly, "Perfectly intelligible, Headmistress."

"Thank you both." Pteria sat back in her chair. "Now, I am sure you are brimming with questions. What would you like to know?"

Millie felt as though she was about to explode with questions, but before she could say a word, Max asked,

"Why are you the headmistress if Quercius is the school? Why isn't he the headmaster?"

"AHEM," said Master Quercius, his face appearing on a large branch above Pteria's desk. "HEADMISTRESS PTERIA AND I SHARE SOME RESPONSIBILITY FOR THE SCHOOL. AS A TREE, I HAVE CERTAIN STRENGTHS AND CERTAIN RESTRICTIONS. I CARE FOR THE SCHOOL, PROVIDE ITS PHYSICAL SPACE, AND MAINTAIN ITS MAGICAL WARDS. I ALSO TEACH A BIT, BUT ON THE WHOLE PTERIA IS FAR MORE QUALIFIED AN ADMINISTRATOR."

Pteria smiled and nodded agreement. "Thank you, Quercius."

A slow smile spread across Max's face. "That makes excellent sense," he said, leaning forward. "How many students do you have? How many classes? Will I be in Millie's class? Do you teach thaumaturgy? Do you have an alchemical laboratory? Will we go on field trips? Will we visit other schools and other Realms?"

Pteria chuckled. "Oh, you're going to be a fun one to keep up with, Maximillian," she said.

"I prefer Max," he told her.

"As you wish, Max," said Pteria. "Let's see if I can answer those questions. We have 414 students in twelve classes. We do indeed teach thaumaturgy, we have a state-of-the-art alchemical lab, we go on many, many field trips, and we have an exchange program between schools.

"As for whether you'll be in your sister's class, I think that's unlikely, since you're two years younger. That depends entirely on the results of your examinations. But first, Ludmilla? Do you have any questions, dear?"

Thoughts and fears raced through Millie's head. What if she couldn't cast any spells? Would she be put in with the youngest children until she caught up? Would she be kicked out of school altogether? Was there any hope for a witch with no magic? But what came out of her mouth was, "Am-am-am... Am I really a witch?"

Headmistress Pteria looked startled. "Well, so far as I know. You're the daughter of a witch, yes?"

Millie nodded.

"Then you are most probably also a witch."

"Probably?" Millie pounced on the word.

The headmistress sighed and sat back in her chair. "Well, I am not a witch, but I have studied the history of the Enchanted Forest extensively, and I have read that, very rarely, a girl who has no magical talent is born to a witch."

Millie's heart sank. "I kn-n-new it," she muttered.

"Wait a minute," Max interrupted. "Why do you think you're not a witch?"

Millie glanced at him, embarrassed. "Well, because every time I try to use magic, it goes h-h-horribly wrong. I once turned M-mother's cauldron into a p-pumpkin, and it exploded. It took me hours to clean up that mess. And the last potion M-mother tried to teach me, I turned into ch-ch-chocolate sauce."

Max burst out laughing. "Pumpkin!"

"AH," said Master Quercius. "YOU'VE ANSWERED YOUR OWN QUESTION."

"I have no t-talent, and I'm not a w-w-witch." Millie bit her bottom lip, trying not to cry.

Headmistress Pteria snorted, smoke trailing out her nostrils. "Quite the contrary. What Quercius means is that, in both those cases, you clearly used magic. Otherwise, no pumpkin, no chocolate."

A tingle went through Millie's body. "I never thought of that," Millie admitted. "Then, I am a witch?"

"You have talent," Headmistress Pteria said. "Whether you use it to become a witch is entirely up to you. Witchcraft, like any magical practice, takes more than talent. It requires craft, discipline, and most importantly, persistence. If you are willing to work at it, I am sure we can help you to develop your talent. Is this acceptable to you?"

Millie thought they were probably mistaken. Just because she'd done things with magic didn't mean she could ever control it. But she thought it would be impolite to argue. "I think so," she said slowly. "I want to learn to use magic. It would make M-mother so happy."

Headmistress Pteria looked at her sharply. "Your mother is not here, Ludmilla, and it's not her talent you're using. If you wish to harness your talent, you must find your own reasons for doing so."

Millie nodded doubtfully. "I'll t-try. But, could you please call me Millie? Only M-mother calls me Ludmilla."

"Millie, it is," Pteria said. "Now, let us proceed to your examination." She paused to take out two slates and two pieces of chalk.

"At this school," the Headmistress continued, "we do our best to place students in classes according to their abilities and prior experience. You will learn with other students, but you will progress at your own rate and in your own time. In order to determine which class you will join and which special subjects you will take, we need to assess your abilities and knowledge with an examination. Please don't worry about this. Wrong answers are just as valuable to us as right ones. Answer as honestly and completely as you can. Do you understand?"

Max and Millie nodded, the scones in Millie's stomach feeling more like stones.

"If you are both ready, you may take your slates and begin. There is no time limit; take as long as you like."

Max took his slate and chalk eagerly, and Millie took her own. At the top of the slate, it said, "Entrance Examination." Below it was a question:

Q. When did the Three Hundred Years' War begin, and which of the Realms were affected?

Millie's heart sank. She had no idea. In shaky letters, she wrote, "I don't know." The slate cleared itself. A new question appeared.

Q. What are the magical properties of mugwort?

Millie relaxed. This she knew. Her mother had instructed her in all the ingredients she used for her potions. She quickly wrote, "Mugwort is a cure for parasites such as worms. However, if harvested at midnight during a new moon, it has the opposite effect, infecting the victim with worms. This is known as midnight mugwort." She went on to explain details of harvesting and dosage, then added her favorite recipe for mugwort tea, blended with rose hips, lemon balm, and lavender.

The slate cleared again.

Q. What are the seven sigils of Simerical?

That was a tough one. Millie thought hard and recalled seeing a sigil marked "Simerical 3" in one of her mother's spellbooks. She drew it as carefully as she could and labeled it.

And so it went. Some of the questions Millie could not answer at all. For these, she simply wrote, "I don't know," and went on. When it came to magical ingredients, she knew nearly every answer and made guesses on two she wasn't quite sure of. She also did well in languages, which she had learned from her recipe books and her mother's spellbooks.

Suddenly, the slate said:

Examination complete. Please return slate to your examiner.

Millie looked up. Max had disappeared, and so had Headmistress Pteria.

Chapter 5
The Power of Scones

"H-h-headmistress? M-max?" Millie called out.

"AH, MILLIE. HAVE YOU FINISHED?" Master Quercius replied.

Millie sighed with relief. "Um, yes. What should I d-do?"

"JUST PLACE THE SLATE ON HEADMISTRESS PTERIA'S DESK. SHE AND MAX HAVE GONE TO LUNCH. YOU MAY PROCEED OUT TO THE GLADE."

Lunchtime? Already? Millie's stomach suddenly growled. She put the slate and chalk on the desk and picked up her lunch cauldron.

"Thank you, Master Quercius," Millie said politely.

"YOU ARE QUITE WELCOME," the tree replied.

Millie pushed out through the moss curtain and went down the stairs to the glade. Under the branches, tables had been set up where the students were eating lunch. Each table had a pitcher of water and glasses on it. Millie noticed that the students were all still the same size. A hush fell over the crowd as Millie entered the glade. Then a leprechaun threw an apple at a centaur, and everyone began talking again.

Millie spotted Petunia waving madly at her from a table full of other pixies. Millie waved back and began to weave her way through the tables. Halfway there, she tripped and fell sprawling on her face, mercifully without spilling her cauldron.

"Oopsy." A much taller Grumpkin stared down at her, a sneer on his face. "That's for getting Titchy in trouble."

"Titchy got himself in trouble," Millie pointed out, getting to her feet.

Grumpkin frowned. "Quercius can see anywhere in the school, but he can't see everywhere. Not all the time. Remember that."

Millie refused to respond, pushing past him to Petunia's table. Petunia met her halfway, her hands balled in fists. "Oooh, that nasty-fatsy-patsy Grumpkin! I wish I could kick him!"

"Not allowed during school, right?" Millie asked.

"Right, but just wait until after school."

"Don't you get in t-trouble because of me," Millie told her.

Petunia grinned at her. "Nah, pixies and goblins are old, old enemies, aren't we? We have to show them who's best of the Underforest!" They had reached the pixie table, and all the pixies cheered, casting jeers at the goblins, who hooted and threw stinking food back at them. Millie had to duck several times until a fairy in a green cap — a teacher, Millie realized — hurried up and put a stop to the impromptu food fight.

"Now, Millie, let me introduce you to my brothers and sisters and cousins," Petunia said. "There's Daisy and Cowslip and Vetch and Primrose and Clover and Holly... and here's my little brother Peaty!" She hugged a young pixie boy and pinched his cheek while he squirmed and hollered "Leggo!" at her. Millie instantly forgot nearly every name Petunia told her. She'd never been near so many pixies in her life. She wondered how Petunia managed to keep track of them all.

"Hey, guys," Petunia said, "how many goblins does it take to make a sandwich?"

All the pixies groaned. "Aw, come on, Petunia!" Peaty whined.

"None! Goblins are too stupid to make bread!"

Petunia's family began pelting her with berries. "Yikes! It wasn't that bad. Quick, Millie, retreat!"

Millie spun around and nearly collided with Max.

"Oh, Max!" she said. "Petunia, you remember my brother, Max."

"Introductions later!" Petunia hollered as a giant blackberry smashed into her shoulder. "Right now, run!"

"This way," Max said, leading them away. "I found a mostly empty table."

As they approached a table near the edge of the glade, Millie paused. The other student at the table was an elf girl, maybe a little younger than Millie, who pointedly ignored them. She was wearing the strangest clothes Millie had ever seen: dark blue trousers and a tight-fitting shirt with an odd symbol, π, centered on a picture of a pie. A white elf robe hung loosely over her shoulders. The elf munched slowly on a leaf while studying a scroll and making occasional notes.

"Have a seat," Max said to Millie and Petunia.

Millie sat, then set her bedraggled hat on the table. The lovely black velvet was torn in several places, and the peak had been crushed in. "I don't know how I'm going to explain this to my mother," she said.

"Obnoxious goblins," said Max. "I'd attempt to repair it, but I'm not allowed to use magic at school yet. And also, I'm really not very good at fixing things." He looked uncomfortable, and an enormous rumble sounded from his stomach.

"Haven't you eaten yet?" Millie asked.

Max looked embarrassed. "I, er, neglected to bring a lunch."

"Oh, that I can fix," Millie said.

Pulling the napkin off the top of her lunch, she spread it between Max, Petunia, and herself and began laying out her lunch. Scones, of course. Deep-fried frog legs wrapped in wax paper. Mushrooms sautéed in butter with marjoram and thyme in a small crock. Shaved beet and fennel salad. Cheese and bacon sandwiches. As she pulled out the food, Max's eyes grew bigger and bigger.

"I'm sorry," Millie said. "I only brought one fork and one spoon. We'll just have to make do." She handed him the fork.

"Mother made all this for you?" Max asked a bit wistfully.

Millie giggled. "Mother burns toast. She hasn't cooked a meal in years."

Petunia gaped at her. "*You* made all this? It smells delicious."

"Help yourself," Millie said. Max took a sandwich and nibbled it suspiciously. His eyes widened, and he began to devour it. Petunia grabbed a scone.

Millie took some frog legs and salad. "Does your father cook for you?"

"Sort of," Max mumbled around a mouth full of food. "He buys the ingredients and then makes it look and taste as though it's cooked using illusion spells. This sandwich is amazing!"

"Better than your father's illusions?" Millie asked.

"Muh bedda!" Max said through a mouthful of food. He swallowed. "I mean, much better. I've been suspecting for a while that Dad has eaten illusory food for so long, he's forgotten what it's supposed to taste like. Except for the Thai food. That's pretty good. But he doesn't make it very often, and I still don't understand why he insists on serving it in little paper boxes."

The elf glanced up at Max with an odd expression, then quickly turned back to her scroll.

"What's Thai food?" Petunia asked. "I've never heard of it."

"It involves lots of peanuts and noodles and cilantro, and sometimes it's really spicy. I think it's from some other Realm." Max took a spoonful of mushrooms.

"So you're brother and sister, but you don't live together?" Petunia asked.

"Half-siblings," Max corrected. "We have the same mother, but I live with my dad."

"That's how it usually works with witches and wizards," Millie added. "Only we usually visit a lot more. Mother had a fight with Max's father about five years ago, and I haven't seen him since."

Petunia sniffed. "It must be nice, having your parents all to yourselves. I have to share mine with a dozen brothers and sisters and way too many cousins. Half the time, my mum doesn't even remember my name."

Millie noticed the elf sneaking glances at them and the spread of food. "Excuse me," Millie said. "Do you like scones?"

The elf raised an eyebrow. "Oh, you're talking to me? I thought I was invisible," she said sarcastically.

"*Y pelraelle*," Millie said, which meant "I'm sorry" in Elvish. "You were reading, and I didn't want to disturb you."

"Yet here you are, at my table, which I find quite disturbing. Especially your pidgin Elvish," said the elf, rolling her eyes.

Max snorted. "First you're mad because we didn't notice you, and now you're mad because we did? That's essentially inconsistent."

"What are you, a walking dictionary?" The elf glared at him. "You're new here, so I will lower myself and explain a few things. This. Is. My. Table. No one else sits here. No one bothers me. No one."

Max half-rose from his seat. "I don't see your name engraved on this table. What gives you the right...?"

Millie broke in hastily. "I am t-t-terribly sorry," she told the elf. "As you said, we are n-new here, and we didn't mean to offend you. Here," she said, handing the elf a scone. "A peace offering."

The elf studied the scone, then sniffed it suspiciously. "What's it made of? Are those real or illusory raisins I smell?"

"Real raisins," Millie assured her. "I got them in Pixamitchie."

"Where's that?" Max asked.

"It's my village," said Petunia. "It's near the Sleeping Castle. A lot of pixies live in the briar hedge there, and there's a group of centaurs who herd goats, and some fairies and leprechauns and gnomes. You know, the usual." She shrugged.

Millie nodded. "Mother and I live just outside the village. We shop in Pixamitchie for things like milk and cheese and butter, fruits and vegetables. I catch frogs and toads and fish with nets in the swamp in my backyard. A dwarf named Baragad brings a lot of our supplies by cart once a month, including most of Mother's spellcrafting supplies," Millie said.

Max nodded. "Baragad supplies us, too, but with pretty much everything."

Millie cocked her head. "So you never go out shopping with your father?"

"My stepmother does all the shopping, but she never takes me anywhere," Max grumbled. "Dad takes me to the monthly wizard convocations, and occasionally we go visit another wizard, but otherwise, he keeps to his laboratory. It's soooo boring. I bugged Dad mercilessly until he gave me the magic carpet for my birthday last month." His face lit up. "Now I can really start exploring."

"Don't you have any brothers to play with?" Petunia asked.

Max scowled. "I have a stepsister, and she's horrible. Always criticizing me and playing mean tricks on me and telling me I'll never amount to anything."

Millie thought of the last Coven meeting. "Wait a minute. Who's your stepmother?"

Max looked surprised. "Didn't Mother tell you? My father married Hepsibat last spring, and she and Cretacia moved in with us."

Millie jumped to her feet. "Aunt Hepsibat? Cretacia? But... but that's terrible! No wonder M-m-mother's been in such a bad mood." She looked at Max with deep sympathy. "I can barely stand Cretacia at Coven meetings. I don't know how you can stand having her around all the time."

"Well, I hide a lot," Max grumbled, stuffing another scone into his mouth.

"Ohhhhhhh..."

Millie glanced at the far end of the table. The elf had dropped her scone. "Oh," the elf moaned. "Ohhhhhhh!"

"W-w-what's wrong?" Millie asked. "Is it the scone? Is it t-terrible?"

Tears were streaming down the elf's face. "It's wonderful," she whispered. "It's so, so wonderful. It reminds me of my mother's elfcakes." Suddenly, the elf jumped to her feet and ran away.

"Oh, dear," said Petunia. "Poor Sagara."

Millie was confused. "D-d-did I do something wrong?"

"No, it's not you," Petunia told her. "Sagara's father was killed in the Elf-Gnome Wars, and her mother has been missing for nearly three years. Some say she wandered into the Dragon Vale and was eaten by velociraptors. Others say she went into the Logical Realm and lost her magic."

"Is that why Sagara comes to school?" Millie asked.

"Oh, no," Petunia said. "She's here because the elf school was fed up with her. All Sagara wants to study is arithmancy."

"The magic of numbers?" Max asked. "That's tricky stuff, and not terribly elvish. Elves usually specialize in nature magic." Max considered a fourth sandwich and the pile of scones, then glanced up at Millie. "You packed an awfully big lunch."

"Well, it's my first day of school," Millie said. "I thought perhaps sharing my lunch might help me make friends."

"Well, I'd say it worked," said Petunia, who nodded at something behind Millie.

Millie turned around and found a teary Sagara standing right behind her.

"I'm sorry," said Sagara. "I didn't mean to run off like that. May I... um, may I have another scone? Please?"

"Of course," Millie said, handing her two.

Sagara sat down gratefully next to her. "I'm sorry," she said again, between bites. "I'd forgotten how much I missed my mother's cooking. I live with my grandmother now, and she insists that cooking destroys the potency of your food. We eat everything raw."

Millie frowned. "That's, um, interesting."

"That's awful!" Petunia exclaimed. "It can't be good for you."

Sagara shrugged. "It's impossible to argue with my grandmother. She's always right."

"She sounds like my m-mother." Millie sighed. "I understand. My father is dead, too. He died when I was very little. Cooking yummy things helps me feel a little better. So don't worry, Sagara. I can bring you scones every day if you like."

"Really?" Sagara smiled happily. "That would be wonderful. Oh, um, do you ever make things with chocolate?"

Millie laughed. "All the time. Our house ghost Horace loves chocolate." Which reminded her that Horace was still a frog, thanks to her chocolate.

Max, about to stuff another scone into his mouth, paused. "Your house ghost. Eats chocolate."

Millie nodded, helping herself to some mushrooms. "Actually, it's a big problem. Maybe you can help me..."

The gong rang.

"LUNCH IS OVER. PLEASE PUT AWAY YOUR LUNCHES SO THAT WE MAY CLEAR THE GLADE FOR RECESS."

All the students promptly picked up the remains of their lunches. Max nabbed one more scone, as did Sagara and Petunia. Millie took the last sandwich and packed her containers into her lunch cauldron.

"Wanna play Freeze and Leap, Millie?" Petunia asked.

"Oh, yes, thank you," Millie said, standing up hastily before their chairs vanished, too.

Max looked annoyed. "What about me?"

"Sure, anyone can play. How about you, Sagara?"

"Ha," said the elf. "That's a baby game. I've got better things to do." Sagara sauntered off.

As she did, Millie noticed a bunch of goblins and imps pull away from the crowd of students to block Sagara's path. Sagara's shoulders stiffened. She lifted her chin, turned, and tried to go around them, but the group spread out, blocking her again.

"Uh oh," muttered Petunia.

"Snooty elf doesn't wanna play," one of the goblins said to Sagara. "She's too good for us."

Despite being the same height, Sagara somehow managed to look down at him. "I have better things to do than bicker with you."

Grumpkin stepped forward. "Why don't you go back to your uppity elf school? Oh, right, they threw you out."

"Reject, reject," Titchy began chanting. The others took up the chant.

"Like I care about your opinions," Sagara said, but she had taken a step back.

Millie rushed up to Sagara. "Come on, Sagara!" she said brightly. "You don't want to miss the game, do you?"

Grumpkin turned to her. "Oh, look. It's the not-a-witch," he said, grinning. "Of course you'd choose to be friends with the school's biggest freak."

Petunia popped up beside them. "Hey, have you heard the latest news about the gnomes?"

The goblins stared at her. "No," one said shortly.

"Of course not!" Petunia replied. "Gnome news is good news!"

Several of the younger goblins and imps giggled. Grumpkin glared at them. "That's sooooo old."

"How many trolls does it take to shoe a horse?" Petunia asked.

"Before or after they eat the horse?" Grumpkin countered, but Petunia plowed onward: "Five! Four to put on the shoes, and one to lift the horse!"

Several goblins guffawed, the imps giggling helplessly. Even Millie and Max started laughing.

"Why can't you borrow money from a leprechaun?" Petunia asked. "Because they're always a little short!"

"Hey!" yelled a nearby leprechaun as the goblins collapsed in helpless laughter.

Even Grumpkin had started chuckling. Then he glanced around sharply. "Where'd that elf go?" Sagara had disappeared. Grumpkin stomped off in a huff.

"Sheesh," Max said. "Not even a thank you. That was

pretty clever, Petunia."

Petunia shrugged. "That's nothing. I was just getting warmed up. Now, do you want to play Freeze and Leap or not?"

"I don't know how to play," Millie admitted. "Can I just watch this time?"

"Suit yourself," Petunia said, and she dashed off into the crowd, yelling, "I'm in, I'm in!" Freeze and Leap seemed to involve teams chasing players from other teams. If you touched someone from an opposing team, they were rooted to the spot and could not move unless another player leaped over them. There seemed to be other rules involving turning invisible, teleporting from place to place, casting illusions, and flying, but Millie couldn't really figure them out. The teams largely formed along race lines, though the pixies and fairies were working together, as were the dryads and sprites. The goblins, imps, and bogeys formed one large team. Gnomes and brownies formed another.

Millie noticed Max standing beside her, looking just as confused. "You've never played before, either?" she asked.

"No, I've played with Cretacia and her cousins," he said, "but when I get caught, I get pummeled or turned green or covered with warts."

Millie winced. "Cretacia has a gift for warts."

"That reminds me." Max turned to her, lowering his voice. "Please don't tell Mother or any of the other witches that I'm here."

"What? Why not?" Millie asked, startled.

Max lowered his voice to a whisper. "Because they don't know I'm here. I forged my entrance papers."

"Why would you do that?" Millie asked.

"When Dad told me you were coming to school, I knew it was my chance to come see you. Besides, I'd do just about anything to get away from Cretacia," Max told her. "She's horrible! She constantly plays nasty pranks on me. She tells me I'm a useless, hopeless, miserable excuse for a wizard."

"I know," she said. "Cretacia d-d-does the same thing to me at every Coven meeting." Millie suddenly pulled Max into a hug. She felt Max sag with relief.

"Then you do understand." He hugged her back. "She makes my life unbearable. I've had to get very good at wards and security enchantments to keep her out of my room. I spend most of my time hiding from her."

"Have you told your father? Why doesn't he put a stop to it?"

Max sighed. "Dad says that every wizard has to learn to cope with witches and that this is a good learning experience for me." He pulled back and looked at Millie desperately. "But he doesn't understand how bad it is! Cretacia is very good at covering her tracks. Half the time, she makes it look like it's all my fault! So when Dad mentioned that the Forest Council was asking for wizards to go to school, I sneaked into his laboratory and forged the papers."

"Why didn't you just ask him if you could go?"

Max pulled away from her and held up three fingers. "One: my father wants me to have a normal wizard's education, which seems to consist of an occasional lesson and then ignoring me the rest of the time. Two: my stepmother would never let him live it down. Three: Cretacia would know where I am." He glanced around nervously. "You don't know what she's capable of. So please, please don't tell Cretacia."

Millie nodded solemnly. "Never. I promise."

Max searched her face, then slowly smiled. "Thank you."

"But," said Millie, "won't your family notice you're gone all day?"

"Cretacia will notice eventually," Max said, "but since I spend most of my time hiding from her, it should take her a while to become suspicious. As long as I show up for breakfast and dinner, no one will have any idea."

"And when they do find out?" Millie asked.

Max stared at his toes. "I don't know. I'm hoping I'll have learned so much here that I'll be able to convince my father that it's worthwhile. But if that doesn't work... well, at least I'll have escaped for a little while, and," he glanced at her, "I'll have spent some time with my sister. By the way, I'm pretty sure your father isn't dead."

Millie was shocked. Her mother had told her, clearly and firmly, that her father had died before Millie could walk and that there was no point talking about it. "Why do you think that?"

Max shrugged. "I could be wrong, but my dad talks about your dad like he's still alive."

"Your father knew my father?" Millie sucked in a breath. "Could... could you ask him? I don't know anything about him, not even his name."

"It's Dean," Max told her. "Dad has mentioned him a few times. I'll try to find out more, but I'll have to be careful. If I get too curious, he'll want to know why I'm asking."

Millie swallowed her excitement. Max was probably wrong. Why would her mother lie about her father being dead? But it would be nice to know more about her father. "I understand. Anything you can find out would be great."

The gong sounded again.

"RECESS IS OVER," Quercius announced. "PLEASE PROCEED TO YOUR CLASSROOMS. MAX AND MILLIE, PLEASE REPORT TO HEADMISTRESS PTERIA."

Chapter 6
Amounting to a Hill of Beans

Max and Millie climbed back up the stairs to the Headmistress's office, where Pteria was waiting for them.

"Please be seated, children," she told them. "I have the results of your examinations."

Millie crossed her fingers and tried hard not to squirm in her seat.

"First off, let's start with your strengths," said the Headmistress. "Max, you are advanced in spoken spellcraft and security magic. Millie, your linguistic skill is impressive, and you have extensive knowledge of spell components." She gave Millie a slightly puzzled smile. "I am surprised that you know so little healing magic, since that is your mother's specialty."

It is? Millie wondered. Bogdana was frequently called on to perform healing magic on the residents of Pixamitchie, but her mother always complained about having to treat her patients, as though it were a distraction from her real work. Millie had always assumed that healing potions were just a sideline for her mother.

"However," Mistress Pteria went on, "you are both shockingly ignorant of the history and cultures of the Enchanted Forest and the Realms in general. I am afraid you will both have to take Remedial History."

Pteria reached into a cabinet and took out two vials. She handed one to Max and one to Millie. The label on the vial read *Remedial History*.

"Interesting," said Max, leaning forward. "Liquefied information?"

Pteria looked pleased. "I brewed them myself. Now drink up."

Millie hesitated. Her mother had warned her again and again never to drink a potion not made by Bogdana herself (especially not any Millie had made), but Baba Luci had sent her to school and so must have trusted Headmistress Pteria. Besides, she had so many questions about the Enchanted Forest and the other Realms. Next to her, Max had already gulped down the contents and closed his eyes. Millie pulled off the stopper and drank.

For a moment, she felt perfectly normal. Then an image formed in her head, a map of the Enchanted Forest. It was beautifully detailed. She could see Pixamitchie, where Petunia lived, the Faerie Vale, the dwarf mines to the east, the Centaur Flats, the Sylvan Woods where dryads and fauns lived, even a small speck marking her own home.

She saw another map, this one of the Dragon Realm. Another, the Celestial Realm with its k'ilin and kami. The Realm of Infinite Sands, djinni and sphinxes. The aquatic realm of Atlantis, and more and more. They flashed through her mind, and with them, histories unspooled themselves in her head. The Three Hundred Years' War. The War of Dragonkin. The convoluted and improbable history of the Logical Realm. The Sundering, when the many Realms were formally separated from the Logical Realm, removing all magic from that strange, human-dominated place. The Great Accord.

Images and information flashed faster and faster in her mind, so much that Millie couldn't grasp it all. It was too much, she felt like she was drowning. Just as Millie opened her mouth to scream, it stopped.

"Oh!" she said, opening her eyes.

Pteria smiled at her. "Easy now. That was rather a lot to take in all at once."

"Oh!" said Max beside her. "That was marvelous! I never knew that our great-great-grandfather was involved in the Great Accord."

"Indeed he was. Another day, I will tell you all about it," Headmistress Pteria said. "Now, however, you should proceed to your assigned classes. Max, you will be joining Mistress Numina's third level class. Millie, I've assigned you to Master Augustus's fourth level class for the time being."

"Oh," Millie said sadly, just as Max asked, "We won't be in the same class?"

"Not every day, no," the Headmistress told them. "But you will both take Elementary Potions with Mistress Pym and Thaumaturgy with Master Bertemious. Here are your schedules." She handed them each a sheet of parchment. "During that time, Quercius and I will monitor your progress. After that, we may adjust your classes."

Millie looked at her schedule:

Onesday

8:30 – 9:00	Morning Meeting
9:00 – 10:30	Reading Group
10:30 – 11:30	Scrolls & Inscriptions
11:30 – 12:30	Lunch and Recess
12:30 – 1:30	Forest Cultures
1:30 – 2:30	Nature Study
2:30	Dismissal

Twosday

8:30 – 9:00	Morning Meeting
9:00 – 10:30	Independent Work
10:30 – 11:30	Math & Arithmancy
11:30 – 12:30	Lunch and Recess
12:30 – 1:30	Elementary Potions
1:30 – 2:30	Exercise and Health
2:30	Dismissal

Threesday

8:30 – 9:00	Morning Meeting
9:00 – 10:30	Reading Group
10:30 – 11:30	Charms & Enchantments
11:30 – 12:30	Lunch and Recess
12:30 – 1:30	Forest Cultures
1:30 – 2:30	High Mystery
2:30	Dismissal

Foursday

8:30 – 9:00	Morning Meeting
9:00 – 10:30	Independent Work
10:30 – 11:30	Math & Arithmancy
11:30 – 12:30	Lunch and Recess
12:30 – 1:30	Thaumaturgy
1:30 – 2:30	Arts & Crafts
2:30	Dismissal

Endsday

No School

She shook her head in confusion. Headmistress Pteria noticed this. "Don't worry," she said. "Master Augustus will guide you through it. Now, allow me to escort you to your classes."

Max looked up from his schedule, a silly grin on his face. "I can hardly wait!" Millie felt the same smile on her own face. She lifted her hands to cover her mouth, then stopped. It felt right, smiling here. And no one objected to Max's dimples.

Headmistress Pteria led them first up the spiral staircase to a small class with about eighteen raucous younger students. Millie spotted Petunia in there, tongue sticking out of her mouth as she pored over a faintly glowing slate. Mistress Numina, a middle-aged wyvern of a delicate pink shade, hurried over and greeted Max, drawing him into the classroom.

"Come, Millie," said Pteria. "Let's take you to your class."

They went further up the staircase to a higher branch. Millie was dismayed to see that most of the students in this rather large class were younger than her. Pixies and goblins chased each other around the room, while young brownies clustered around a map of the Enchanted Forest, placing pins in specific locations.

Master Augustus turned out to be a chestnut faun in a neatly tailored waistcoat and the green teachers' cap with spectacles perched at the end of his pointed nose. "A new student! How exciting!" he exclaimed. "Welcome to our class, Millie."

"A word, Augustus?" Pteria asked.

"Oh, certainly, Headmistress," Master Augustus replied, bobbing a little bow. "Millie, you can leave your things in this empty cubby here. Then why don't you head over to the book nook and make yourself comfortable until I call for you?"

"Yes, Master," Millie said politely. She placed her cauldron and hat in the cubby alongside a bewildering array of outer clothing and lunch boxes and buckets, then headed to the corner she'd already spied, the one full of scrolls and books.

There were two other students seated in the book nook, a young fairy with fluttering orange wings and a leprechaun boy. Both children were completely absorbed in their books and ignored Millie, which was something of a relief.

Millie turned to the bookshelves. There were dozens — no, hundreds of books here that she'd never seen or heard of. Most of the books in her house were spellbooks, books of witch history and heritage, dictionaries, and her many cookbooks. The shelves here had nothing but books for children, written in good, familiar Canto, rather than English or Elvish or High Mystery. *The Polite Sasquatch.* *The Dragon's Handkerchief. Letitia's Letters. Don't Give an Ogre an Orange.*

Millie liked the sound of that last one, so she pulled it out, sat on the floor, and began to read. The book was clearly intended for much younger children, but it was so whimsical and funny that Millie loved it. She read it right through and went looking for another. And another. And another. When Master Augustus called all the students to gather in a circle, Millie had a small pile of books around her.

"My twining ivy, Millie!" Master Augustus said. "Headmistress Pteria told me your reading skills were good, but I think she rather underestimated you. Please put these away and come join us."

Hastily, Millie put the books back, more or less where she'd found them, and walked over to Master Augustus. Most of her classmates were sitting in a ring on a wide rug. A few latecomers ran up and scooted into place. Millie hesitated, wondering where she should sit.

"Remain standing, Millie," Master Augustus said. "Class, we have a new student today. This is Ludmilla Noctmartis, but she likes to be called Millie."

"Hello, Millie," the students chorused.

"Now, would you please introduce yourselves, starting with Poppin?"

"Hi, I'm Poppin!" said a young brownie girl in a pretty pink frock. Next to her, a goblin boy cried, "Hi, I'm Snot-Nose!"

"Snorri, that's inappropriate," Augustus corrected.

"It's what my mum calls me," Snorri declared, and everyone giggled.

"Hi, Millie," said the goblin sitting next to him. "I'm Grumpkin, but you already knew that." He sneered at her.

Millie's lunch turned to stone in her stomach. Grumpkin would make her life miserable, she just knew it. Two more names went by while she fought down her panic, and then Millie heard another familiar voice. She glanced up and met Sagara's eyes.

A smile spread across Millie's face. "Hi, Sagara!" she said. For just a second, Millie thought she saw Sagara smile back.

The rest of the names went by in a blur. Millie was so happy to have a friend in class that she spent most of the introductions beaming happily at Sagara. At the end, everyone chorused, "Welcome, Millie."

"Millie, this period is usually when we discuss Enchanted Forest cultures," Master Augustus said. "Since you are the first witch to attend this school, could you tell us a little about witches and what they do?"

Millie froze. "Um, sure, I g-guess. What do you want to know?"

Instantly, half a dozen students raised their hands. Master Augustus pointed to a pale green imp in a frilly blue dress. "Allie?"

"What kind of magic do witches do?" Allie asked.

Millie twisted her hands. "W-well, we do all kinds of magic but mostly enchantments, charms, and potions. My m-m-mother is a healer," she said slowly, still getting used to the idea, "so she makes a lot of healing potions."

"Snorri?" Master Augustus pointed at the young goblin.

Snorri grabbed his ankles, rocking back and forth. "I

thought witches mostly did curses and hexes," he said.

"Well, sometimes," Millie said. "Curses and hexes are just types of enchantment."

"What's the difference between a curse and a hex?" Snorri asked.

Millie thought for a moment. "A curse affects you personally, like if you're cursed with warts. A hex affects the world around you, like a bad luck hex."

Sagara raised her hand, and Master Augustus pointed at her. "Witches work together to create larger enchantments, don't they?"

"Yes," Millie said, nodding. "Covens meet once every month at the full moon to renew enchantments that help the health and strength of the Forest."

A shy brownie raised her hand. "Are all witches girls?"

This made Millie blush. "Y-yes, all witches are girls. If a w-witch has a boy child, he lives and studies with his father and becomes a wizard. Sometimes a witch and a wizard will m-marry and live together, but in general they live apart."

Millie answered several other questions, like where she lived and why witches wore hats and had green skin, but most of her answers ended up being, "Well, it's traditional."

Finally, Master Augustus said, "All right, let's not wear Millie out. Anyway, it's time for Nature Studies. This week, we're going to work on botany. Who knows what botany is?"

Three or four students raised their hands. "Izzy," Augustus said, pointing to a young green-skinned dryad in a dress made of patchwork maple leaves.

"Botany is the study of plants, like me," Izzy said proudly.

"That's correct," Master Augustus said. "So over this week, I'd like you to collect samples of plants from around your home. Please be certain not to collect samples from thinking plants, and to ask trees politely before plucking their leaves.

And please do not bring in any poisonous plants, such as poison ivy, nightshade, or mandrake. If you don't know what these look like, come see me after class."

"Yes, Master," the students said.

"We will also be growing our own plants in pots here in class. I have brought in some beans, pots, and soil, so we can try sprouting them using magic. Let's all move over to the worktables, and we'll begin. Please be gentle in your work and try not to make an excessive mess. In particular, no throwing soil, seeds, or pots. Do you understand?"

"Yes, Master!"

Augustus smiled. "Then you may proceed."

The students got up, the goblins, imps, fairies, and pixies dashing for the worktables at the rear of the classroom, followed closely by eager leprechauns, sprites, brownies, and the young dryad. Millie followed Sagara over. A large tub of soil lay in the center of each worktable, along with a small pile of beans and several trowels. Master Augustus passed out small clay pots.

Millie took hers, picked up a trowel and began filling the pot with soil. Sagara took a pot and used it to scoop up the soil from the pile. She poked a bean in the soil with one finger. Then Sagara closed her eyes and held her hands over the soil. Instantly, a bean plant sprouted out of it. Sagara sighed. "Booooooooring."

"That was amazing," Millie said. As she watched, the plant unfurled its stubby first leaves, then two more larger deep green leaves.

"Excellent job, Sagara," Augustus told her, patting her shoulder. "And how are you getting on, Millie?"

"Just getting started, Master," Millie said, reaching for a bean.

Carefully, Millie evened out the soil in her pot. Then she

made a small hole in the soil, placed her bean in it, and covered it up. Taking up a watering can, she gave it a bit of water. Millie glanced around. The pixies had gotten into a soil sculpting contest, ignoring the beans, while the goblins were all busily stuffing the beans up their noses and snorting them out, which was technically not throwing them. One of the fairies had sprouted a bean, but it instantly withered, turned brown, and died. The leprechauns, brownies, and dryads had all done as Millie had, and now they were variously chanting and waving their hands over the pots. One by one, small sprouts began to emerge. Millie sighed enviously. "I wish I could do that."

"You don't know how?" Sagara asked. "But it's so easy. What kind of witch can't sprout a bean?" She touched a leaf, and the vine shot up, sprouting more leaves and bursting into flower. "In elvish schools, we do this in kindergarten."

"My mother never taught me any nature magic," Millie said. "I would have liked that. Maybe I could grow my own vegetables and herbs."

"Want me to help?" Sagara said, reaching for Millie's pot.

"No, d-don't," Millie said hastily. "I appreciate it, but I want to learn to do it myself. How do you do it?"

Sagara shook her head. "I don't know. I've never thought about it. I just sort of do it."

"Think about it," Millie urged. "How did you feel when you made the bean sprout?"

Sagara closed her eyes. "It's like... deep inside me, I can feel my life. How I'm breathing and growing all the time. I sort of share that feeling with the bean." She opened her eyes, frowning. "It's not very precise."

"Hmm," Millie said. "M-mother never described magic that way. She always talks about power and channeling and bending things to your will."

Sagara snorted. "Maybe that's how it feels to her."

Millie closed her eyes and felt inside herself. She could feel her heart beating, the air moving in and out of her chest. She tried to feel how she was alive, but she just felt like the same old Millie, who never gets anything right. Millie the dud. Millie the mistake.

Cautiously, Millie opened one eye and peeked at the pot. It looked exactly the same. Nothing had sprouted. Nothing at all.

"Oh, no," Millie whispered. She had known deep down that it would never work.

Sagara snorted. "See what I mean. So imprecise. Try this," she said, taking a second pot. She filled it with soil, poked a bean into it, and frowned at it, concentrating. Then she said, "Let g be the rate of growth. Set g to one inch per three seconds. Produce a figure, two-pi-r, where r is a radius of three inches, proceed an additional pi-r, and then follow the z-axis for a total of one minute. Go."

Instantly, the bean sprouted, the vine curving slowly and beautifully into a perfect circle, then curving halfway around again and growing straight up. It stopped after exactly one minute. Several of the students burst into applause.

"There," Sagara said with satisfaction. "Precise."

Millie's head spun. She had no idea what pi-r meant or how that could make the bean grow in a circle. "I don't think I could do that."

"Not to worry, Millie," Master Augustus said. "Sagara has a rather, um, unique perspective on magic. Would you rather try reciting a common brownie sprouting spell?"

"Oh, y-yes," Millie said.

"Repeat after me," Master Augustus told her.

Little seed, time to wake,
Roots to grow and soil to break.

Leaves unfurl and flowers make.
Little seed, time to wake.

Hesitantly, Millie repeated his words, but the pot remained stubbornly bare.

"How about some gestures?" suggested a leprechaun. "Watch how I wave my hands." Millie imitated him as best she could. No sprout. She tried a fairy's wand. No sprout. She tried singing a dryad song. No sprout. Before long, half the class was trying to help Millie sprout her bean, but none of their suggestions worked. Grumpkin snickered and whispered to the other goblins. Millie bit back tears.

Master Augustus saw this. "That's enough, class. Remember, we needed a control for our experiment. Thank you, Millie, for providing one. Now everyone mark your pots and line them up on the windowsill."

Millie picked up her pot and got in line for the windowsill. *If only this had been a baking lesson*, she thought. *Something with chocolate. I know what to do with chocolate.*

At that moment, Millie felt a tingle go through her, from the top of her head right down to her fingertips. She glanced down at the pot, half expecting to see a neat green sprout rising up from the soil. But no, the pot remained bare. Sadly, she placed her pot beside the others and tried to take comfort from the fact that her pot wasn't the only empty one.

The gong rang. Millie's first day of school had ended, and she'd accomplished nothing. She trudged back to her cubby to retrieve her cauldron and her hat and followed the other children down the stairs and out to the glade. As they stepped off the staircase, they returned to their normal sizes.

Sagara grew several inches taller than Millie. As Millie spotted Petunia and started off to walk home with her, Sagara put a hand on Millie's shoulder and said, "Tomorrow

will probably be better." And she hurried off.
But it wasn't.

Chapter 7
Snickerdoodles and Sunchokes

On Twosday, Millie woke up with her ears still ringing from her mother's screaming fit over the damage done to the new hat. Bogdana had confiscated the hat and made Millie dust the entire house, covering every surface in a thick layer and adding plenty of dust bunnies under the furniture.

Bogdana slept late, as she usually did, so Millie put the mud in her hair and slime mold on her skin again, dressed in a blood-red gown, and made a huge frittata with scrambled eggs, onions, potatoes, peppers, tomatoes, and spinach, topped with a good hard cheese, grated fine so that it would melt into the eggs. She packed half of the frittata for lunch and left the rest for her mother's breakfast and lunch. To her own lunch, she added a mixed green salad and some leftover snickerdoodles from dinner, plus some extra plates and forks.

No one saw her off or told her to have a good day, so she told herself and walked out to the Path to greet the elm tree and meet up with Petunia.

Grumpkin was delighted at her lack of hat and managed to trip Millie twice before school started. In class, he glued her dress to her chair so that when she tried to stand up, the chair came with her. Master Augustus dispelled the glue and sent Grumpkin off to see the Headmistress, which gave Millie a little peace during Arithmancy. She rather liked the math but couldn't manage even a simple addition spell.

When the lunch gong sounded, Millie breathed a deep sigh of relief and ran for her cubby to retrieve her cauldron. Sagara, who hadn't said so much as a word to her all morning, popped up behind her and asked, "Did you bring more scones today?"

"Snickerdoodles," Millie told her.

Sagara considered. "Okay, I suppose I can allow you to sit at my table again."

Max and Petunia were already there, waiting for them. Petunia had brought a meat pie and apple slices. Sagara had elegant little bundles of raw vegetables wrapped in mint leaves and chard. Max pulled out a pile of ham sandwiches made with the strangest bread Millie had ever seen. She picked up a sandwich and studied it.

"Your bread has no holes," she said, poking it with a finger. "It's just a solid slab of white."

Max nodded. "That's what I was telling you. It's wizard bread, made out of my father's vague idea of what bread should be. Go on, try it."

Millie bit into it and nearly spat it out. The bread had no taste at all, though the ham was quite good. She recognized the flavor. "Baragad's ham?" she asked.

"Of course," Max said. "We get all our meat from him."

Millie sniffed. "Well, the ham's good, but the bread is pretty awful. Have some of my frittata."

Max grinned. "Thanks! And, um, could I have some cookies?"

"They're snickerdoodles, and I brought them to share," Millie told him.

"I'll give you some *melthas* if you give me some frittata," Sagara offered.

"Sure," Millie said. She put a slice of frittata onto a plate and took the mint bundle in exchange. Millie bit into it and gasped in surprise. "Ginger? Mmm, jicama and honeydew and... and straw mushrooms? And what's that other flavor?"

"Sunchoke," Sagara told her.

Millie studied the layers in the *melthas*. "I've never had sunchokes before. Y'know, these are really very good."

Sagara lifted a fork full of eggs in response. "So are these."

"No, I mean, I've never eaten Elvish food before. It's yummy." Millie cocked her head. "Could I borrow a cookbook from you?"

Sagara took a moment to swallow. "Well, I suppose it might be interesting to someone who doesn't know any better. I'll bring it tomorrow, but it'd be written in Elvish."

"That's fine; we have an Elvish-Canto dictionary at home."

Sagara laughed. "Sure, that'll make it easy."

"So will you play with us today, Sagara?" Petunia asked.

The elf shook her head. "I've got research to do. Sorry."

"What do you call an unathletic elf?" Petunia asked.

Sagara grimaced. "Annoyed."

"No, a shelf!" The pixie dashed off, giggling.

The gong rang, and Millie got her first taste of Freeze and Leap, playing with Max and Petunia on the pixie team. She spent most of recess frozen, but Millie didn't really care. It was so much fun just playing with other children.

After lunch, Millie had Elementary Potions with Max, which was taught by a cheerful but easily distracted brownie, Mistress Mallow. Normally quite small, about the height of Millie's knee, Mistress Mallow had dark brown skin, like soft, supple bark, dark brown hair pulled back into a neat bun beneath her green teacher's cap, and warm golden brown eyes. She wore a saffron orange dress with a neat apron over it that made Millie miss her own aprons.

Mistress Mallow refused to let Millie and Max sit together, so Millie shared a worktable with a young gryphon named Terrence.

"For today's lesson, we shall be brewing sleeping potions," Mistress Mallow announced. "Please light your braziers and set your flasks on them to heat. Now, we will be working with shadow juice, month-old cobwebs, and dream dust. Be very, very careful not to inhale any dream dust, or you will spend the rest of the day napping. Oh, dear," she said, glancing at Millie's worktable, where Terrence was already snoring deeply. "Too late."

Millie did her best to follow Mistress Mallow's instructions, but they reminded her too much of lessons with Bogdana. Instead, her mind drifted, thinking about what she did when she needed help sleeping. And then she caught a whiff of her potion.

Mistress Mallow caught it, too. "What is that? What's that I smell? *Chamomile?*" She bustled over to Millie's worktable. Millie shrank in her seat and considered hiding under the table. But Mistress Mallow had moved too quickly. She tapped the glass flask bubbling away over the brazier. The liquid inside was a pale yellow, translucent and tempting. Mistress Mallow sniffed it. "Chamomile tea? How on earth did you do that?"

"I'm s-s-sorry," Millie blurted out. "I didn't m-mean to do that. I followed all your instructions, r-really I did. Please don't be m-m-mad at me."

Mistress Mallow cocked her head. "Whyever would I be mad at you? This is an interesting result, a far cry from the usual broken crockery and explosions. Now, how did you manage this? We didn't even use chamomile among the ingredients, though that might have been a useful addition."

"I- I don't know how I did it," Millie said, her stomach twisting into knots. "This is always what happens when I try to make p-potions. I m-m-mess everything up."

"Hmm... we'll see about that," the brownie said. "I'll just take this for analysis." She pulled on a mitt and took the flask. "And blow out that brazier, if you please."

Millie did so, just as a flask across the room exploded. Mistress Mallow sighed. "Really, Snorri? That's the third flask this month."

⤳

After Elementary Potions, Millie had exercise class. She hadn't known what the word meant until they assembled in the glade. She was woefully unprepared. Master Schist, a gargoyle, started off by making them run ten laps around the glade. Millie had worn her formal shoes, and her feet burst into blisters before she had completed a single lap. But Master Schist allowed no excuses and simply instructed her to run barefoot, which was admittedly much better.

Then they did twenty push-ups, except for the four-legged students who alternated pushing up their fronts and their rears. Then the students without hooves climbed ropes hung from Quercius's branches, and no flying was allowed. Grumpkin excelled at everything, Sagara scaled the ropes like a squirrel, but Millie had never climbed anything steeper than her staircase and fell off the rope several times.

At the end of school, Millie had rope burns on her hands, bruises on her knees, and blisters so bad she could barely walk. Max spotted her staggering through the glade with her shoes in her cauldron, Petunia pacing in agitation at her ankles.

"Let me give you a ride home," Max suggested, rolling out his carpet.

"Won't that make you late getting home?" Millie asked.

Max shrugged. "Honestly, I usually hide out until dinnertime anyway. Please, allow me." He gave her a deep bow as he rolled out the carpet.

"Well, as long as I won't get you in trouble." Gratefully, Millie settled herself on the carpet.

Petunia danced excitedly beside them. "Can I come, too? Pleeeeease?"

"She does live near me," Millie said.

"Oh, sure, why not?" Max said. "Take a seat." He sat cross-legged next to Millie.

Petunia leaped aboard and climbed onto Millie's lap. "Hey, what do you get if you cross a fairy and your pet carp?"

"Um, a scaly fairy?" Max asked.

"Nope, a flying carp-pet!" Petunia laughed so hard, she fell into Millie's cauldron. "Mmm," her voice echoed up. "Cookie crumbs."

Max and Millie laughed, too. "I have to tell that one to Sylvester, another wizard I know. His dad keeps giant carp in the moat around their tower."

Petunia climbed out of the cauldron. "C'mon, let's go!"

Millie gripped the edge of the carpet tightly as Max twisted a tassel, and they zoomed out from under the branches of the oak tree. Petunia whooped with joy.

"Ohhh, d-darkness," Millie moaned, squeezing her eyes shut.

"What's wrong?" Max asked.

"I don't like heights," Millie gasped out.

"I'll decelerate and even it out," Max told her.

Petunia sighed. "Too bad. That was fun."

The carpet leveled out and slowed down, so that it felt to Millie like a light breeze was blowing. Cautiously, she opened one eye. And then she opened both of them wide.

The whole of the Enchanted Forest was laid out before

them like an enormous green quilt. To her surprise, Millie saw that it wasn't completely flat. There were rolling hills and broad valleys. Here and there she saw the silvery glimmer of a river or the mirror expanse of a lake.

"There's the Faerie Vale," Petunia called out, pointing to a valley riotous with flowers. "About a dozen of my aunts and uncles and a bazillion of my cousins live there."

Millie spied a patch of forest where all the leaves were tinged with silver and gold. "That must be the Sylvan Wood," she called out.

"And over there's the Schwarzwald," Max said, gesturing at a place where a shadow seemed to lie over the forest, the trees dark and twisted. "That's where goblins, ogres, and trolls live."

"And there's Pixamitchie!" Petunia cried out.

"My house is just on the edge of the fen, there," Millie told Max. "Oh, but you'll have to land at least a hundred feet away. Mother has strong wards up and won't let anything fly near the house except for her and Baba Luci."

"I can feel them from here," Max told her. "Coming down now." He twisted another tassel, and the carpet glided gently down to land on the Path without so much as a bump.

Petunia leaped out. "That was amazing!" she screamed. "Can we do that every day?"

Max winced, rubbing his ears. "Um, tomorrow I have a lesson with Dad, so I must decline. My apologies. Will you be able to walk, Millie?"

"M-mother will patch me up," Millie said, hobbling off the carpet.

"Oh, good. Well, see you tomorrow."

Millie limped the rest of the way home, where Bogdana complained loudly as she smeared healing ointments on Millie's feet. "What a useless school, damaging children like this. And now I have to brew more ointment. I'd make you do it," she said, glaring at Millie, "but I'd probably end up with raspberry jam instead. So do try not to damage yourself from now on." Bogdana glanced at Millie, then said casually, "You know, you can quit school anytime. You've fulfilled the Baba's request. You don't have to go back."

Millie gritted her teeth. "N-n-no, I want to keep t-trying. I'm sure it will get better soon."

Chapter 8

The Backwards Witch

On Threesday, Millie woke up with her feet completely healed. She made oatmeal bread, scrambled eggs, and sweet maple sausages for breakfast, then went through the morning ritual of mud and slime mold. She packed leftovers from last night's dinner in her cauldron and headed out to the Path. Petunia met her by the kitchen gate, a large box balanced on her head.

"What did you bring for lunch today?" Petunia asked.

Millie grinned. "Butternut squash soup, grilled asparagus, and oatmeal bread."

Petunia's face fell. "No dessert?"

Millie smacked her forehead. "Dessert!"

"Awwwww..." Petunia said.

"Just kidding. Chocolate chip cookies."

Petunia squealed and did a wild dance around Millie's ankles, the box tipping dangerously. "Come on!" she said. "The sooner we get to school, the sooner we can have lunch. I brought some goodies today, too. Mutton sandwiches and raspberry-rhubarb crumble."

"That sounds great," Millie said. "I love rhubarb."

They got to school just as Max came zooming in on

his carpet. "I thought I'd be late," he told them. "Cretacia followed me, and it took me eons to lose her in the forest." He rolled up his carpet and headed up the stairs. "See you at lunch?"

"Of course," Millie replied.

Before circle time, Millie snuck over to the bean pots, then gasped. Something had sprouted in her pot, but it looked different from the others somehow. She took the pot down from the windowsill. The sprout was bigger than most of the others. It pushed up a much darker bean husk, a sort of purplish brown, and it smelled sort of fruity, like bananas.

Master Augustus trotted over. "Your bean sprouted, Millie?"

Millie nodded. "But it looks different, and it smells funny. Is it sick?"

The faun frowned over the pot. "I'm not sure. Let's give it a few more days and see how it does."

That morning, they had Reading Group, in which everyone talked about a book they'd read. Millie had read the book during Independent Work the previous day, and now she listened, amazed at how everyone talked about what the characters were feeling, and why they did what they did, and what would happen next. Embarrassed, Millie realized that she was only supposed to read the first two chapters of the book.

After Reading Group, Millie went off to Charms and Enchantments. It was held in the same lab room as Elementary Potions and taught by a very formal and proper unicorn, Mistress Pym, her glossy coat the color of fresh snow. To Millie's delight, Petunia was also in the class. Unfortunately, so was Grumpkin.

"Today, class, we'll be making insect repellent charms. Many sections of the Enchanted Forest are approaching their summer season, so this is both timely and practical.

Please open your scrolls. Note that the charm lasts for only twenty-four hours. Longer insect-repellent charms require more potent ingredients and can have unpleasant side effects such as skin rashes and noxious odors."

Petunia nudged Millie. "On goblins, how could you tell?" she whispered, loud enough for Grumpkin to hear. He glared back at her.

"To effect this charm, you must grind the ingredients in the mortars, sprinkle them on your skin, and recite the incantation on your scroll. You will need frankincense, beetlebane, condensed cedarwood smoke, and alum. Who can tell me why we use alum?"

Several hands and forelegs shot up, and Millie tentatively added hers.

"Millie, isn't it? Nice to see initiative from a new student. Go ahead."

"Alum is a binding agent," Millie said in a tiny voice.

Mistress Pym shook her mane. "What's that? Speak up so everyone can hear you."

Millie cleared her throat and said, a bit too loudly, "Alum is a binding agent, Mistress Pym."

The class giggled, but the unicorn nodded. "Quite right, quite right. And if you don't have alum on hand, what other binding agents could you use? Grumpkin?"

Grumpkin, who had been mimicking Millie, stopped and scratched his head. "Um, glue?"

Mistress Pym snorted. "I suppose that would do for goblins, but what about something less, er, messy?"

Millie raised her hand again, and Mistress Pym nodded at her. "Arrowroot is also a good binding agent," she said.

"Correct!" said Mistress Pym. "Well done. Now, let's get busy. Measure out your ingredients into the mortar and get grinding."

Grumpkin scowled at Millie.

Millie took up her measuring spoons and carefully measured out each ingredient. Beside her, Petunia simply pinched or scooped out the ingredients with her fingers, littering the table with bits of beetlebane and trickles of condensed smoke.

"Aren't you going to measure?" Millie asked.

"Nah," Petunia said. "Pixies never bother. Come on, get grinding before Picky Pym gets after you."

Millie turned back to her mortar, but out of the corner of her eye, she saw Petunia sneak a tiny pinch of glittering white powder from a pouch at her waist, then add it to her mortar. The pixie quickly began grinding.

Millie ground at her ingredients, too, having some difficulty with the condensed smoke. It looked like a black powder, but it clumped and flowed, rather like honey. As she beat it into the other ingredients, Millie thought about beating honey into batter. *Perhaps I'll make honey-glazed chicken for dinner*, she thought. Eventually, Millie managed to grind everything together into an even grey powder.

"Everyone ready?" Mistress Pym asked. "Now, sprinkle a bit of your mixture onto your skin and recite the charm. Millie, can you read High Mystery?"

"Of c-course, Mistress Pym," Millie said, trying to sound more confident and less terrified than she was.

"Very good, carry on."

Millie glanced around her. Everyone else was sprinkling their mixture on a bare bit of skin, a forearm or shoulder or knee, and reciting the charm in halting High Mystery, which was always challenging. Sometimes Millie thought it didn't want to be said. Carefully, she sprinkled some of her powder on her left arm. Then she read the charm aloud. "*Karkoita hyönteiset*," she read. *Skin to insects forbidden be.*

The powder sank into Millie's skin, and to her astonishment, a golden shimmer enveloped her. *Did I actually do it right?* she wondered. Then she glanced at the other students and saw that their shimmer was more silvery or grey. Mistress Pym gave her a puzzled look, then turned to Petunia, whose charm glittered brightly.

"Using pixie dust again, Petunia?" the unicorn asked.

Petunia blushed a bit. "That's how pixies do it."

"I have told you not to use pixie dust in this class. It encourages sloppy practice, which can be dangerous in more advanced enchantments. Ten points off your grade."

Petunia groaned.

"Now let us see whether you have succeeded," the unicorn said. She trotted up to a small wooden box on her desk and tapped it with her horn. The box sprang open, and a cloud of buzzing mosquitos sprang out. They hovered in the air for a moment, then immediately attacked Millie.

"Eeek!" Millie cried, slapping at them frantically. "Help, they're all over me!"

Petunia jumped forward, waving her arms wildly around Millie, which just caused the mosquitos to move to less protected parts of Millie, like her legs.

Mistress Pym rushed forward, her nostrils flaring. "What have you done? You smell like honey. You've made an insect-attracting charm, Millie!"

Grumpkin broke out in howls of laughter. "Some witch!" he cried. "You do everything backwards. You're a backwards witch!"

"Backwards witch! Backwards witch!" the other students began chanting.

"Oh, yeah?" Petunia yelled back at Grumpkin. "Why do goblins never wipe their noses? Because they think a runny nose is exercise!"

Grumpkin laughed. "Think I'm stupid? You're the one who's friends with a backwards witch."

Covered with mosquito bites, desperately slapping at her face and arms, humiliated again, Millie got angry. Why did people have to rub it in? She knew she was a terrible witch, she knew she did everything wrong, it really didn't bother her anymore. But why did they have to go after her friends? If Grumpkin only knew how it felt.... A tingle came over Millie, from her fingers to her toes, and suddenly, Grumpkin's shimmer changed, from a dark grey to a pale gold. Half the cloud of mosquitos careened away from Millie and attacked Grumpkin.

"Geroff!" he howled. "Get 'em off me!"

"Midnight moonbeams!" Mistress Pym cried. "It's spreading! Millie, get over by Grumpkin. I'm going to have to douse you both."

Millie stumbled across the room to stand by Grumpkin. Mistress Pym waved her horn, tracing a water sigil in the air. "*Sada,*" she said, in a voice like thunder.

A raincloud formed in the air above Millie and Grumpkin, and it opened up, drenching them both to the skin. The golden shimmer faded and then disappeared. The mosquitos fled the rain and dispersed. All of the mud and slime mold had washed off Millie, making a mess of the smooth stone floor.

"I'm so sorry," she told the Charms teacher.

Mistress Pym glared down her horn at Millie. "Explain to me what just happened. I have seen many a charm go wrong, but I've never seen one corrupt other charms."

Millie stared at her sodden shoes. "I d-don't know, M-m-mistress. I always get ch-charms wrong."

"And where did the honey come from?" Mistress Pym asked. "Did you bring some to class with you?"

"N-no, Mistress. Only..."

The unicorn stamped in annoyance. "Only what?"

"Well, as I was g-grinding the ingredients, I was thinking about making d-d-dinner."

Mistress Pym looked thoughtful. "And this dinner included honey?"

Millie nodded miserably.

"Interesting. Did you intentionally change Grumpkin's charm?"

"Oh, no, M-m-mistress," Millie said hastily. "I never m-meant to do that. I d-d-don't know how that happened."

"Hmm, I can guess," said Mistress Pym. "I will have to consider this. Meanwhile, you owe Grumpkin an apology."

Millie bowed her head. "I'm very sorry, Grumpkin. I didn't mean to charm you."

"Grumpkin, do you accept this apology?"

Grumpkin frowned, shaking water out of one ear. "Yah, sure," he muttered.

"Very good," said Mistress Pym. "Millie, you will clean up this mess, and you will launder Grumpkin's clothing for him. Right now, you and Grumpkin should get changed. Go to the Lost and Found box and find some suitable clothing, then go to the bathrooms to change. After that, you may proceed to lunch. Millie, you will return during recess to clean the floor." The unicorn lifted her head to survey the room. "Everyone else, good job. Class dismissed."

"Do you always think about food?" Petunia asked her as they filed out.

Millie hung her head. "Pretty much."

Petunia showed her to the Lost and Found box just outside the bathrooms, where Grumpkin was extracting some tattered trousers.

"You'll pay for that, witch," he told her, heading for the boy's bathroom.

Petunia sorted through boots, hats, scarves, shirts, pants, and jackets and pulled out a plain brown dress, slightly stained. "I think this is the best we've got."

Millie took it. "Any towels?"

The pixie plucked out a fleecy vest. "Will this do?"

Millie nodded. A few minutes later, she emerged from the girls' bathroom, mostly dry and completely free of mud, slime, and shoes. "Do you think it's all right to go barefoot?"

Petunia looked pointedly at her own bare feet. "Suits me fine." She cocked her head. "You look better without all the mud. Your hair is shiny."

"Darkness, I must look awful." Millie frowned. "Come on, let's go get our lunches."

Chapter 9

Mashed Asparagus and Cookie Crumbs

When she returned to class, Millie went to her cubby and got a nasty shock.

"M-m-master Augustus?" Millie cried.

Augustus looked up from lining up the other students. "What is it, Millie?"

Millie's lip trembled. *I must not cry, I must not cry.* She took a deep breath. "Master Augustus, my lunch is gone."

Augustus trotted over and saw that her cubby contained nothing but Grumpkin's sodden trousers. He frowned. "Class, Millie's lunch has gone missing. Does anyone know where it is?"

Several giggles and snickers erupted from the line, swiftly silenced by a glare from Master Augustus. "Let me make this very clear," he said slowly. "No one, not even I, will go to lunch until Millie's cauldron is found and returned to her." He folded his arms, waiting.

After a long and awkward moment, a leaf sprite raised his hand. "Um, Master Augustus? I think I saw something odd in the paints cupboard."

"Go fetch it, Bay, if you please."

The sprite dashed off, then returned with Millie's

cauldron. The flask of soup was still there, though it had been opened, and some had spilled. The grilled asparagus had been mashed into a sticky paste all over the inside of the cauldron, and the bread and cookies were gone.

"Which of you stole Millie's lunch?" Augustus asked. "We are not leaving until I find out." He looked carefully at each of the students. "Grumpkin, you seem to have crumbs in your hair and on your pants."

Grumpkin shrugged, not the least bit embarrassed. "I found it in the paint cupboard, same as Bay did, and helped myself."

Augustus trotted over to his desk and retrieved his wand. "I think we'll try that again with a truth spell in place."

Grumpkin raised his hands. "Okay, okay, I took it. 'Twasn't fair, them cookies smellin' so good. They tempted me."

"Then I believe you owe Millie an apology and your lunch in compensation."

Grumpkin looked disgusted. "I don't owe her nothing. She sent those skeeters after me."

"I'm sorry," Millie told him. "I didn't mean to do that. It was an accident."

Master Augustus said, "Now, Grumpkin, apologize to Millie and give her your lunch."

Grumpkin growled out, "Sorry." He handed her a dirty sack filled with what looked and smelled like mashed earthworms.

"Ugh," Millie said. "No, thanks."

"Now, Grumpkin, I think you should visit Headmistress Pteria's office," said Augustus.

Grumpkin grimaced at Millie, then stumped down the stairs.

"Everyone else, back in line," Augustus said. "Down to lunch we go!"

Max and Petunia were waiting anxiously for Millie at the bottom of the stairs. Max looked Millie over, surprised, and said, "What happened? You don't look like a witch anymore." And Millie burst into tears.

"I'm sorry!" Max said. "I'm sorry, I didn't mean it. What did I say?" he asked Sagara, who had followed her.

Sagara rolled her eyes at Max. "Grumpkin stole her lunch, and you're insulting her, you pompous idiot."

"But she *doesn't* look like a witch," he said, bewildered.

"You must have brushed your teeth with gunpowder this morning," Petunia said, rolling her eyes, "because you just keep shooting your mouth off."

"He's right, I don't look like a witch," Millie choked out. "What kind of witch can't keep her hat or make a simple charm or sprout a bean or prevent her lunch from being stolen? I don't think I'm actually a witch at all."

Max looked mournfully at Millie's cauldron. "Stolen? Does that mean no lunch today?"

Sagara smacked the back of his head. "Yeah, that's the important thing here, your stomach. Millie, of course you're a witch."

"But I never get anything right, not one single spell, ever," Millie wailed.

Max looked confused. "Well, that's not true. You used to be fantastic at magic when we were little. You made mud pies so real, you'd trick me into eating them every single time. And the thing is, I didn't mind because they were so delicious."

Millie stared at him. "I did? I don't remember that."

"You did, though." Max nodded vigorously. "You were like the opposite of my dad. He makes food boring and awful. You made boring, awful things into food. You'd turn sticks into pretzels, rocks into rock candy. And they were all so yummy."

Petunia looked thoughtful. "Today, when your charm went wrong, you were thinking about honey. What about other spells that have gone wrong?"

Millie told them about the cauldron she turned into a pumpkin, and the elephant egg quiche, and the chamomile tea in Elementary Potions class on Twosday. "And then there's Horace," she said, explaining about the chocolate sauce.

All three of her friends stared at her. Millie turned bright red and considered crawling under the table.

"That's... that's..." Petunia began.

"Impossible. Unbelievable. Inconceivable," Max said.

"Very interesting," said Sagara.

The others turned to stare at her. She shrugged. "It should be impossible for a ghost to eat physical food, so ghosts are generally immune to potions of any kind. But Horace can eat your food. You said he was getting fat."

"Well, that's what Mother says, anyway," Millie said.

Sagara sat down at the table, plunking down her lunch bag. "So somehow, you have the power to affect spirits, allowing them to interact with physical matter. And it's always food?"

Millie nodded.

"Then I think you're definitely a witch. You just have an unusual talent," Sagara told her, "and it has something to do with food. You just have to figure out what it is."

Millie thought it just proved she couldn't get anything right, but it was nice of Sagara to say otherwise, so she smiled.

"Speaking of food, can we eat?" Max asked, glancing at Millie's messy cauldron. "Did Grumpkin steal everything?"

"He ate the oatmeal bread and chocolate chip cookies, and he ruined my asparagus. There's still some butternut squash soup, though," Millie told him, pulling out the flask.

Max groaned. "Chocolate chip? Awwww..."

"I should have known better," Millie said. "Chocolate always gets me in trouble."

"Well, I brought some kale salad and carrot rolls," Sagara offered.

"Mutton sandwiches and raspberry-rhubarb crumble," Petunia added, laying her box on the table.

Max pulled out more not-bread sandwiches, the bread smeared with jam and a nut paste, along with some wrinkled apples.

"That looks awful," Millie said.

"I'm used to it." Max bit into a sandwich and chewed slowly.

"Have some soup," Millie offered, pushing the flask over to him. "And from now on, I'm going to bring you lunch."

"We can all bring some extra lunch," Petunia said, "and we can share recipes."

"Speaking of which," said Sagara, "here's the cookbook you requested." She pushed a parchment scroll over to Millie.

Millie took the scroll and unrolled it a bit. "Oh, this isn't too hard," she said. "I don't know all the ingredients, though. I wish I'd brought my Elvish-Canto dictionary."

"You could just check one out of the school library," Sagara said.

Both Max and Millie turned to stare at her. "There's a library here?" Max said, his eyes round with greed.

"Where do you think I go every day during recess?" Sagara asked.

Petunia slapped her forehead. "Research! Of course you'd be in the library."

"What are you researching?" Max asked.

Sagara scowled. "You're awfully nosy. I happen to be researching the Logical Realm for an independent project.

Millie's head suddenly filled with information. The Logical

Realm was the strangest of all the many Realms of Earth because it had no magic at all. About six hundred years ago, people began to notice that magic seemed to be disappearing there, possibly due to the rise of logic and reason. Worried that this problem might spread to other Realms, the greatest wizards, witches, enchanters, sorceresses, demons, djinni, and other magicians of all kinds formed a coalition and separated the Logical Realm from all the other Realms in a vast, world-changing enchantment called the Great Sundering. All magic had been removed from the Logical Realm in the process.

There were some interesting side effects. Magic in all the Realms got stronger, but travel between the Realms got harder. Instead of being able to slip from one Realm to the next anywhere, anytime, people now had to use portals to move from Realm to Realm. There were portals that led to the Logical Realm, but they were sealed and guarded to prevent people from accidentally wandering across. Many people couldn't live without magic and would die there.

"Millie? Max? What's wrong?" Petunia took Millie's arm and shook her.

Millie blinked a few times. "I'm all right," she said. "Headmistress Pteria gave Max and me Remedial History potions. I think it just activated. I got a lesson on the Logical Realm, right inside my head."

Max was shaking his head. "Wow, what a weird place."

Sagara looked jealous. "Liquefied information. That's tricky magic. Headmistress Pteria is the leading expert on it. I wish she had a Logical Realm potion. Then I wouldn't have to do all this research." She considered that a moment. "But then I'd only get the information the Headmistress thinks is important. She might miss something. I'm better off doing it myself. But what I was saying, Millie, was that you should come with me to the library. Maybe you can figure out how to change Horace back into a normal ghost."

"Do you think so?" Millie asked.

The elf shrugged. "Couldn't hurt, could it?"

"It sounds like a good idea, and maybe I could help you with your research, too. That's only fair." Then Millie slumped. "I wish I could go with you, but I have to clean up the lab during recess."

"I'll help you," Petunia said. "It'll go faster with two of us, and then maybe we'll have time for the library before class."

Millie smiled at her. "Thanks, Petunia."

"I'll go to the library with Sagara," Max said eagerly. "I have some things I want to look up, myself. And I'll get you some books on transformations."

"If you're going to the lab, you might try asking Mistress Mallow. I bet she'd know how to change Horace back," Sagara pointed out. "Hmm, can I have some of that soup?"

Millie grinned. "Trade you for some kale."

When the lunch gong rang, all four of them headed for the stairs. Millie and Petunia stopped at the lab.

"The library's just a little farther up the stairs," Sagara said. "Come join us if you finish before recess is over."

"We'll be right there," Petunia said.

Millie followed her into the lab. None of the teachers were there, just a bucket of sudsy water and a mop. Millie grabbed the mop.

"Oh, don't bother," Petunia said. "I can fix this right up." She pulled a bit of the sparkling white powder from her pouch and sprinkled it over the mud and slime on the floor. "Slime of green, mud supreme, make this floor be squeaky clean!"

There was a faint pop, and the mess vanished, leaving a shiny, sparkling clean floor.

"More pixie dust?" Millie said. "I thought that was terribly rare."

"Not for pixies, silly," Petunia said.

"So, it just makes things happen?" Millie asked.

Petunia thought for a moment. "Nah, it sort of helps magic along. If I hadn't used the cleaning charm, nothing would have happened. Pixie dust just sort of, well, makes it easier, like oiling a door hinge."

"I wish I had some," Millie said. "Maybe I could actually get something right for once. I don't suppose you could spare any?"

Petunia shook her head. "I'm not allowed to give it away. Pixie code of honor. Besides," she said with a wink, "you'd probably just turn it into powdered sugar or something. Now, do you want to go to the library or not?"

They went a bit farther up the stairs and through a large arched entrance. Millie's mouth fell open as she entered. She hadn't known this many books existed. The walls of the room were lined with tall bookshelves, all full to bursting with books and scrolls. Shorter bookshelves formed a ring around a large scrying pool in the center of the room, and tables and desks were scattered between the ranks of shelves. Max and Sagara each sat at a table, poring through books. Next to the door, a dryad sat behind a very large desk, her hair a long trail of green leaves slightly lighter than the green teacher's cap on her head.

"Hello, Petunia," she said. "Who's your friend?"

Petunia gave her a short bow. "Hello, Mistress Willow. We've come to do some research. This is Millie. She just started school on Onesday."

"Welcome, Millie," said Mistress Willow. "Let me give you a tour."

"M-maybe another time," Millie said. "I would love one,

but right now, I need to research transformation potions."

Mistress Willow smiled. "Please come with me."

She led Millie over to a bookshelf marked Potions and Possets. "I'm not sure how much information you need. Here is an elementary text on potions, and here is another on potions that affect the material world, and here's a specific text about transformations, although it's rather advanced."

Millie took them gratefully. "Thank you, Mistress." She sat at a nearby table and began flipping through the elementary text, but it was all basic stuff that Millie had already learned from her mother. She tried the advanced text book and was almost immediately lost in explanations of what existence and transformation meant and the conversion rates between different materials. But the material potions book made a kind of sense, and she delved into it. Before long, she found a section on animal transformations, particularly frogs.

The classic frog prince potion is especially tricky, as it must cause two transformations: once into a frog, and again to regain the subject's original form. Thus, the potion must be left in an unfinished state. By adding the final ingredient (for example, true love's kiss), the second transformation is triggered, and the spell is completed. This elegant solution is what makes a frog prince enchantment so hard to dispel. Because the spell is ongoing, it is exceedingly difficult to cancel.

"Oh," Millie breathed. *A bit of orange peel to season chocolate sauce.* Maybe all she needed to change Horace back was orange peel.

The recess gong rang. "Time to go back to class," Mistress Willow called out. "Please bring me any books you'd like to check out."

"You mean we can take these home?" Max asked.

"For a few days," Mistress Willow told him.

Millie brought the material potions book to the librarian's

desk. Petunia was checking out a book of riddles and giggling to herself. Max put down a book on magical methods of storing information. Sagara hung back, waiting for the others to finish.

As Millie left the library, she paused and peeked back through the archway. Sagara had a large book with an intimidating title: **Portal Mechanics and the Practical Aspects of Realm Travel.** Sagara quickly tucked the book into her robe, out of sight.

Millie spent the afternoon in Forest Cultures class, talking about fairy culture and flower husbandry. Fairies ate only nuts, berries, and flower nectar, and their techniques for harvesting and processing the nectar were fascinating. After that, High Mystery was downright boring. Millie knew a fair amount of High Mystery already, and she could care less about verb tenses and mystical grammar.

The final gong rang. Millie collected her cauldron, still stuffed with dripping wet clothes, tucked the Elvish cooking scroll and the transformation book under one arm, and started down the stairs. Halfway there, Grumpkin blocked her way.

Millie froze. "Grumpkin, I said I was sorry, and I'm out of cookies for you to steal."

Grumpkin touched a finger to his lips, looked nervously up the stairway, then behind him. Finally, he grunted and looked Millie in the eye. He seemed confused, terrified, and... concerned? "Be careful," he whispered. "She's watching. She knows about your brother. Tell him to take the long way home."

"Who's watching?" Millie asked loudly.

"SHHHHH!" Grumpkin motioned for her to come closer. "You didn't hear this from me, understand?" the goblin said.

Millie nodded and leaned closer to him.

Grumpkin put his mouth close to her ear and whispered, "*Cretacia.*"

Millie's stomach clenched. Cretacia? Here? She opened her mouth to speak, but Grumpkin shook his head vigorously, then turned and dashed down the stairs.

"What was all that about?" asked Petunia behind her. "Was he being mean to you? I'll go kick him in the Salivary Swamp."

"No," Millie said, not quite believing it herself. "I think he was trying to help me."

Petunia's eyebrows shot up. "He *what?* No goblin ever helps anyone unless there's something in it for him."

"It was weird," Millie admitted. "I don't think he actually wanted to. It was almost as if he couldn't help himself."

"Who couldn't help himself?" asked Max, shouldering past a centaur.

"Grumpkin. He says that Cretacia is watching us and knows you're here at school."

Max's face turned the color of chalk. "I thought I was so careful. I was sure she didn't follow me. What am I going to do? I don't want Dad to pull me out of school."

"You need a likely explanation for being here," Petunia said. "Something other than going to school."

"Me!" Millie squeaked. "You came here to see me, since Mother won't bring me to see you. That's a plausible explanation. It's even mostly true."

Max nodded. "That might work. In fact, it'll be even better if I give you another ride home today."

Petunia jumped up and down, clapping her hands. "Flying carpet, flying carpet!"

"But don't you have a lesson with your father?" Millie pointed out.

He shrugged. "I'll be late. That's pretty normal."

"Then, sure," said Millie, grinning. "I'm happy to help with your cover story."

They made their way down the stairs and into the glade, where they returned to their normal sizes. Max unrolled the carpet, and they climbed aboard. This time, Max took them at a pleasant pace, following the Path.

"Thanks for taking it slow this time," Millie told him.

He gave her a slightly terrified smile. "I'm not just doing it for you. I want to be sure Cretacia sees me, in case Grumpkin was lying."

"You think he was trying to fool us?" Petunia piped up from Millie's shoulder.

Millie shook her head. "That doesn't make sense. How could he tell us about Cretacia if he didn't already know her? My guess is that Grumpkin's family has a contract with Aunt Hepsibat. Basically, that would make Grumpkin Cretacia's minion."

"Hey, am I your minion?" Petunia asked.

"Nope, there's no contract between us," Millie said. "You're my friend, which is much better."

The flying carpet slowed to a stop just up the Path from Millie's house. "Thanks, Max. And good luck with Cretacia."

Max nodded. "I think I'll go visit my friend Sylvester instead of heading home, just in case Cretacia wasn't watching the school. That should confuse my trail a bit."

Petunia slid down Millie's arm. "See you tomorrow!" she cried, and she dashed down the Path to Pixamitchie.

"Tomorrow, then," Millie said. "Good luck, Max." She watched Max take off, soaring up and over the Forest. And for just a moment, she thought she spied someone on a broomstick, flying low through the leafy canopy. But when she blinked, it was gone.

Millie gave her neighbor the elm tree a curtsy before she

went through the kitchen gate. "Horace," she called as she opened the kitchen door. "Horace, I think I can fix you."

Horace hopped through the pantry door and croaked, "Really? You think so?"

"Maybe," said Millie, showing him the book. "I've been studying transformations." She hurried over to her cupboard and pulled out a slice of dried orange peel, then knelt down and offered it to Horace. "Here, this might do it."

"Orange peel?" Horace said dubiously. "Well, all right." His long tongue darted out, licking right through the peel and Millie's hand. Horace tried several times, then sat back. "How long should it take?" he asked.

"I'm not sure," Millie replied. "I thought it was supposed to happen immediately." She waited a few more moments, then sighed. "Oh, Horace, I'm sorry. It must be more complicated than I thought. I'll read more of the book tonight and see if I can figure it out."

Horace puffed out his cheeks, then blew out a long breath. "Well, at least you're working on it. Bogdana won't even try. Thanks, Millie." He looked up at her. "I don't suppose you could bake something yummy for dinner?"

"Of course," Millie said, relieved that Horace was talking to her again. "What would you like?"

Horace smiled at her. "Something chocolate, of course."

Chapter 10
Cretacia and Cacao

Millie and Max expected Cretacia to show up at school at any moment, but over the next two weeks, she never appeared. Gradually, Millie slipped into a routine. Realizing that everyone had seen her without her mud and slime mold, Millie stopped bothering to dress up and went to school looking the way she normally did, in a simple dress with an apron and her comfortable clogs. She combed out her hair and trimmed all her nails with relief. When Grumpkin teased her for giving up all pretense of being a witch, she ignored him. And he let her, which was a little weird.

Millie continued bringing extra food for her friends, especially baked goods such as blueberry muffins, apricot bars, and cinnamon rolls. Sagara brought Elvish delicacies for her to try, and Petunia brought fresh fruits, the most important part of the pixie diet. Gradually, Max gave up bringing lunch; it was so horrible no one would eat it, including him.

Millie's sprout continued to grow, gradually shrugging off its husk and putting out new leaves. It was obviously not a normal bean plant, but Millie had grown fond of it and watered it faithfully every day. Millie got better at her classes, though she continued messing up her spells, turning a courage potion into chicken soup and coating the stone she was trying to levitate in meringue. It didn't surprise her that she was starting to get a reputation among the teachers as "that witch girl who turns everything into food."

The one bright spot in her classes came from Master Augustus. During Independent Work period on her second Twosday, he brought her a small notebook. It was labeled, "Millie's Journal."

"Millie, I'd like you to start writing in this journal every day. You can write about whatever you like," he told her.

Millie thumbed through it, loving the feel of the blank pages. "Can I write down my favorite recipes?" she asked.

Master Augustus laughed. "Somehow, I'd be surprised if you didn't."

Encouraged, she began experimenting with the Elvish recipes she'd gotten from Sagara. After a week or so, she thought she was ready to tackle the hardest recipe in the book.

Foursday dawned bright and clear with the fresh scent of the previous night's rain. Millie slipped into a pale blue dress and tied on an apron over it, as she usually did. Ignoring the bubbling jar of green slime in the bathroom, she washed her face, brushed her hair, and tied it back with a token bit of black lace. Then she skipped down to the kitchen to check on the dough she'd left rising overnight.

There was no sign of Bogdana, as usual, but Horace hopped anxiously next to the bowl, draped with a towel to keep it fresh, which had risen like a bubble about to pop. "What is this, Millie?" the ghost asked. "I've never smelled anything like it."

"You'll see," Millie said with a smile. Pulling off the towel, she worked quickly, rolling and shaping and smacking cakes onto baking sheets. She felt her fingers tingling with happiness as she slid the sheets into the oven. While they baked, she poached some eggs and sautéed some mushrooms and tomatoes.

At last, Millie pulled the sheets from the oven. Horace gaped. "Breccckkk! Are those what I think they are?" Millie nodded. "Elfcakes! I made them especially for my friend Sagara."

"I thought only elves could make elfcakes," Horace said. Millie shrugged. "Here, try one." With a spatula, she lifted a crispy cake off the baking sheet and slid it onto a plate, then set it on the floor. Horace's tongue darted out, tearing chunks out of the cake. "Mmmmmm..." he croaked.

Millie made herself a pot of tea and had an elfcake with eggs, mushrooms, and tomatoes. The elfcake was light and fluffy yet flat, unlike any cake or scone or muffin she'd ever made. More like a pancake, but richer, more full of flavor. Still, Millie thought she could improve upon it with practice.

"That was delicious, Millie," Horace said. He hesitated, then asked, "Do you think you can fix me today?"

"I'll do my best," Millie said. "I'm going to try to talk to the potions teacher today. Mistress Mallow might know what I did wrong. She's been out sick for the past two weeks, but I heard that she'd be back today."

Horace nodded. "That sounds good." He watched her pack her lunch, frowning at the number of elfcakes she packed into the cauldron on top of her slice of leftover eel pie. "You're not going to take all of those, are you?"

"Don't worry," she told him, tucking a layer of wax paper over the elfcakes to keep them dry. "There are plenty more for you and M-mother today. And if you eat them all, I'll just make more tomorrow. No school on Endsday, you know."

Horace nodded. "Good. I miss you when you're at school."

"Millie! Come on!" came Petunia's voice from the kitchen gate.

"See you tonight, Horace," Millie said.

"Have a good day," he replied as she dashed out the door, cauldron swinging.

Max was waiting nervously in the glade when Millie arrived at school, Petunia perched on her shoulder. "Cretacia's up to something," he said, clutching his flying carpet. "She was nice to me all morning, and she only does that when she's got something really wicked planned for me."

Millie glanced around the glade, but she saw no sign of a witch's pointed hat or Cretacia's signature braids. She did, however, spy Grumpkin. He was surrounded by a cluster of goblins, all chattering away, but he kept glancing over his shoulder, as though he was waiting for something.

The gong rang. "Come on," Petunia said. "She can't get to you in school."

They hurried up the stairs to their classrooms. Petunia and Max peeled off and headed into their class. Millie went farther up the stairs to Master Augustus's room. She could hardly wait to tell Sagara about the elfcakes. She walked through the archway and stopped short.

There, chatting amiably with Master Augustus, was Cretacia in her full witchy finery: hat, dress, braids, warts and all.

"Ah, good morning, Millie," Master Augustus called out. "It seems word has gotten out about you attending our school, and it inspired Cretacia here to visit our school for the day."

Cretacia looked Millie over from head to toe, a delighted, horrible grin cracking open her face. "Well, Millie. How *nice* to see you." Millie's stomach tied itself into knots.

"Since you are cousins, Millie, I thought you could

be Cretacia's buddy today and show her around," Master Augustus went on.

"Um, of course," said Millie, determined not to let Cretacia see how upset she was. "I'd be happy to."

"Good, good," said Master Augustus. "Now, put your things away, and let's get ready for circle time." He hurried off.

"Well, well," said Cretacia. "It seems that school has been good for you, Millie. You've clearly given up any pretense of being a witch and accepted your fate as a talentless nothing."

Millie clenched her fists. "I'm a p-perfectly good w-witch, Cretacia, and I'm doing f-fine here at school."

"That's not what I hear," said Cretacia, glancing at Grumpkin as he came in. Grumpkin ducked his head, throwing his lunch sack in his cubby and hurrying over to the growing circle of students. "I understand you've done absolutely nothing right since you got here."

Millie had to unclench her teeth to say, "It's circle time. Come on, we're going to be late."

Millie found Sagara and sat next to her, while Master Augustus called Cretacia over to him and introduced her to the class.

"This is Max's evil stepsister?" Sagara whispered to Millie as the rest of the class called out, "Hello, Cretacia!"

Millie nodded. "She hasn't said anything about Max yet, but I'm pretty sure Grumpkin's her minion. He must have told her about Max."

"Grumpkin," Sagara said in a voice that would have curdled milk. "Did I ever tell you how miserable he made me when I started here?"

"No, but I can imagine," Millie said.

"Now, Cretacia, why don't you tell us about yourself?" Master Augustus asked.

Cretacia plastered a sweet smile over her face. "Well, as

you know, I'm a witch, the best of all the apprentice witches in our Coven. I started riding my broomstick when I was six, and I enchanted my own hat when I was eight. The *true* mark of a witch is her hat, you know." She stroked the brim of her hat for emphasis. "I am also *exceptionally* talented at curses." She met the eyes of each student in the circle, and Millie watched them wither under her gaze. But Millie met her eyes defiantly, and so did Sagara. Cretacia just smiled a little broader, recognizing a challenge.

"Millie has already told us a bit about witch culture," Master Augustus said, "so why don't you tell us about your family?"

"Oh, of course," Cretacia said. "My mother, Hepsibat, is an extremely talented witch who specializes in animation spells. She makes the best golems in the Forest. I'm sure she's next in line to Baba Luci, the leader of our Coven."

Millie wanted to throw her clogs at Cretacia's head, but she kept herself still.

"I live with my mother," Cretacia went on, "and with my stepfather Alfonso Salazar, a pasty, old wizard, and his idiot son, Max."

Millie shot to her feet. "He is NOT an idiot!" she yelled. "He's got more talent in his little finger than you have in your whole body!"

"Millie, sit down!" Master Augustus ordered. Millie sat in a huff. "And Cretacia, insults are not appropriate in school."

"My apologies," Cretacia said. "It's quite normal in witch culture to trade insults. It's like a friendly handshake."

"Very interesting," said Master Augustus, "but please be more considerate of others."

"Yes, yes, certainly," Cretacia agreed.

"You may sit down," Master Augustus told her. Cretacia walked around the circle and chose a spot next to Grumpkin, glaring at the imp next to him until she scooted over and made space for Cretacia to sit. Grumpkin looked as miserable as Millie felt.

"All right, class," Master Augustus continued. "It's Foursday, and that means finishing up your independent work today." A groan rose from the circle. "Now, now. If you've been keeping up with your lessons, you'll be done in plenty of time. I expect all of you to have completed your journal writing and vocabulary exercises. We'll have a short spelling quiz before Arithmancy." More groans. "All right, class. Let's get busy!"

The students variously leapt or tumbled to their feet and dispersed around the room to pick up their work. Cretacia sauntered over to Millie. "Well, Millie? Are you going to give me the grand tour?" She glanced at Sagara. "You're an Arela, aren't you? What a fall for you — a princess among swine."

A dizzy spell came over Millie as Remedial History unspooled in her head, explaining that the Arela clan of elves was a ruling clan, once quite important but waning in power. Sagara wasn't quite a princess, but she was close.

Sagara drew herself up and opened her mouth to speak, but Millie shook her head in warning. So Sagara said, "Indeed. And here you are with us." And she turned and marched stiffly away.

Cretacia frowned. Quickly, Millie said, "Over here are the map boards, where we learn the geography of the different realms."

"How *cute*," Cretacia said. "Does it include the Logical Realm?"

Millie shook her head. "Too weird, I guess. Over here is the book nook, where you can do your reading work or just read for fun."

Cretacia sneered. "Who would ever read for fun?" She glanced over at the pots on the windowsill and smiled. "Now what's that over there?"

"Oh," Millie said, embarrassed. "That's a botany project. We're growing beans."

"And which one is yours?"

Millie shoved her hands into her apron pockets to keep from hitting her cousin. "It's the brown one."

Cretacia eyed it critically. "It looks different from the others. What's wrong with it?"

"NOTHING IS WRONG WITH IT."

Cretacia nearly jumped out of her shoes.

"Ah," said Master Augustus, trotting over, "allow me to introduce our Caretaker, Master Quercius."

Quercius's face had appeared in the large branch forming the top of the window frame.

"GREETINGS, CRETACIA NOCTMARTIS. BE WELCOME IN MY BRANCHES."

Millie had never seen Cretacia so thoroughly disconcerted. "Um, thank you, Master Caretaker."

"NOW, THE BEAN. MILLIE, YOU'VE DONE SOMETHING I HAVE NEVER SEEN IN THIS SCHOOL BEFORE, AND THAT IS SAYING SOMETHING," Quercius told her. "LOOK CLOSELY AT YOUR SPROUT. WHAT IS DIFFERENT ABOUT IT?"

Millie peered at her pot. "It's larger than the other sprouts were. And darker. It smells different, too. More like," she sniffed briefly, "like bananas."

Cretacia had regained her composure. "You planted a banana tree instead? Well, that's just like you, always messing things up."

"IT IS NOT A BANANA TREE," Quercius told them. "IT IS STILL A BEAN, JUST A VERY DIFFERENT BEAN. TELL ME, MILLIE. WHAT IS YOUR FAVORITE TYPE OF BEAN?"

"Cacao," Millie answered promptly. Then she covered her mouth with her hands. "No," she mumbled. "It couldn't be." "YOU ARE CORRECT. THAT IS A VERY YOUNG AND SOMEWHAT CONFUSED CACAO SPROUT. I HAVE BEEN REASSURING HER ALL MORNING, LETTING HER KNOW THAT SHE WILL BE WELL CARED FOR AND LOVED." Cretacia frowned. "Why would you plant a cacao bean? I'd expect you to make chocolate out of it first."

"I d-didn't plant a cacao bean," Millie said. "I'm s-s-sure of it. I planted a regular b-bean like everyone else."

"And you tried quite a few different spells and charms to help it grow," said Master Augustus. "But none of those would have transformed a regular green bean into a cacao bean. Did you do anything else? Anything related to cacao?"

Millie thought back to that first Onesday. It seemed like years ago. "I... I just remember thinking that I wished it had been chocolate. I'd have known what to do with chocolate."

"AND DID YOU FEEL ANYTHING WHEN YOU THOUGHT THAT?"

Millie gazed down at the little sprout. "I felt a little, um, tingly."

Cretacia threw her a disgusted look. "And that didn't tell you anything? Idiot."

"Cretacia," said Master Augustus. "Remember our talk about insults."

"Oh, yes, sorry," she replied distractedly.

"MILLIE, I BELIEVE THAT YOU TRANSFORMED YOUR ORDINARY GARDEN BEAN INTO A CACAO BEAN."

"I did?" Millie said in a small voice.

"YOU DID. AND BECAUSE SHE SPROUTED HERE, IN MY BRANCHES, SHE WILL BE A SPECIAL

KIND OF CACAO TREE. SHE IS ALREADY SELF-AWARE, WHICH MOST TREES DO NOT ACHIEVE UNTIL THEY ARE SEVERAL YEARS OLD. IN TIME, SHE WILL DEVELOP THE ABILITY TO USE MAGIC. SHE WILL WALK AND TALK. IN SHORT, SHE WILL BE A DODONAS, LIKE ME. HER NAME IS THEA." Remedial History flared in Millie's mind. The Dodonoi were an exceedingly rare race of intelligent, powerful tree-like beings. Very little was known about their culture or habits because there were so few of them, and young Dodonoi were precious and closely guarded. Quercius was the best known Dodonos in the Enchanted Forest, and he was — Millie gasped — over two thousand years old.

Millie glanced up at him, startled. "You can walk?"

Quercius laughed. "I DID, ONCE. I WANDERED ACROSS ALL THE MANY REALMS. NOW, HOWEVER, I AM TOO LARGE TO TRAVEL EASILY. I HAVE SETTLED HERE, AND HERE I WILL LIKELY REMAIN UNTIL THE END OF MY DAYS." The great Dodonos sighed, and a little ripple ran through his branches. "I NEVER THOUGHT I WOULD HAVE A CHILD. THANK YOU, MILLIE, FOR PRESENTING ME WITH THE OPPORTUNITY, UNUSUAL AND COMPLICATED AS IT IS."

"Complicated?" Cretacia butted in. "She messed this up, too, didn't she?"

"HARDLY," said Master Quercius. "IT MERELY LEAVES ME WITH A QUANDARY. CACAO TREES NEED CERTAIN CONDITIONS IN WHICH TO GROW AND THRIVE. ORDINARILY, THE SHADE OF MY BRANCHES WOULD BE IDEAL, BUT MY GLADE IS A BUSY, MUCH USED PART OF THE SCHOOL AND NOT SUITED TO RAISING AN INFANT DODONAS.

THERE ARE THREE OTHER DODONOI IN THE ENCHANTED FOREST, BUT TWO ARE SIMILARLY OCCUPIED WITH IMPORTANT BUSINESS, AND THE THIRD IS STILL IN HER JOURNEYMAN PHASE, WHEREAS THEA MUST REMAIN STATIONARY FOR AT LEAST THE FIRST TWO YEARS OF HER LIFE. WE MUST FIND HER A SUITABLE HOME."

"Can't she just go live with other cacao trees?" Cretacia asked.

"I CAN MAKE ARRANGEMENTS TO SEND HER TO A CACAO FARM IN ANOTHER REALM, BUT I WOULD PREFER THAT SHE STAY NEAR TO ME, SO THAT I MAY INSTRUCT HER IN THE WAYS OF THE DODONOI."

Millie reached out and gently touched a tiny leaf, and she felt a tingle go through her again, and a feeling of quiet joy. Considering carefully, Millie said, "Well, we have a nice big backyard, and it's shaded by a lovely, kind elm tree. Mother's wards are very strong, so no one would bother her, and I could keep her company when I'm not at school. It would be a little like having a sister." Millie liked that idea. "I'd have to get Mother's permission, though."

"YOU ARE KIND TO OFFER. I THINK THIS IS A GOOD SOLUTION. WITH YOUR PERMISSION, I WILL SCRY YOUR MOTHER TO INQUIRE WHETHER THIS IS ACCEPTABLE."

Millie gulped. "Could I t-talk to her first, please?"

"CERTAINLY," said Quercius. "PLEASE INFORM ME OF YOUR DECISION ON ONESDAY."

Cretacia sniffed. "Millie will probably kill it. She messes everything up."

"Well, if this is how Millie messes up," Master Augustus said, "I hope she keeps on doing it. The world needs more

Dodonoi and more unusual results."

"Hmph," said Cretacia. "She still didn't do it right." And she stomped off.

Master Augustus cocked his head. "Rather competitive, your cousin."

"You have no idea," Millie said.

"MILLIE, COULD YOU PLEASE BRING THEA TO MISTRESS MALLOW? SHE IS SKILLED IN GARDEN MAGIC AND HAS PREPARED A PLACE FOR THEA UNTIL YOU HAVE OBTAINED PERMISSION TO KEEP HER."

"Of course, Caretaker," Millie said.

"Please come back in time for Arithmancy at ten-thirty," Master Augustus said.

"I will." Millie picked up the pot. "Hello, Thea. We're going to be friends, you and I."

In response, the sprout unfurled a new leaf.

Millie carried the pot up the stairs to the laboratory, where Mistress Mallow was waiting. "Goodness gracious me," said the brownie. "I never thought I'd live to see a Dodonas sprouting. They're terribly rare and secretive, you know. Bring her over here."

Millie brought Thea to a small side table in a shadowy corner of the room. A slab of black slate lay on the table, and when Millie set the pot down on it, she found it was pleasantly warm.

"Eighty degrees," Mistress Mallow said. "Just the right temperature for a cacao tree."

Millie thought she could hear Thea sigh in contentment, and the little sprout stretched up a bit more.

"Growing fast," Mistress Mallow said. "We'll have to repot her soon." She turned to Millie. "Now, suppose you tell me just what's going on with your magic."

Millie blushed. "I don't know, really. I always get things muddled."

"Hmm, that's so, but muddled in the right way, I'd say. I tried that chamomile tea you made in class nearly two weeks ago. Slept so deep I didn't wake up until yesterday."

Millie clapped her hands to her cheeks. "Oh, I'm so sorry, M-m-mistress!"

The brownie smiled kindly at her. "Don't be. I tested the tea quite thoroughly first, you know, and determined that it was, in fact, a sleeping potion. It gave me the best sleep I've had in months, soothing and restful as sleep is meant to be, rather than just knocking me out. That's subtle magic."

"Oh," said Millie. "But I didn't mean to."

"So I gathered," Mistress Mallow quipped. "Now tell me what happened in fussy old Pym's class. You turned your insect repellent charm into honey, correct?"

"Yes, that one really didn't work at all," Millie said sadly.

"But it's very similar to what you did with both the tea and the bean. In just about every case, you transform what you're supposed to be doing into a food. Tell me, Millie. Do you like to cook?"

Millie couldn't help it. She started laughing. And laughing. When she couldn't stop, Mistress Mallow made her sit down and thumped her on the back. Gasping, she nodded, tears streaming down her face. "Yes, Mistress. I like to cook. I LOVE to cook. It's what I love doing most of all."

Mistress Mallow glanced up at the clock on the wall. "Bother. It's time you went back to class. But I want more time to talk to you, and to the Headmistress. Something curious is going on with your magic. Can you meet me in Pteria's office during recess?"

"Yes, of course," Millie said. "I had a question for you anyway."

"Then off you go," Mistress Mallow said. "And don't worry. I'll take good care of Thea for you."

Chapter 11
Elfcakes and Pizza

Millie thought that Arithmancy would never end. Cretacia mercilessly mocked everyone in class. Under Master Augustus's watchful eye, she didn't insult anyone, but she was bitingly sarcastic. "Oh, poor little dryad," she cooed at Izzy. "You should be careful about thinking so hard, your wooden head might catch fire." Millie wished that Sagara was there to put Cretacia in her place, but of course Sagara studied arithmancy with the more advanced students in another classroom.

By the end of the lesson, Millie was completely wrung out with anger and worry. As soon as the lunch gong rang, she ran to her cubby, grabbed her cauldron, and dashed down the stairs, not even waiting for Master Augustus to dismiss them.

Somehow, Sagara had contrived to reach their table first. "Arithmancy's still too easy in the advanced class," she said. "They aren't even up to basic algebra yet." Her eyes narrowed. "How's Cretacia at math?"

Millie blinked. "I don't actually know. She was too busy making fun of everyone else."

"Ha!" Sagara said. "She's probably terrible at it and just covering herself."

"I can't imagine Cretacia being terrible at magic. She's the best apprentice witch in our Coven."

"I'll bet you she's not nearly as good as she pretends to be," Sagara said. "Wait. Do I smell elfcakes?"

Max and Petunia dashed up. "Millie, I saw Cretacia! She's here!" cried Max.

"I know," Millie told him. "She's been in my class all day."

"Oh, no, here she comes," Max groaned. Cretacia was stalking through the lunch tables, headed right for them. "Quick, everyone sit down. I'll put up a ward."

Hastily, they all took their seats. Max pulled out his wand. *"Hiljaisuuskupla,"* he intoned dramatically, waving the wand in a circle around his head before pointing straight up. A shimmering curtain extended from the tip of his wand, surrounding them in a faint dome. All sounds from the crowded glade abruptly stopped.

"Dome of Silence," said Sagara, looking grudgingly impressed.

Cretacia ran up to them and pounded on the dome, shouting something, but none of them could hear her. Her face turned bright red, and she made menacing arm motions at Max.

"I can see why you're good at this," Petunia said.

Max put his head down on the table, slightly crushing his hat. "I'll pay for it, I always do. Usually, she just gives me hives, but this time, I am doomed. Finished. Defeated. Cretacia's going to go straight home and tell my father everything, and I'll never be able to come back."

Petunia balled her fists. "I'll take care of that nasty Cretacia."

Millie shook her head. "Trust me, that just makes it worse. I've found the best thing to do is just ignore her." She pointedly turned away from Cretacia.

The others followed suit. After a few more minutes of silent rage, Cretacia folded her arms and stalked away. Max heaved a sigh of relief. "It worked."

Petunia eyed the shimmering dome. "I wish I could do this sometimes, when I have ten brothers and sisters all pouncing on me."

"Doesn't your mother stop them?" Millie asked.

Petunia shook her head. "Mum expects us to solve our own problems."

"Ahem," Sagara said. "Millie, I believe I asked you a very, very important question."

"About Cretacia and math?"

Sagara rolled her eyes. "No, about ELFCAKES."

Max's head popped up. "I thought I smelled something good."

"Mmm, me, too," Petunia said.

Millie dropped her cauldron on the table, took off the wax paper, and pulled out handfuls of elfcakes, about a dozen in all.

Sagara gasped. "Oak and ash. I thought I was dreaming. Where did you get them?"

Millie smiled at her. "Come on, Sagara. You gave me the cookbook. I made them."

Sagara stared at her. "Only elves can make elfcakes," she declared. "You can't possibly have done this."

"It was a tough recipe to translate, but I think I figured it out. Why don't you taste them and tell me if I got it right?"

Hesitantly, Sagara reached out and took a cake. Then she bit into it, closed her eyes, and sighed. "They're a little sweeter than my mother's but, yes, they're real elfcakes." And she devoured the whole cake and licked her fingers after. Max and Petunia looked at Millie pleadingly. "Go ahead," she said. "Help yourselves."

Everyone sat down and began the serious business of eating. Petunia passed around strawberries and watercress sandwiches. Sagara offered a mix of nuts, seeds, and dried fruits along with a green salad. Max pulled out a wax paper packet containing bizarre, triangular pieces of flat bread coated with tomato sauce and topped with melted cheese. "Surprise!" he said. "I brought something to share for once." Petunia eyed them dubiously. "What is that stuff?"

Max shrugged. "Dad calls it pizza. It's not bad, better than a lot of his food."

Sagara finished her third elfcake and sat back with a contented sigh. "Those were marvelous," she said. "But I still don't understand how you could have made them. Who taught you elf magic?"

"No one," Millie said. "I just followed the recipe."

Slowly Sagara said, "Millie, that wasn't just a recipe. It was a spell. Elfcakes rise by magic, and complex magic at that. Even I haven't mastered it, or I'd have been making my own cakes ages ago."

Millie gaped at her. "I thought it was an odd recipe," she said. "All that clockwise stirring and rhythmic kneading. But it didn't seem magical to me at all."

"Millie!" Petunia squealed excitedly. "Do you know what this means! You cast a spell, and you got it right!"

Millie's stomach expanded, feeling light as air, despite all the elfcakes. Could it be true? Had she really done magic, correctly and properly? Millie looked down at the elfcake crumbs and blushed. "Actually, I don't think it was my first success." And she told them about Thea and the chamomile tea.

"You see?" Max said. "I knew it all along. You're a kitchen witch. You do food magic."

Petunia scratched her nose. "Except sorta backwards. My mum does some kitchen magic. Usually, you take food and turn it into something else or make it do more than just fill you up. Millie takes other stuff and turns it into food."

"That is weird," said Sagara, picking up elfcake crumbs with her fingers. "Transformation is a pretty advanced skill, but that's what you've started with."

"Hmm. We have Thaumaturgy this afternoon," Max pointed out.

Everyone groaned. Though it was the one class they all had together, Millie dreaded it because Master Bertemious was the most boring teacher ever. He droned on and on about thaumaturgical principles and philosophy. "Thaumaturgy is the magic of likeness. How is a mushroom like a moonbeam? How is a raven like a writing desk? Understanding these connections is the key to powerful magic, which you will learn to channel and control."

"Hey, it could be an opportunity for Millie to figure out her talent," Max said. "In thaumaturgy, you use water drops to call rain and push rocks to move mountains, because on some level they're the same. Millie seems to find how something is like food and then changes it into that food."

Sagara raised her eyebrows. "You're right. That will be interesting. Now, about this pizza of yours."

"Oh, would you like some?" Max offered her a slice.

"No, thanks, full of elfcakes," Sagara said. "But I've had pizza before. Guess where."

Max shrugged. "A friend's house?"

Sagara glanced around her, then leaned forward. "No. I ate pizza in the Logical Realm."

Stunned silence fell on the table. Max actually stopped eating for a moment.

Petunia set down her watercress sandwich. "You've been to the Logical Realm? That is so not allowed. How did you do it?"

"I'll tell you, but only if you swear not to tell anyone else," Sagara said.

"Fine, I swear," Petunia replied.

Sagara held out her pinky. "Swear for real."

"What do you call a paranoid Sagara?" Petunia asked. "A stealth elf."

"Swear," Sagara growled.

Quickly, Millie linked her pinkie with Sagara's. "I swear." She felt a weird tingle go up her arm as she let go.

"Fine," Petunia said, linking pinkies. "I swear, too."

Max looked dubious. "How do I know you're not dissimulating?" he asked.

Sagara grinned at him. "Now *you're* prevaricating. Don't you want to know about the pizza?"

Max fidgeted, turned red, and finally reached out his pinky finger. "Curiosity will be my doom. Fine, I swear."

"My irritating, perfect brother brought me to see my mom. He actually blindfolded me, the jerk." Sagara stabbed at elfcake crumbs with her finger.

"Then the rumors are true?" Millie asked. "Your mother lost all her magic and had to go to the Logical Realm?"

Sagara rolled her eyes. "She didn't lose her magic. She went there on purpose."

Max's mouth fell open. "Why would anyone do that? Who'd want to live in a place with no magic, powerless?"

"Better ask your dad that," Sagara said, nodding at the pizza. "I'm pretty sure he goes there all the time."

"What?" Max screeched. "That's absurd. Impossible. Inconceivable!"

"Then why do you keep bringing Logical Realm food to lunch?" Sagara asked sweetly. "Peanut butter on white bread, pizza, and you mentioned Thai food in little boxes. That's called take-out. My brother told me all about it."

"Your brother goes to the Logical Realm?" Millie asked.

Sagara nodded. "He's part of the species preservation team. Without magic to help them, many of the plant and animal species there are dying out. My brother collects endangered plants and brings them here, or even to other Realms."

Petunia's eyes grew big as saucers. "He does that without magic? Sounds dangerous!"

"Oh, puh-lease," Sagara said. "Not you, too. My whole family goes on and on about what a hero he is. But none of them know that he's really doing it so he can see Mom."

Millie was confused. "Sagara, why are you telling us this? Aren't you putting both your brother and mother at risk?"

"Well, I made you swear. Also, we're in a Dome of Silence," Sagara pointed out. "Thanks for that, by the way," she told Max. "I know Quercius is different, but every other tree I know is a terrible gossip. They'd spread the news faster than you can fly."

"My pleasure," Max murmured, staring at his pizza.

"Also, well..." Sagara bit her lip. "I need your help."

"Uh oh," Petunia said. "To do what, exactly?"

Sagara straightened her back. "I want to go to the Logical Realm to be with my mother."

"To visit?" Millie asked.

"No. I want to run away from home."

Chapter 12

The Chocolate in Trouble

Petunia snorted. "You just want to get away from your grandmother."

"Well, yes, duh," Sagara said. "And I want to be with my mother. But also, there are some really interesting things happening in the Logical Realm. They've learned to do things without magic that we've never imagined, most of it using math. That's why my mother left to live there. And I want to learn about it, too."

"But, you'll be infected! You'll become logical and lose all your magic!" Petunia cried.

"Indubitably," Max added.

Sagara laughed. "Doesn't seem to affect your dad. I checked up on him. He's one of the most powerful wizards in the Enchanted Forest and several other Realms." She put her palms down on the table. "I don't think logic and magic are incompatible. They're just two different ways of getting things done. What I want," and the elf's eyes began to gleam, "is to find ways to combine them, to use the strengths of both disciplines, together."

"Hmm, sort of like combining two recipes," Millie said. She enjoyed doing that.

Sagara shook her head violently. "No, more like using recipes to... to build bridges. Or using music to plant crops."

Petunia shrugged. "Just sounds like more magic to me."

"Regardless, travel to the Logical Realm is very dangerous," Max insisted. "You can be lost between Realms! And even if you do get there, you'll lose all your magic, and there's a good chance you'll never get home."

"I think it's worth the risk. Will you help me?" Sagara looked at each of them, pleading.

Millie nodded. "What do you need us to do?"

"Right now, I need help with research," Sagara said. "I need to figure out where the nearest portal to the Logical Realm is. Max, your dad probably knows. I'd like you to look through his notes, see if you can find anything out."

"Gadzooks!" Max exclaimed. "If Dad finds me going through his notes, he'll skin me alive. Besides, all his notes are in..." He paused, thunderstruck. "They're all in English."

"Told you so," Sagara said smugly. She turned to Millie. "Millie, you're one of the fastest readers I've ever met. Could you help me read through books on Realm travel and figure out how to open the portal?"

Millie nodded. "Sure, that sounds interesting."

"What about me?" asked Petunia.

"Two things," said Sagara. "I need you to keep an eye on our enemies. If the goblins figure out what we're doing..."

"Or Cretacia," Max added gloomily.

"I'm on it!" Petunia said, looking fierce. "What's the other thing?"

Sagara looked embarrassed. "Well, um, you're a pixie. So perhaps you could give me some pixie dust? To make it easier to open the portal?"

Petunia frowned. "You know I can't do that. Pixie code of

honor." She thought for a moment. "But if I go with you to the portal, I can use it myself."

"I can't ask you to do that," Sagara said. "It's much too dangerous. Max and Millie are human, and I'm close enough to human to be able to survive without magic. But pixies are an inherently magical race. If you accidentally slip through the portal, I don't know what would happen to you. You might turn into a bird, or a flower, or you might simply cease to exist."

"Hmph," said Petunia. "Then I'll just have to be careful."

"Won't you need clothes from the Logical Realm?" Max asked.

Sagara looked pointedly down at her shirt, which was yellow with a drawing of triangles inside triangles inside triangles. She was also wearing the odd blue trousers again.

"Oh," Millie said. "You've been wearing Logical Realm clothes all along."

"My brother brings them back for me," Sagara confirmed. "But actually, it wouldn't matter. The local portal to the Logical Realm connects to one of the few places where I could dress like an elf or a wizard or a witch without anyone noticing at all." She pulled out a book, written in English, titled **Welcome to Witch City**.

"There's a city of witches?" Millie gasped. "How is that even possible?"

Sagara laughed. "It isn't. There are no witches there anymore, but the humans in the Logical Realm remember when there used to be. About three hundred years ago, some people in a place called Salem went kind of crazy and started accusing each other of being witches, which was considered evil and dangerous. They actually killed several people before they finally calmed down and remembered there's no magic."

"Muck and muddle," said Petunia. "And that's where you want to go?"

"Oh, it's all different now," Sagara explained. "Today, people think it's fun to pretend to be witches and wizards and pirates. Salem has become a gathering place for people who do this, so it's completely normal to walk around dressed as a wizard or a witch."

"Ingenious," Max said. "Place the portal where you're least likely to be noticed."

Millie noticed other students getting up and clearing their tables. "I think the recess gong just rang," she said. Fortunately, they'd consumed every last crumb of lunch already, so clearing up was easy.

"Excuse me," said Millie. "I have an appointment with Headmistress Pteria and Mistress Mallow during recess."

"Oh, is this about the cacao tree you sprouted?" Sagara asked.

Millie nodded. "And because Mistress Mallow thinks something funny is going on with my magic."

"I'll say," Sagara replied. "Make sure you tell them about the elfcakes."

Max took a quick look around, but Cretacia was nowhere to be seen. Pulling out his wand, he tapped the dome lightly, and it burst like a soap bubble. The babble of the schoolyard washed over them again.

"See you at Thaumaturgy!" Millie told her friends, and she started off for the stairs.

When she reached the Headmistress's office, she heard voices chattering, hushed but excited. She caught a few words: *tampering* and *exceptional* and *motives*. Not wanting to eavesdrop, Millie knocked politely on the doorframe.

The voices hushed, and Millie heard hasty footsteps. Headmistress Pteria pulled aside the curtain.

"Ah, Millie, my apologies," the dragon said. "I know you expected to meet with me and Mistress Mallow now, but I'm afraid something urgent has come up. Can you come to school a little early on Onesday?"

Millie swallowed her disappointment. "Yes, of course, Headmistress."

Pteria smiled kindly at her. "Thank you for your patience, my dear. Now, if you'll excuse me." And the Headmistress turned and let the curtain fall behind her. Then Millie heard her pronounce the words she'd just heard Max use for the Dome of Silence, and all was still.

Millie stood for a moment, at a loss for what to do. She'd never been alone in the school before. Sagara and Max were undoubtedly in the library, Petunia out in the glade watching for Grumpkin and Cretacia. But Millie wanted to check on Thea, and to see if Mistress Mallow was in the lab, where she might be able to help Millie turn Horace back. She headed up the stairs to the lab.

The lab seemed deserted at first, but then Millie heard a small, familiar voice grumble from the dark corner where Thea's table was. "No," said Grumpkin. "I won't let you."

Quickly, Millie hid behind one of the workbenches, then peeped out at the corner. Grumpkin stood in front of Thea, his arms folded and his jaw set. Before him stood Cretacia.

"You are my minion," Cretacia hissed, "and you will do as I say."

Grumpkin shook his head stubbornly. "I agreed to spy for you, and I agreed to harass your cousin. That was fun, actually. Good cookies. But I won't kidnap someone for you, and I won't let you kidnap someone, neither."

A chill ran down Millie's spine. Cretacia wouldn't, would she?

"Moron," Cretacia said. "I just want to study it, to see

what trick Duddy's trying to pull, convincing everyone she's special when she's got no talent to speak of."

Grumpkin stood firm. "I know how you study things," he said. "I've helped you often enough. You're going to hurt that little baby tree. Do you know what Quercius will do to you? What he'll do to me?"

"No one will ever know," Cretacia said soothingly. "If the stupid tree gets hurt, we can blame Duddy. She messes everything up, doesn't she?"

"If your mother knew," Grumpkin began.

"If my mother knew that you were disobeying me," Cretacia growled, her fingers twisting into claws, "she'd send her golems to trample your home and grind your family into paste. Now get out of my way."

Grumpkin turned pale. He glanced over his shoulder, clearly wavering.

Millie jumped to her feet. "Stop!" she screamed. "You leave Thea alone!"

Cretacia spun around, her angry snarl turning into a delighted grin. "Duddy! How nice of you to join us."

"Step away from there," Millie said.

Cretacia sniggered. "Or what? You'll bake at me?" She doubled over laughing. "There's nothing you can do, except..."

Behind Cretacia, Grumpkin had tiptoed to the little cacao tree. Gingerly, he picked it up, then motioned at the door. Millie needed to keep Cretacia's attention.

"Except what?" she asked warily.

Cretacia put her hands on her hips and thrust up her chin, braids waving about her head like snakes. "Tell me how you tricked them. Just admit what you did, and I'll leave the stupid plant alone."

"I don't know what I did," Millie said, "but it wasn't a

trick. It just happened."

"Oh, come on," Cretacia said. "Everyone knows you lost your magic when you were five."

"I did?" Millie asked. Grumpkin was edging along the wall, Thea cradled in one arm. "I don't remember that at all."

"Of course not," Cretacia said. "I heard it was some spectacular failure, an explosion. It wiped your memory and destroyed your magic. Your mother tried to hush it up, but we all knew."

Millie frowned. "What kind of explosion? What did I do?"

Cretacia threw up her hands. "Oh, how should I know? All I know is, you blew it and ruined your talent forever. So you can't possibly have transformed that bean. *Jäädy!*" she cried suddenly, pointing at Grumpkin. The goblin stopped just steps from the doorway, frozen in place with a look of terror on his face.

"Thought you could sneak past me?" Cretacia said. "I see what's going on. You two are conspiring against me!" She turned back to Millie. "I don't know how you've broken my hold on Grumpkin, but you'll pay for interfering with my minion. *Syyliä!*"

Millie felt warts erupt over her entire body, throbbing and aching. *Oh, won't Mother be pleased*, she thought absurdly.

Cretacia grinned at her. "There, now you look more like a proper witch. Now, let's see about this tree of yours." She reached out a hand toward Grumpkin.

"No," Millie said. "Do what you want to me, but leave Thea alone."

"You really need more practice bargaining," Cretacia crooned. "Don't offer me something I can already do anyway, stupid. Of course I can do what I want to you. Haven't I always?" She turned back to Grumpkin.

Millie thought fast. Cretacia's magic was generally spoken.

If she could prevent Cretacia from speaking... Quickly, Millie pointed at Cretacia and said, "*Hiljaisuuskupla!*" A strong tingle went through her, from the tips of her toes to the top of her head and right out through her finger. The Dome of Silence popped into being around Cretacia.

Cretacia's jaw dropped. She screamed something furiously, but Millie couldn't hear a thing. She breathed a sigh of relief. Thea was safe.

"WHAT IS GOING ON IN HERE?" Master Quercius thundered. Millie looked up, spotting his face in the doorframe. "I DETECTED POWERFUL MAGIC IN THIS ROOM, WHICH SHOULD BE EMPTY. GRUMPKIN, WHAT ARE YOU DOING WITH THEA?"

"He saved her!" Millie cried. "Cretacia wanted to steal her, to figure out what I'd done to transform her, and Grumpkin wouldn't let Cretacia do it."

"IS THAT SO, GRUMPKIN?" asked the Caretaker. "OH, LET'S REMOVE THAT FREEZE SPELL. *KATOA!*"

Grumpkin nearly toppled over, but he held fast to Thea. "That's right," he said, nodding vigorously. "I may be her minion, but I won't kidnap babies, not even baby trees. I ain't that bad."

"WELL," said the Dodonos, raising his mossy eyebrows. "THEN I AM VERY GRATEFUL TO YOU, GRUMPKIN. WOULD YOU PLEASE SET THEA BACK ON HER WARMING SLATE?"

"Yah, sure," said Grumpkin, trotting over and depositing the pot in its place. Millie thought she heard Thea gasp with relief.

"AND YOU, MILLIE," Master Quercius asked, "WHAT WAS YOUR PART IN THIS?"

Oh, darkness, Millie thought. *I'm not supposed to be doing magic, especially not on students.* "I, I came up here to talk to Mistress Mallow about another project of mine. I found Grumpkin trying to stop Cretacia. We got in an argument. She froze Grumpkin, she covered me with warts, and she was about to do something to Thea. So I had to stop her."

"WHICH YOU APPEAR TO HAVE DONE, QUITE EFFECTIVELY," Master Quercius said. Cretacia was beating her fists against the inside of the dome, her green face nearly purple with rage. "I BELIEVE IT'S TIME WE LET HER OUT. WOULD YOU PLEASE TAKE DOWN YOUR DOME?"

"I'm not sure how," Millie admitted.

"TOUCHING IT SHOULD SUFFICE," the Dodonos told her.

Cautiously, Millie stepped forward and touched the dome.

"I will destroy you and all your friends!" Cretacia screamed, launching herself at Millie.

"*JÄÄDY!*" said Master Quercius. Cretacia froze mid-leap.

"Ulp," she said. "Um, I didn't really mean that."

"PERHAPS NOT," said Master Quercius. "NONETHELESS, YOU HAVE ATTACKED TWO OF MY STUDENTS AND ATTEMPTED TO KIDNAP AN INFANT. YOU ARE HEREBY DISMISSED FROM THIS SCHOOL. I AM SENDING YOU HOME. YOUR MOTHER AND THE AUTHORITIES WILL BE NOTIFIED. FAREWELL, CRETACIA NOCTMARTIS. *MENE KOTIIN.*"

Cretacia threw Millie a look of pure hatred just before she vanished. Millie shivered. She knew she hadn't seen the last of Cretacia.

Millie heard a sudden rush of wings and pounding footsteps. Headmistress Pteria swooped in, followed by

Mistress Mallow and Master Schist. "We came as quickly as we could," the Headmistress said. "What happened?"

Master Quercius quickly explained what had happened. The dragon blew an angry snort of flame. "Stormwinds! Is your cousin always this obnoxious?"

Millie shook her head. "She was worse than usual."

"Beggin' yer pardon," Grumpkin said, "but that's not so. She's usually this bad an' worse. She don't like being outdone by anyone. Cretacia always has to be the best at everythin', an' sometimes that means making sure everyone else does worse."

"I must say, I'm surprised," said Headmistress Pteria. "You were very courageous, Grumpkin. Cretacia is likely to want revenge upon you and your kin."

Grumpkin ground his teeth. "I know it. But I couldn't just let her go an' take a baby like that. It ain't right."

Headmistress Pteria nodded. "Well said, and well done. I believe we can help you in this regard. I will speak to Cretacia's mother on your behalf and explain that you were simply upholding her family's honor."

Grumpkin looked at her, astonished, then up at Master Quercius. "You'd do that for me?"

"It's no more than the truth," Headmistress Pteria pointed out. "By preventing Cretacia from harming Thea, you protected her from more dire consequences. Now, I believe you have class to get to."

"Yes, Headmistress," said Grumpkin, bowing low. "Thank you, Headmistress." He walked out the door, a look of wonder on his face.

"Well, Millie," said the Headmistress. "It seems to me that you were under the impression that you couldn't do magic. Do you still believe that?"

Millie found that she was shaking from the shock of it all. She sat down heavily on a stool. "No, Headmistress. I cast that spell, that Dome of Silence. I didn't even know I could, I just did it."

"Had you ever attempted that spell before?" Mistress Mallow asked.

Millie shook her head. "I'd never seen it before today. Max used it at lunch to shut Cretacia out, and then, um," Millie blushed, "I heard you use it in your office before I left."

"So you just imitated what you had seen and heard today?" the brownie asked. Millie nodded.

"Well, let's see if you can do it again," said Mistress Mallow. "I imagine you don't want to go around covered with warts. Why don't you try dispelling them?"

Millie rubbed the warts on her hands. "Um, how?"

"THINK CAREFULLY. YOU JUST SAW ME DISPEL THE FREEZE SPELL ON GRUMPKIN. DO YOU REMEMBER WHAT I DID?"

Millie thought back. "Yes, I think so."

"Go ahead, then," Mistress Mallow encouraged her.

Millie focused on her warts. She felt a tingle start in the soles of her feet and spread through her body, up to her head. She took a slow, calm breath and said, "*Katoa.*" The tingle washed over her skin. The warts shrank and then vanished altogether. *I did it!* she thought. *I actually did it!*

Mistress Mallow turned to the other teachers. "See, I told you. If she hasn't been able to cast spells before now, something has been interfering with her."

Headmistress Pteria frowned. "Let's leave that discussion until later. Millie, you know that you were forbidden from using magic in the school, especially on another student."

Millie nodded, feeling tears begin to fill her eyes. "I'm sorry. I just didn't think. Am I expelled, too?"

Master Schist snorted. "Hardly."

Headmistress Pteria smiled. "First of all, Cretacia was not

a student. Secondly, you were defending a fragile life. And thirdly, you were upholding the honor of the school. Though you did not formally have permission, I believe under the circumstances, you were fully justified."

"Then I'm not expelled?" Millie asked, trembling.

"No, you certainly are not," Headmistress Pteria told her, "but I must caution you against using magic again until we have a better understanding of what has changed to allow you to cast spells. Also, I would like to meet with you and your mother together. Will you please ask her to come see me on Onesday morning?"

The gong rang. "TIME FOR CLASS," Master Quercius announced. "I BELIEVE THE LAB IS NEEDED FOR THAUMATURGY NOW."

"Oh, yes," said Mistress Mallow. "May I recommend that Thea be moved to a safer location?"

"AN EXCELLENT IDEA," the Dodonos replied.

Headmistress Pteria placed a gentle claw on Millie's shoulder. "You've had quite a shock, Millie. Would you like to go home?"

Millie did, desperately. She wanted to be back in her cozy kitchen, baking something soothing and delicious. But she had to tell Max what had happened. "Thank you," she said, "but I've really been looking forward to Thaumaturgy. May I stay?"

The Headmistress laughed, a soft roaring like the first rumble of a thunderstorm. "Of course you can stay. Mallow, please take Thea to my office. I'll stay and have a word with Bertemious."

"Certainly, Headmistress," said Mistress Mallow. She swept out of the room with Thea and the warming slate.

An elderly salamander in yellow robes and a green teacher's cap bustled in. "What's all this? I have class now!"

"Simmer down, Bertie. We're just leaving," said Master Schist. "A word, Bertemious?" said the Headmistress. She took the salamander aside. Master Schist stomped out, and Master Quercius's face faded from view. After a moment, Headmistress Pteria nodded to Millie and left.

Chapter 13

Mud Pies and Cupcakes

The other students filed in. Sagara rushed up. "Where were you? You didn't come to the classroom."

Max and Petunia came over. "You're pale as a ghost," said Max. "What happened?"

Quickly, as the other students filed in and took their seats, Millie told them what Cretacia had tried to do and how the teachers had reacted.

Petunia whistled. "What do you call a humiliated witch?" she quipped. "A snitchy witchy."

Millie nodded miserably. "I'm sorry, Max. She's sure to tell on you now."

Max looked crestfallen. "You couldn't help it, Millie. You did the right thing." He poked her. "Hey, can I come to your house for dinner? I don't think going home is a very good idea right now."

Millie brightened and nodded. "Of course! I'm sure we can convince Mother to let you in."

"Quiet!" yelled Master Bertemious. "You snivelling mob of miscreants. Sit down and shut up."

Max sat with Millie, and Sagara and Petunia took the workbench next to them.

"Today," the salamander boomed, "we shall discuss the properties of that very flexible material, mud, and how it can be applied to a wide range of spells."

"Mud?" Max muttered. "Really? Could this be any more boring?"

Master Bertemious glared at him. "Tell me, Mister Salazar, what are the properties of mud?"

Max sat up straighter, rising to the challenge. "Mud is a proto-material, imbued with infinite possibilities, endlessly mutable..."

Millie hardly listened. Her mind was spinning. She'd done magic, real magic! And without any food involved at all. She actually was a witch, after so many years believing she wasn't. It was such a tremendous relief, and yet Millie surprised herself by feeling a little disappointed. Did this mean she'd have to give up on cooking and focus on magic now? Still, she could hardly wait to go home and tell Mother.

But then she'd have to tell her about Cretacia, and Max. Millie was sure Cretacia would exact her vengeance on Millie's brother, which was so unfair it made Millie beat her fists on her thighs. But what could she do?

PLOP. Millie jumped. A large lump of mud had landed on the workbench in front of her. Master Bertemious chuckled and dumped another lump in front of Max.

"What are we doing?" she asked Max.

"We're supposed to turn the mud into marble," he whispered back.

Millie raised her hand. "Um, Master Bertemious? Headmistress Pteria said I wasn't to do magic until she said so."

Master Bertemious harrumphed. "The Headmistress meant that you should not do magic unsupervised. I am present to prevent any more of your, ah, catastrophes."

The class giggled.

Millie bit her lip. "I'm pretty sure that's not what she meant, sir."

The elderly salamander glared at her. "This is my class, and while you are in my class, you will do as I say."

"Just pretend," Max whispered to her.

Millie nodded. "As you say, Master Bertemious." But she had no intention of using any magic. She sunk her hands into the great messy glob and began kneading it absently. Marble was a ridiculous assignment anyway. The only marble she'd ever worked with was marble cake, chocolate and vanilla dough swirled together so that when it was baked and sliced, it revealed lovely marbled pattern. Frosted with chocolate buttercream frosting and dotted with white chocolate curls, it was both beautiful and delicious.

A heavenly aroma wafted through the room. Heads began to turn. Max nudged Millie. "What are you doing?" he hissed.

Startled, Millie looked at her mud blob. She had sculpted a layer cake, complete with frosting. As she watched, the frosting changed from the dull brown of mud to the rich, creamy color of chocolate.

"Oh, no," she whispered.

Master Bertemious's head swiveled around. "What is that?" he demanded, marching over to Millie's workbench. "Is this meant to be a joke, Miss Noctmartis?" he demanded.

"No, Master," Millie said. "I just made the wrong marble. This is a marble cake."

"An illusion? This is thaumaturgy, girl," the salamander spat. "I expect a physical change."

"It's no illusion, sir," Max assured him. He was starting to drool, just a bit. "Millie used to do this all the time, making mud pies that were really pies. Taste it, you'll see."

"Max," Millie hissed. "What are you doing?"

"Hmph." Master Bertemious picked up a small knife and cut a slice of cake. All the students sighed as the aroma of cake rose and filled the room. Bertemious lifted the slice, examining the swirls and veins of chocolate and vanilla sponge, prodding it with one webbed finger, lifting it to his small slit nostrils.

Finally, he took a nibble. His golden eyes closed, and he breathed a sigh of pleasure. "Light, moist, rich. Subtle tones of vanilla countered by the bitter tang of chocolate. Excellent. One of the finest cakes I have ever eaten. Transformed from mud." He opened his eyes. "I have never seen or tasted anything like it."

"May I have some?" Max asked.

Master Bertemious's eyes narrowed. "Is this a class or a party?"

"Why can't it be both?" Sagara suggested. "We can give everyone a slice."

The salamander looked unconvinced, but then he took another bite of the cake. His shoulders relaxed, and he began to smile. "Oh, why not?" he said. "Here, Miss Noctmartis. You do the honors." He handed Millie the knife.

"This is a bad idea," Millie said, but Master Bertemious seemed so happy, and the other students looked so eager, she didn't have the heart to refuse.

Millie gave a slice to Max as the other students lined up, Sagara and Petunia first in line. One by one, she gave generous slices to each of her classmates, leaving just enough for herself at the end.

For a few glorious moments, the room echoed with the perfect silence of contentment. And then, someone said, "Can I have some more?"

"Sorry," Millie said, swallowing her last bite. "There's none left."

"But you could make more," said Terrence, the gryphon Millie partnered with in Elementary Potions.

"Hmm, yes. An excellent idea," Master Bertemious said. "Please demonstrate your technique to the class. Use Mr. Salazar's mud." He swept away the last remaining crumbs of the cake and shoved Max's mud over to her side of the worktable.

"Um, sure, I'll try," Millie said. "But I don't really know what I did in the first place."

"Come now, your brother says you've been doing this for years," said Master Bertemious. "Just walk us through it. What do you do first?"

Millie considered. "Well, I think about a food I want to make, like the marble cake."

"Could you make cookies?" asked Izzy the dryad.

"Yes, probably." Millie began to knead the mud, trying to think of a good cookie recipe. Maybe gingerbread?

"What about fudge?" called out another student. "You could turn my mud into fudge."

"I want fried chicken!"

"Cherry pie!"

"Meatloaf!"

"Elfcakes!" Sagara called out, then, "Ouch!" as Petunia elbowed her in the ribs.

Millie froze. "Wait!" she said. "I can't make everything at once. We need to agree on something."

"Start with more cake," said Master Bertemious.

"No! I want fudge!"

"Croissants!"

"Toadstools!"

"Cupcakes!" Millie cried out desperately. "I'll make cupcakes, all right?" She seized the mud in front of her and began shaping it. *Cupcakes for everyone*, she thought.

As Millie transformed her mud, some of the mud in front of each student began to transform. At each workbench, the mud reshaped itself into a cupcake for each student, and for each student, it was their favorite cupcake. White, golden, strawberry, peanut butter, butterscotch, red velvet, dark chocolate, pineapple, and carrot cake with cream cheese frosting. For Master Bertemious, there was a molten chocolate cupcake with buttercream frosting dotted with candied flies, and Sagara got a cupcake-shaped elfcake. Millie's was maple bacon.

A reverent hush fell over the class. Then everyone immediately devoured their cupcake. Max smiled at her, and Millie giggled at his blue frosting mustache.

But then, someone said, "More."

"Yes, more!"

"Please, Millie, that was wonderful."

"You're wonderful, Millie. Can I be your friend?"

"Millie's the best!"

The students began to crowd around Millie's workbench. Even Master Bertemious pressed forward. "Most impressive, Miss Noctmartis. You are clearly one of the finest students in this school, and I discovered you. Oh, they will sing our praises, you and I. Now, you must teach me your technique." He reached for her.

Millie shrieked. Everyone was reaching for her, snatching at her hands, her hair, her clothes. "Stop, please," she cried, batting away and picking off their hands.

"Back off!" Petunia cried. "Everyone stand back."

Max tried to push the crowd back far enough to pull out his wand, but they pinned him against the workbench.

Sagara began doing rapid calculations on her fingers. "If x is the number of students and f is the force required to repel them..."

"No time!" Petunia shouted. Picking up a leftover lump of mud, she threw it hard, and it splatted against Izzy's face. "Hey!" Izzy shouted. She scooped up some mud and fired back at Petunia, who ducked. The mud hit a goblin instead, who scraped it off and fired it back. It sailed across the room and smacked Max in the shoulder, splattering several other students. Before he could even protest, the air was full of flying mud. Swiftly, Millie scrambled down and ducked under the worktable.

"Stop it! Stop throwing mud this inst-ARGLE!" cried Master Bertemious as a mudball hit him right in the mouth.

Max got under the worktable, too, smeared with mud. "What did you do?" he gasped. "It's a mudtastrophe out there!"

Sagara scuttled over to join them. "I suppose elfcakes are out of the question now?" she asked.

"Yes!" Max and Millie yelled together.

"Where's Petunia?" Millie added.

"TAKE THAT!" Petunia roared beside them before ducking under the table as well. Her acorn cap had been knocked off, and her hair, face, and dress were all thoroughly plastered with mud. "What do you call a mud fight in school?"

"Umm, earth science?" Millie guessed.

"FUN!" Petunia scooped some mud off the floor and ran off, hurling mudballs.

"THAT IS ENOUGH!" Master Quercius thundered. "*KATOA.*"

The screaming and mud-slinging died down, stopping altogether when Headmistress Pteria swept back into the room. "Great scales! What happened? Master Bertemious?"

The salamander scraped mud from his mouth, spat, and said faintly, "Bogswater. What was I doing?"

"You were under the influence of a powerful charm," the Headmistress told him.

Master Bertemious looked confused. "Absurd. No charm has gotten past my wards in over twenty years."

"Nonetheless, you were charmed." The dragon glanced over the classroom. "Do you know who's responsible?"

"Noctmartis. It's all that Noctmartis girl's fault."

"Millie?" the Headmistress called out.

Millie felt the blood drain from her face. She crawled out from under the workbench. Her classmates began to stare at her and mutter, some angrily. Sagara looked shocked and hurt.

Petunia raised her hand. "This is my fault, Headmistress. I started throwing the mud."

The Headmistress raised an eye ridge. "And why did you do that?"

Petunia began twisting the muddy ends of her hair. "Well, because everyone was rushing at Millie. I thought they were going to crush her!"

"And you couldn't have come up with a better way to stop them, such as summoning another teacher or Master Quercius?"

"Oh," said Petunia in a small voice.

"Exactly. Detention today, Petunia," the Headmistress said.

Millie cried out, "No, don't! It's not Petunia's fault. She was just trying to help me."

Headmistress Pteria frowned. "Petunia is responsible for her own actions, just as you are responsible for yours. Come with me, Millie. It's time we had a serious talk."

Max patted Millie on the back and Petunia clenched her fists, but Sagara refused to look at her. Millie trailed after the Headmistress to her office.

"What a day! Sit down, Millie," Headmistress Pteria told her, taking her own seat and coiling her tail neatly around

its legs. Millie sat gingerly, wringing her muddy hands. The
Headmistress stared down at her, golden eyes focused intently.
"I believe I told you not to use magic anymore,"
Headmistress Pteria said.

"I tried not to," Millie said. "Master Bertemious insisted
that I could if he was supervising, but I didn't want to take
the chance. I wasn't going to do anything, but it happened
anyway. I'm sorry."

"I'm not sure what to make of you, Millie," the dragon said
slowly. "When your mother came to fill out your paperwork,
she told me you were utterly hopeless. Yet, in just three short
weeks, you're creating charms so powerful, even your teacher
was affected." Pteria cocked her head. "That's rather unusual.
In fact, to my knowledge, Master Bertemious has never been
bespelled by one of his own students, though he did catch
the Polka Pox along with the rest of us a few years back, but
that was let loose by a far more advanced student.

"So, I wonder if is this a hoax, some strange attempt by
your mother to curry political favor by implying that school
was a roaring success, when in fact you were a perfectly
competent witch before you came here? Or are you honestly
just coming into your power? Hmm?" She drummed her
talons on the desk.

Millie gulped. "M-mother's not trying to fool you,
Headmistress. Honestly, I *was* hopeless before I came here.
And I really didn't mean to charm everyone. I just made
cupcakes out of the mud because Max told me I used to do
that when I was younger. I didn't even know I was casting a
charm." She explained exactly what had happened in class.

"Let me get this straight," Headmistress Pteria said.
"Before you started at the Enchanted Forest School, you
had never cast a spell successfully. Since then, you've had
a few minor missteps, but also some impressive successes,

such as Thea and the Dome of Silence. Now you're making powerful charms."

Millie shrank down in her seat. "Um, I guess so."

The Headmistress sighed, then drew out her wand. "In general, I dislike using magic to get answers, but this muddle needs straightening out before you start turning people into cupcakes."

Millie blanched. "I would never do that!"

"Not intentionally, perhaps." The Headmistress pointed the wand at Millie and intoned, "*Totuus*." Truth. A tingle washed over Millie, but otherwise she felt no different.

"Now then," Headmistress Pteria began, "has everything you just told me been the truth?"

"Yes, Headmistress," Millie said.

The dragon sat back and breathed out a small puff of smoke. "Well, then. It's good to know my judgment is not impaired. Now, are you certain you've never been able to cast spells?"

"No," Millie replied. "Max said I used to cast spells all the time, and Cretacia said I lost my magic when I was five in some kind of accident."

Headmistress Pteria's eyes narrowed. "Interesting. Did she say what kind of accident?"

"No," said Millie. "I wondered that myself."

"Do you remember this accident?"

"No, Headmistress. But Cretacia said the accident affected my memory."

The dragon tapped a talon on the desk. "That is not unheard of, but it seems rather convenient." She looked at Millie. "Tell me, Millie. Do you enjoy using magic?"

Millie opened her mouth, but so many different things had popped into her head that she struggled to get them out. "Yes. No! Sometimes. I'm not sure. I don't care. I want to..."

"That's enough. I'm asking the wrong question. Millie, what do you want to do?"

Relief poured through her. That was easy. "I want to cook. I love cooking. And I want to make Mother happy."

"Why do you want to make your mother happy?"

"So that she'll finally love me," Millie said, and then she gasped. Tears stung her eyes, and her stomach flipped.

"Ah," Headmistress Pteria breathed out. "I see. You don't think your mother loves you."

"Of course not. I'm useless," Millie whispered.

"Enough," Headmistress Pteria said, waving her wand. Millie felt the tingle fade. "Quercius, what is your opinion in this matter? Quercius?"

"I BEG YOUR PARDON." The Caretaker's face appeared over the doorway. "I HAVE ALSO BEEN KEEPING AN EYE ON CLEANUP EFFORTS IN THE LAB.

"NOW THEN, MILLIE, IT IS MY OPINION THAT YOU HAVE CONSIDERABLE MAGICAL ABILITY WHICH HAS BEEN FRUSTRATED FOR A LONG TIME. YOU HAVE SINCE DISCOVERED HOW TO USE THAT ABILITY, BUT YOU HAVE NOT YET DEVELOPED THE CONTROL NEEDED TO PREVENT, ER, LET'S CALL THEM UNFORTUNATE ACCIDENTS. I BELIEVE, HOWEVER, THAT YOUR INTENTIONS ARE GOOD. YOUR DEFENSE OF THEA IS STRONG EVIDENCE IN YOUR FAVOR."

Headmistress Pteria nodded sharply. "I concur. Millie, I think you've started leaking magic, even when you don't intend to. You may have been leaking for some time, but your mother's wards have been sufficiently strong to diffuse the effects until now." She sighed. "Until further notice, I must ask that you stay out of magic classes and refrain from sharing your food with anyone. I will also write a letter to your mother, explaining today's events. We can discuss this when we meet with her on Onesday."

Millie's stomach churned. *Mother is going to kill me*, she thought.

"DURING ENDSDAY, I WILL STRENGTHEN THE WARDS AROUND THE SCHOOL, PARTICULARLY IN MILLIE'S CLASS," said Quercius.

"Yes, good idea," the dragon replied. "Now, Millie, while I am convinced that your charm was not intentional, you need to know that I will not accept that as an excuse. You are responsible for your own magic, and you must understand the consequences of your actions." She took a slate from her cupboard and tapped it briskly with her claw. "Millie shall write, '*I will not charm my classmates or teachers*,' one hundred times." Then she handed the slate to Millie, along with a piece of chalk. "There you are. Get going."

Millie took the tablet and began scratching out I will not charm my classmates or teachers, over and over. After ten lines, her hand began to cramp up. She had never written so much, at a single sitting, in her life. By twenty lines, she began to garble the sentence. *I will not clarm my chassmates...* she began, and the slate swiftly corrected her. She rubbed out the chalk with her sleeve and started again.

By the time she finished the final line, Millie was sure that school had let out, everyone had gone home, and the sun had gone down hours before. Her hand was shaking and would not unclench. Still she added, *I'm very very sorry*, before placing the slate on the desk.

Headmistress Pteria looked up from scribbling on a scroll, one claw dripping purple ink. "Finished?" she asked.

Millie gulped and nodded, handing her the slate.

The Headmistress looked it over, then nodded with satisfaction. "Very good. Here is the letter for your mother."

She handed Millie a scroll tied with a green ribbon and sealed with wax. "It's quite close to the end of school, so go down to your classroom and fetch your things. You are dismissed. I recommend that you think long and hard this Endsday about your goals here at the Enchanted Forest School, and I hope that you exercise better judgment in the future."

"Yes, Headmistress," Millie said in a small voice. "Thank you, Headmistress." Scroll clutched in her hand, she left the room.

Chapter 14

The Promise of Orange Peel

As she went down the stairs to her classroom, Millie met Mistress Mallow going up with a large pot filled with soil. "Oh, Millie," she said cheerfully. "You'll be pleased to know that Thea has outgrown her pot. I'm just about to transplant her, but I can wait until after school if you'd like to help." The brownie blinked, finally noticing the mud caking Millie and the dejected look on Millie's face. "Good gravy, what happened to you?"

"I charmed everyone in thaumaturgy, even Master Bertemious. But I didn't mean to!" Millie burst into tears.

"There, there," Mistress Mallow said. She set down the pot and gathered Millie into a gentle hug. "It's all right. Accidents happen."

"I'll never be a witch. Never ever," Millie sobbed. "I never do anything right."

"Dear girl, you're already a witch," said the Potions teacher. "You're just going about it differently than most. And you shouldn't be so afraid of making mistakes. We learn more from our failures than our successes."

"We do?" Millie asked, surprised.

"Certainly. For example, you charmed that old

curmudgeon Bertemious, didn't you?"

Millie nodded ruefully. "Yes, but..."

"But you didn't mean to," Mistress Mallow finished for her. "You did, though, and that's quite impressive. You somehow slipped in under his wards, and that means you're either very clever or very strong. Possibly both. Either way, you've got talent. It just needs proper training, that's all."

"Really?" Millie asked.

Mistress Mallow smiled at her. "Oh, yes. I'm sure of it."

"Well," Millie said slowly, "there's another failure I've been meaning to talk to you about." And she told Mistress Mallow about Horace.

The brownie's smile turned to a frown, which deepened considerably as Millie's explanation went on. "That shouldn't be possible," Mistress Mallow said at the end. "Potions shouldn't work on ghosts. But you say Horace has been eating food for years?"

Millie nodded. "He especially loves chocolate."

"Good heavens, hasn't your mother taken any notice? If Horace is actually eating your food, then you've been transforming your food into spirit food for him. That's complicated. What's more, you can still eat it, so it's somehow both normal AND spirit food, which is terribly complicated." Mistress Mallow thought for a moment.

"All right, I can't be sure of this, but I think you were on the right track with the orange peel," said the brownie. "Your problem is that you hadn't transformed it into something Horace could eat. If you just bake him something with orange peel in it, he should be able to eat it."

"Of course!" Millie blurted out. "I'll make him orange-cranberry scones." She paused. "But what if it doesn't work? What if I mess up again?"

Mistress Mallow smiled gently. "Then you'll have

learned something new. Now, do you want to help with Thea or not?"

Millie's face fell. "I can't. I have to go straight home and take this letter to my mother."

"Best get moving then." The brownie gave her a last, reassuring squeeze before letting Millie go.

"Say hi to Thea for me?" Millie asked.

"Of course!"

Millie continued down the staircase to her classroom. Quietly, so as not to disturb the class, she crept in, gathered her cauldron, and left.

She had never walked home alone before. Millie had always wanted to do that, to have time to really look at things and explore, maybe try some of the Path's side branches. Today, she just felt lonely. She missed Petunia's happy chatter and bad jokes. She missed Max's pompous talk and dimpled smile. She missed the flying carpet. She even missed Sagara's sarcasm. Millie couldn't forget the look on Sagara's face at the end of Thaumaturgy, that look of hurt betrayal.

Her stomach hurt. She stared at her feet, shuffling slowly along the Path. Millie felt so alone; she'd have been glad of any company right then, even Grumpkin's. Anyone except...

"Well, well. If it isn't Duddy."

Millie looked up. Cretacia was standing in the Path, broomstick in one hand, blocking Millie's way home.

"What're you doing out here during school?" Cretacia leered at her. "Playing hooky? Or did you get kicked out? The way you got me kicked out." Cretacia's hands twisted into claws.

"What? Now you want to go to school?" Millie asked.

"That's beside the point. I do the rejecting, not the other way around."

"You got yourself rejected," Millie told her. "Even if I

hadn't stopped you, Master Quercius would have known it was you who took Thea and hurt her. You would have been kicked out for sure."

"Hah! Think I'm that stupid?" Cretacia glared at her. "I was going to pin it all on Grumpkin. That's what minions are for. Only you corrupted him somehow. Did you try to recruit him?"

"No, of course not. Why would I do that?" Millie asked. Then suddenly, Millie remembered: Grumpkin had stolen and eaten her lunch, including those chocolate chip cookies, back during the first week of school. *Did I charm him, just like the thaumaturgy class?*

Cretacia saw the look on Millie's face. "You did! I knew it! Did you bribe him somehow? Offer him a better deal than mine?" She stomped her foot. "Ooh, when I get my hands on him..."

"You leave him alone!" Millie said. "It wasn't his fault. I charmed him."

Cretacia's face twisted into a mocking leer. "Oh, come on, Duddy. You can't even grow your own warts. Do you expect me to believe that?"

"I stopped you in my Dome of Silence, didn't I?" Millie flung back.

Cretacia grew rigid with rage. "Yes, you did. How dare you? How dare you interfere with my plans? Did you know they scryed my mother? That I'm to be tried before the Coven? All because of your interference!"

"You interfered first!" Millie yelled. "You only came to school to mess with me! You had no intention of enrolling, you just wanted to make me feel horrible, the way you always do. If you'd just left me alone, you wouldn't have been there to get in trouble in the first place."

Cretacia smiled her glittering crocodile grin, and Millie

took a step back, alarmed. "Oh, but then I would never have found out about Max," she purred. "Poor little Max, he misses his big sister soooooo much, he actually cheated his way into school. I was wondering where he'd been hiding. I had a lovely spider charm I wanted to try out on him. But I couldn't find him, got bored, and went looking for you instead. And there he was! I can't imagine what his father will say when I tell him what Max has been up to."

"Stop it!" Millie said. "Why do you do that? Why are you always so mean all the time?"

"Because I'm the best," Cretacia answered. "I'm the top of the apprentice witches, everyone knows it. And I intend to stay that way. Baba Luci chose to send you to that stupid school, and everyone assumed it was out of pity. I just had to make sure. And Mom has been spending entirely too much time with that stupid brother of yours."

Millie's jaw dropped. "You were *jealous*?"

"Of him? Of you?" Cretacia laughed, clutching her ribs. "You've got to be kidding. Of course I'm not jealous. But no one gets what they want by just being nice. I know how to get what I want, and if that means I step on some idiots along the way, so be it. Really, that's what being a witch is all about. Which is why you'll never be a witch."

"Fine, I'm not a witch," Millie said. "Now will you leave me and Max alone?"

Cretacia considered. "I could, I suppose. If you made it worth my while."

Millie got a sinking feeling in her stomach. "What do you want, Cretacia?"

Cretacia smiled. "See? You can be smart when you want to be. I want you to testify on my behalf before the Coven."

"What? But I'll just confirm the school's charges against you."

"No, you won't," Cretacia said. "Instead, you'll explain that you framed me for the whole thing, and that it's all your fault."

Millie gasped. "You want me to lie?"

"Through your teeth."

"You want me to lie to the Baba?" Millie asked incredulously. "But, but she's the Baba! She can always tell if you lie."

Cretacia smiled. "Then you'd better do a very, very good job. You convince the Baba, or I will make life miserable for Max, and he'll hate you, too."

"But, if I tell the Baba it was my fault, I'll be punished," Millie said. "They might pull me out of school!"

"Mmm, yes," Cretacia said, resting her chin on one hand. "I suppose that's true. But your brother will still get to go to that stupid school. Think about it, Millie. The next full moon is in three days. You have until then to decide."

Cretacia straddled her broomstick and zoomed off, cackling.

Chapter 15

The Crack in the Kitchen

When Millie got home, she found a note on the kitchen table.

Ludmilla,
I've been called to an emergency Council meeting. I hope to be home for dinner.
Mother

"Oh, darkness," Millie said, tossing her letter onto the table next to the note.

Someone knocked on the front door. Startled, Millie jumped out of her chair and hurried to open it. "Max!" she cried.

Despite all the mud, Max looked like he'd been in a hurricane, his hair blown straight back and his eyes watering. He was still rolling up his carpet. "I came as soon as school let out, as fast as I could go. Where's Mother?"

Millie stepped outside. "M-mother had to go to an emergency Council meeting. She won't be home until much later. I'd ask you to come in and wait, but I can't let you in through the wards."

Max's face fell. "Just as well," he lied. "She might ask

awkward questions."

"You're not afraid I'll charm you again?" Millie asked.

He grinned at her. "Preposterous. You can't charm someone to like you if they already do." He hugged her. "Now tell me all about what happened with the Headmistress."

They sat on the front step, and Millie told Max all about it, and about what Mistress Mallow had said.

"She's clever, and she's right," Max told her. "I blunder frequently, and I learn something every time I do."

Millie stared at him. "You do? But you're so good at magic!"

"I'm good at some things, like wards and countercurses, thanks to Cretacia," Max replied. "But I struggle with potions, and transformations are quite difficult for me. Most people specialize in one or two things, not every aspect of magic."

"Hmm, like Mother with healing magic," Millie mused.

Max sighed. "Well, I guess I should go home and face the music. I can still come and visit, though, even if I can't attend school anymore."

"Oh, I don't think Cretacia will tell on you just yet," Millie said quickly. "I ran into her on the way home. She's going to hold off a while to torment us both."

Max rolled his eyes. "Fantastic. Dinner at home is going to be soooo entertaining. But hopefully I'll see you at school on Onesday. Let me know how it goes with Horace."

Millie nodded. "Be careful. Cretacia may not tell, but that doesn't mean she won't try to hurt you. She mentioned some spider charm."

Max shuddered. "I *despise* spiders. I shall double my wards tonight." He gave Millie a last hug. "See you soon!"

"Bye," Millie said, squeezing him back.

Back inside, Millie tossed her mother's note in the oven firebox. Millie briefly considered throwing the Headmistress's letter in, too, but instead she set it on a shelf next to the peppermint. She glanced around the kitchen, her kitchen, the place she loved most in all the world. *Time to see if they're right about me,* she thought.

And Millie started baking. Flour, baking powder, salt, butter, eggs, cream, dried cranberries, and grated orange peel. Millie sifted together the dry ingredients and cut the butter into them, all the while thinking, *for Horace.* But this time, she paid attention to the tingle of magic she felt. It was so faint, she had trouble finding it. But it was there, a low vibration in the soles of her feet. It felt heavy, forced, like she was pushing frosting through a tiny pastry tip. Something was holding her magic back, something smooth and hard, sort of like a ward. It was in her way.

So Millie pushed at it. As she mixed and rolled the scones, she pushed at the wall holding back her magic, but it just kept pushing back. Finally, Millie poked at the hole, the tiny crack through which she could reach, a crack meant, she realized suddenly, for Horace. Taking up the knife to slice the dough into individual scones, she imagined prying into that crack.

The wall parted, then crumbled, and the tingle washed right through her from her toes to the top of her head. *Slow down,* she thought. *I'm just baking scones for Horace.* Millie pulled the tingle back into herself, where it lay quiet inside her. She knew she'd always be able to find it now.

She laid out two dozen scones on her baking sheets and popped them into the oven to bake. A few minutes later, the aroma of baking citrus began to fill the air. Horace hopped through the pantry door.

"That smells delicious, Millie," he croaked. "Can I have some?"

Millie knelt down next to him. "Those scones are especially for you, Horace. I talked to Mistress Mallow today, and I think I know how to change you back."

"With scones?" the ghost asked, flicking out his tongue.

"Why not?" she replied. "It was chocolate sauce that got us into this mess, wasn't it?"

"How soon will they be ready?" Horace asked.

Millie peeked into the oven. "Another five minutes."

"Breek!" Horace said. "I hate waiting." He blinked at her. "Why are you covered in mud?"

"I'll take a bath later. Let me put on a kettle for tea, and I'll tell you all about it."

Millie told Horace about her day until the scones were ready. As she pulled them out to cool, Horace said, "I'm sorry, Millie."

Millie set down the second baking sheet. "It's not your fault."

"I don't mean about your day." Horace flicked his tongue out a few times, then said, "I've been a jerk to you. It's my own fault I'm a frog. I knew better than to eat that chocolate sauce. But I was so ashamed, I didn't want to think about that. I wanted it to be your fault, not mine."

"There's a lot of that going around," Millie said, scraping scones onto the cooling rack.

"But you've been having all this trouble at school, and I had no idea," Horace said. "I've been punishing you for my problems when you have problems of your own. I should have been helping you. What are you going to do about Cretacia?"

Millie sighed. "I don't know, but I've got a few days to figure that out. Here, the scones are ready." She put one on a plate for him. "Now let's see whether I should pour your tea into a cup or a saucer."

Horace hopped up to the table and cautiously flicked his tongue out. It sank deep into the scone and came back out covered in crumbs. "Mmm... delicious," Horace said, sliding the lids shut on his slitted eyes.

Suddenly he gave a great, deep moan. "BRRRRREEECCCCCKKKKKKK!" His shape turned misty, expanded, and reformed as an indistinct human, standing in the middle of the kitchen table. He looked at himself, raising his arms, draped in his old chains. "I'm back! Millie, you did it!"

Millie's stomach felt warm and happy, but maybe that was just the tea. "Cup it is," she said and began to pour.

↛

The problem with Endsday was that there was no school. On the other hand, Millie got to dawdle in bed that morning. She really didn't want to face her mother just yet. But her stomach grumbled loudly, so she threw off her black patchwork quilt and padded down to the kitchen.

Millie stoked up the oven. She took down the bread dough she'd left to rise the night before and formed two loaves, put them in pans, and left them to rise. She boiled potatoes for hash browns, then put them in the sink to cool and popped the bread in the oven. In a skillet, she laid three thick slices of bacon, and she put on a pot of water for soft-boiled eggs. As the bacon finished, she pulled the slices out, tossed in chopped onions, and grated the cooled potatoes right into the skillet.

It was easy to feel her magic this morning, as though it had always been there, a part of her, but she worked on not letting it spill into her cooking this time. She just made the change so that Horace could eat her food as usual.

Bogdana finally came down as Millie pulled the bread from the oven. "You were out late," Millie said. "Soft-boiled egg?" At her mother's nod, she gently dropped three eggs into the boiling water.

Bogdana settled herself at the kitchen table, not even bothering with the dining room. "Do you know what the Council discussed last night? Your cousin Cretacia."

Millie nearly dropped the jam jar she was setting out. "I thought that would be a Coven matter."

"I had to argue long and hard to make it so. The Dodonoi delegate was quite angry. Dodonoi children are rare enough without people going around and trying to kidnap them." She rubbed her temples. "In the end, I convinced her that the Coven would be best suited to mete out justice.

"Now, what's your involvement in all this?" Bogdana looked at Millie with an odd mix of bewilderment and hope. "You sprouted this treeling?"

Millie nodded.

"And where did you get the cacao bean? I thought you'd stopped trying to grind your own chocolate."

"I transformed it," Millie said, "from a regular bean."

Bogdana blinked. "You did? You performed a successful transformation?"

Millie nodded. "Apparently, I'm pretty good at it."

"Then Horace...?"

"Back to normal," Millie said. "Horace! Breakfast!"

Horace slid through the pantry door. "Mmm, bacon and fresh bread," he said. "Good morning, Millie, Bogdana. Look, I'm my old self again!" He twirled happily through the wall and back again.

Bogdana spluttered. "I don't believe it. How did you do that?"

"I just had to transform the completion element into spirit food so Horace could eat it," Millie explained.

"Oh," Bodgana said, at a loss. "It seems you've learned quite a lot at school. What else have you learned?"

Millie set out the soft-boiled eggs in their cups, then

took the letter down from its shelf and, with a trembling hand, gave it to her mother. "Here, I think you should read this first."

As Millie cracked the top off her egg, Bogdana broke the seal on the letter and unrolled it. "Chamomile tea?" she muttered, munching hash browns as she read. "Insect repellent? A Dome of Silence, really? Mud? Charms?" Bogdana put down the letter. "Headmistress Pteria informs me that I have probably been charmed." She stood up and looked herself over. "Greatest dark darkness, where did all these come from?" Millie's mother began brushing herself off with her hands, and Millie felt little cracklings of magic skittering off into the corners of the room.

Bogdana gave herself a final shake and blinked twice. "Well, that was a surprise. How long have you been charming me, Ludmilla?"

Millie wanted to hide under the table, but she stayed seated. *Keep calm. You can do this.* "I really don't know. I didn't know I was doing it until yesterday."

A gleam came into Bogdana's eyes. She strode forward and seized Millie by the chin, turning her face from one side to the other. "Hmm, yes, I see it now. Your power has been growing for some time. You charmed your whole class?" Bogdana asked, and Millie nodded sheepishly.

A deep, satisfied smile spread across Bogdana's face. "So. You're a kitchen witch, despite my best efforts."

Millie's jaw dropped in shock. "What? You knew?"

"Oh, darkness, it was so obvious," Bogdana said. "Mud pies, gingerbread men. What a tired old cliché. Kitchen magic went out of fashion at least two centuries ago. I suppose you'll be wanting a gingerbread house next."

"Um, not really..." Millie stuttered.

"I did my best, I really did," Bogdana went on. "I tried

everything I could to steer you onto a path of power. Now it seems I was right. You have developed real power, Ludmilla."

"I have?"

Bogdana gave Millie a toothy grin. "Do you know how powerful the wards at that school are? How powerful mine are? And you overcame them without even trying! You are an exceedingly powerful witch, just as I've always hoped you would be."

Giddy with excitement, Bogdana drew Millie into a bone-crushing embrace. Millie, completely confused, burst into tears, which caused Bogdana to drop her back into her chair. "Why, whatever is the matter with you? You should be exultant!"

Millie shook her head. "I d-don't know," she sobbed. "It's just... it's all so m-much!"

Bogdana plumped herself down beside Millie and put her arm around Millie's shoulders. "Oh, I understand. Great power can be a trifle scary. But just think, Ludmilla! Think of the terror you will strike into the hearts of your enemies! At a mere eleven years of age, you can already overcome the most potent of wards. Who will be safe from you? No one!" Bogdana rose to her feet, triumphant.

"Oh, just wait until the Coven hears about this! I can hardly wait to tell Hepsibat. Thinks her Cretacia's so special. Now Cretacia will be punished, and you'll rise within the Coven's hierarchy to take her place."

Darkness! Cretacia wasn't entirely wrong to be jealous. Are all the witches like this, constantly trying to best each other? "What will happen to Cretacia?" Millie asked.

Bogdana waved her hand. "Nothing serious. We'll bind her power for a while."

"B-bind her power? That sounds awful," Millie said.

"Oh, yes, it will be hard for her," Bogdana said,

gloating. "She won't be able to use a speck of magic until the binding is lifted."

As much as Cretacia deserved it, Millie felt sorry for her. That was just how she'd felt all these years. And then she thought, *that's how I felt in the kitchen yesterday.* "Mother, are there other cases when a person's power might be bound?" Bogdana looked sharply at her. "Generally, it's for misuse of power. Why?"

Millie took a deep breath. "Have you ever put a binding on me?"

Bogdana flushed a deep green. "No! Why would you even think such a thing?"

Millie blew out. "Well, I've been so bad at magic for so long."

"Darkness, no, child. I don't want you to fail, I want you to succeed. If I'd put a binding on you, you would never have learned to use magic, and I so wanted that for you." Bogdana smiled at her daughter. "To have true power, to take your rightful place as a Coven leader."

"Really?" Millie said. She felt a warm glow in her stomach.

"Oh, yes," Bogdana confirmed. "But you couldn't do that as a useless kitchen witch. So I placed a binding on the kitchen."

Millie blinked. "You what?"

"To do kitchen magic, you need a kitchen," Bogdana explained. "I just placed a magical barrier on the kitchen to prevent you from using kitchen magic. That way, you'd be forced to develop your other magical abilities. And it worked!" she cried, leaping to her feet. "You've demonstrated that. Extremely powerful charms! Rare transformations! You're going to be a great power, I can feel it!"

"But... but Horace is magical, and he can be in the kitchen," Millie protested.

Bogdana sighed. "I had to place an exception in the barrier for him, allowing only spirit magic. Doubtless that's the loophole you found and exploited in order to make your charms. I never noticed them because I assumed you couldn't be charming me with your food. Silly me."

Millie stared at her mother. "All this time," she said slowly. "All this time, when you were telling me I was worthless, you knew I could do magic?"

"Well, I had to," Bogdana said. "I couldn't allow you to think that your kitchen magic was acceptable. Every time you turned a potion into jelly or enchanted a corset to become a roast turkey, I had to stop you from thinking that was proper magic." She looked down at Millie. "Believe me, I didn't enjoy it at all."

"You didn't enjoy it?" Millie echoed. "How do you think I felt? I thought I was hopeless, I thought you hated me!" Anger exploded in Millie's stomach, drenching her in rage. "How could you do that to me? HOW COULD YOU?"

"Now, now," said Bogdana, startled. "Don't get so upset. It was all for your own good. And look where it's gotten you! You've done several impossible things just in the last few weeks! Oh, I can hardly wait to tell Hepsibat."

Millie jumped to her feet. "Stop that! I'm not some toy in a game. I'm your daughter! You bound the kitchen and kept me from using what I really love, cooking, to do my magic. Do you have any idea how awful that was? Trying and failing, over and over again? You had no right to do that!"

"I'm your mother," Bogdana replied stiffly. "I have every right. And I've proved that."

"You're wrong," Millie told her. "I nearly gave up. I was convinced I'd be nothing but a cook for the rest of my life, that I'd be banished to the Logical Realm."

Bogdana flushed at that. "Oh, no, I would never have allowed that."

"It would have been better than this!" Millie screamed. "At least there, no one would have thought I was weird or stupid for loving to cook. I'd have been normal, not some freak. That's what you made me, Mother. A freak."

Bogdana's eyes flashed angrily. "I understand that you're upset, but I am still your mother, and I demand that you respect me."

"How can I?" Millie threw back at her. "How can I respect someone who lies to me, binds my power, and tells me I'm worthless when I'm not and never was? How can I ever trust you again?"

Bogdana drew herself up to her full, angular height, and stared down her nose at Millie. "You will respect me, Ludmilla. I am your mother."

Millie clenched her fists. Then, with one sweep of her arm, she knocked all the food from the table onto the floor.

"I hate you," she said. "I hate you, and I will never cook for you again." Millie turned and ran up the stairs to her room.

Chapter 16
Burnt Oatmeal

On Onesday morning, Millie woke to the scent of burning oatmeal. She dressed for school and came downstairs. To her utter surprise, she found the dining room table set with clean plates.

"Good morning, Ludmilla," said Bogdana, her gown smudged with flour. "I made you some breakfast."

"I'm not hungry," Millie said. This was a blatant lie. Millie hadn't eaten a thing since yesterday's breakfast, but she refused to admit it.

"Well, I am," said Bodgana, seating herself with a bowl of burnt oatmeal, liberally doused with milk, and a cup of rather weak tea.

"What are you doing up so early?" Millie asked.

"Headmistress Pteria requested I come in to talk to her today," Bogdana reminded her. "I'm looking forward to discussing your future course of study. I hate to admit it, but Baba Luci was right. School has been good for you." She buttered a bit of toast salvaged from Millie's bread.

"I'm going to make my lunch," Millie said, marching into the kitchen.

"Take your time, dear," Bogdana called after her. "I can

fly us both there in no time at all."

"I'll walk," Millie said through gritted teeth.

There was a fair bit of bread left. Millie made three or four jam sandwiches, wrapped them in wax paper, and put them in her lunch cauldron. She met Petunia at the kitchen gate. Petunia gave a long whistle when she saw her.

"You're in that much trouble, huh?" Petunia asked.

"Nope. My mother's in that much trouble." As Millie set off grimly up the Path, she told Petunia about the binding on the kitchen.

"Slugs and bugs!" Petunia exclaimed. "That's horrible! My mother would never do that to me. If she noticed I existed at all."

"I just can't believe she did that," Millie said. "All these years, I was a perfectly fine witch, but she tried to convince me otherwise just because she doesn't like kitchen magic!"

Bogdana flew up behind them on her broom. "Ludmilla, are you sure you won't ride with me? I could even give your little friend a ride, if you like," she said, offering a slightly disgusted smile to Petunia.

"Exercise is good for me," Millie told her.

Bogdana looked sad but nodded. "I'll see you at school, then," she said, and she flew off.

"Wow," Petunia said. "If I treated my mother like that, she'd give me a whipping."

"I'm the only daughter she's got," Millie said grimly. "Lucky me."

"Hmm. What do you call a witch's quarrel?" Petunia asked. Millie shrugged.

"A rough spell!" Petunia giggled uncertainly, but when Millie didn't join her, she stopped. "What are you going to do?"

"I don't know," Millie said. "I really don't know. I broke the binding on the kitchen, though I don't think Mother noticed. So I can do all the kitchen magic I like now. But how do I know she won't do something else? Something worse?"

"Don't you have a Coven meeting coming up?" Petunia asked.

"Tomorrow night," Millie said. "Why?"

"Well, you could ask your granny for help."

"My granny? You mean Baba Luci?" Millie considered this. "That's not a bad idea. It's going to be a busy meeting, though. We're trying Cretacia for attempting to kidnap Thea. I think that's part of why Mother had to go to school this morning."

"Lilies and ladybugs!" Petunia said. "What will happen to her?"

"Mother says the Coven will probably bind her magic for a while, so she can't hurt anyone else," Millie said. "I almost feel sorry for Cretacia."

"Ha!" said Petunia. "She's getting off easy. If she were a pixie, she'd be whipped and thrown in Bramble Jail."

They arrived at school, where Grumpkin promptly tripped Millie, who fell on her face.

"Grumpkin, I am so not in the mood for this," Millie began, but Grumpkin bent low to Millie's ear.

"Chase me," he muttered in a low voice. Then he took off running across the glade, yelling, "Can't catch me!"

"What was that about?" Petunia said. "I thought he was helping you."

Millie scratched her head. "I think he still is. Come on." She picked herself up, and they ran after him. Grumpkin darted back and forth, weaving between the other students, until he led them to the far side of the glade and stopped beside a bunch of bushes.

"There you go," Grumpkin said to the bushes, and he ran off.

"Thanks, Grumpkin," called the bushes in Max's voice. He cautiously peeped out between branches, hat in his hands.

"Max!" Millie cried. "I'm so glad you're here! Cretacia didn't snitch on you?"

"Shhhh!" Max said. "No, she didn't. I have no idea why not. She's grounded right now, stuck in her room under ward. But Hepsibat and Mother are coming to talk to the Headmistress, so I need your assistance to get me into school."

"Oh, no," Millie told him. "No more unauthorized magic for me."

Max laughed. "Obviously. Just keep lookout, okay?"

"Well, Mother's already here. She passed us on the way in."

"I'm surprised you didn't ride in with her."

Millie clenched her fists. "I am never riding anywhere with her again if I can possibly help it," she declared.

Max's eyebrows shot up. "What happened?"

So Millie told Max her story again.

Max sucked in her breath. "That's... that's abominable! I can't believe Mother did that to you!"

"It's criminal," Petunia said. "Abuse. You should persecute her."

"Prosecute," Max corrected.

"Whatever."

"I'll talk to Baba Luci at the Coven meeting tomorrow," Millie said, then smacked herself on the forehead. "Oh, no, I'll have to ride with Mother."

"I'll take you," Max said. "I think Dad and I are invited on account of being Cretacia's family."

Millie relaxed. "That would be great. Thanks."

"There goes another witch," Petunia sang out.

Millie glanced up in time to see Aunt Hepsibat fly up to the staircase. She stepped off and gingerly set foot on the stairs, shrinking down to Millie's size. This gave Millie a fit of giggles.

"What?" Max said.

"Teensy Aunt Hepsibat. She's heading up the stairs," Millie told him. "Okay, she's probably far enough that you can go on up to class now."

Max popped out of the bush like a frog after a fly, lugging his rolled up carpet and a bulging knapsack. "I can hardly wait for Elementary Potions today," he said. "I'm going to try making my own liquefied information."

Millie looked dubious. "What kind of information?"

"English!" Max said. "I borrowed some books from Dad. If I can learn English, I can read his notes and identify the location of the Logical Realm portal."

Slow respect spread across Petunia's face. "It's a good idea. But do you still think Sagara wants us to help her?"

"Why wouldn't she?" Millie asked.

Max glanced at her. "Um, Sagara was not very happy after Thaumaturgy on Foursday. She thinks you charmed her from the beginning."

Millie's stomach lurched. "Oh, no. Do you think I was? I mean, I might have been. What if I charmed all of you?"

Petunia rolled her eyes. "We're still here, aren't we? Quercius dispelled any charms in class, so if we're here, it must be because we like you anyway, even if you do dress funny."

Millie stuck out her tongue at her. "Still, I'm going to have to find a way to make it up to her. But first, I have to go talk to the Headmistress and my mother."

They reached the stairs and started up, Millie stopping at Headmistress Pteria's office. "See you at lunch!" Petunia called to Millie as she and Max continued to their classroom.

"I'm not allowed to share my lunch with you," Millie warned.

Max grinned. "I brought Thai food."

Millie burst into laughter. "Perfect!" She waited until they were out of sight around the bend of the stairs, and then she knocked respectfully on the door frame.

"Come in!" called Headmistress Pteria.

Millie pushed through the curtain. Bogdana and Aunt Hepsibat sat in one of the chairs, and Thea rested in her pot on the Headmistress's desk.

"Welcome, Millie," said Headmistress Pteria. "I'm sorry to do this to you again, but I'm afraid your mother and your aunt have some deeper discussion to finish. Perhaps we can meet after lunch?"

Relieved, Millie nodded. "Of course, Headmistress."

"Thank you, Millie. You may go."

෴

It was so hard for Millie to concentrate in class. She tried to talk to Sagara, to apologize and explain, but the elf kept glaring at her and slipping away. Millie fidgeted all through Circle Time, and she stared out the window through most of Reading Group. Fortunately, Master Augustus didn't push her.

At last, the gong sounded, and Millie snatched up her cauldron and dashed off to lunch.

When she got to the table, Petunia was waiting for her, but there was no sign of her brother.

"Where's Max?" she asked, setting down her cauldron.

Petunia twisted the ends of her hair nervously. "He got called to Headmistress Pteria's office."

"Oh, that can't be good. Aunt Hepsibat must have found out about him." Millie swallowed hard.

"Ahem," said a voice behind her.

Millie turned to find Sagara looking at her curiously.

"Sagara!" Millie cried. "I'm so sorry. I didn't know I was charming you, and I didn't mean to, really."

Sagara held up a hand to stop Millie's babbling. "I know that," she said.

"Then, you're not mad at me?"

Sagara sighed. "I was at first. I hate it when people mess with me. My brother used to charm me all the time when I was little, made me think I was a bird or a squirrel. It was humiliating.

"So when I found out you'd charmed me, I was furious. I thought you were just as bad as my brother. Then I saw you in class today, and it was obvious that you were really sorry, which my brother never was. I got to thinking about what, exactly, you charmed me to do. And I realized that your charms just made me feel happy and less lonely. Comforted."

Sagara smiled at her. "You don't charm people to hurt them. You do it to help them, to make them feel better."

Millie thought about that. "That's true. I think that's why I love cooking so much. Food makes people happy, and I like feeling like I've helped them."

"Also, yummmmm," added Petunia.

"I realized one other thing," Sagara said. "You were nice to me even before you charmed me, and you were nice to me after, even though you didn't know I was charmed. You're my friend, and I'd like to continue being yours. Also, the occasional elfcake wouldn't hurt." She winked.

Millie broke into a big grin. "Then you accept my apology?"

Sagara lifted her nose, rolled her eyes, and in her old snooty elf voice, said, "Well, I suppose I could do that." And they all laughed.

"Now listen," Sagara said as she sat down. "When I thought I couldn't rely on Millie doing research for me, I stole my brother's notes on the portal, and I know how to open it. We have to face a guardian of some kind who will give us three tests. Then we have to say the proper incantation and use a great deal of magical power to open the portal. That's where your pixie dust will come in handy, Petunia. All we really need is for Max to find the location of the portal, and we can get to the Logical Realm."

"I'm in," Petunia said.

Millie nodded. "I should be able to help with the guardian, now that I've figured out how to charm people."

"Don't overdo it," Sagara said. "I don't need the guardian following me through the portal."

Millie grimaced. "I'll do my best."

"So when do you think you'll go?" Petunia asked.

"That will depend on Max," Sagara said. She looked worried. "I hope he'll be okay. I was finally getting used to him and his silly vocabulary. It'd be a shame if he had to leave school now."

"MILLIE, PLEASE REPORT TO HEADMISTRESS PTERIA'S OFFICE," Master Quercius announced.

Millie's stomach flipped. "I guess I'm about to find out." She put down her cauldron and left the glade, heading up the stairs to the Headmistress's office. She wasn't sure, but Millie thought she heard Aunt Hepsibat saying, "But would you consider enrolling Cretacia?" A shiver ran down Millie's back. Not wanting to hear more, she knocked politely.

"Enter," came the dragon's voice.

Millie pushed past the curtain and stopped short. In the office were Headmistress Pteria, Bogdana, Hepsibat, and a terrified-looking Max.

"It has come to our attention," said Headmistress Pteria, "that your brother Max was enrolled at the Enchanted Forest School under false pretenses."

Hepsibat was grinning triumphantly, while Bogdana looked like she was ready to spit nails.

"Millie," said the Headmistress, "did you know that Max had forged his entrance papers?"

Millie considered. She could lie and potentially save herself, but that felt wrong. And there was always the possibility that Headmistress Pteria would simply use another truth spell on her. Besides, she could never lie to her mother.

"Yes," Millie said.

"What?" Bogdana screeched. "And you didn't tell me?"

Millie squirmed. "He asked me not to."

"I am his mother!" Bogdana stated, standing straight and looking Millie right in the eye, which was a little disconcerting. "I have a right to know information that affects the well-being of my son."

"You're his mother," Millie said, "but you don't make decisions for him. His father does that, just as you wouldn't expect my father to make decisions for me if he were still alive."

Hepsibat looked startled and began to say, "Oh, but he's not dead..." but Bogdana interrupted her.

"That's beside the point," Bogdana said to Millie, glancing sharply at Hepsibat. "Alfonso consults me on Max's upbringing as a courtesy."

Headmistress Pteria broke in. "Councilor Salazar has been notified and will be here shortly."

"And how was I supposed to know that?" Millie said. "I thought you'd lost all interest in Max, since we haven't visited him in five years. Can you really blame him for wanting to enroll? He missed me, and I missed him, and I'm glad he came."

"So you lied to me," Bogdana hissed. "After all your posturing, you're just as untrustworthy as you accuse me of being."

"I did not lie!" Millie insisted. "I told you Max had been

giving me rides home from school. You just assumed he wasn't attending, which is a pretty silly assumption if you ask me."

"Treacherous child! Inconsiderate brat!" She rounded on Headmistress Pteria. "And you! You should have informed me as soon as he enrolled."

The Headmistress eyed Bogdana coolly. "I had no obligation to do so. Nor would I have informed you had the papers been legitimate, unless Councilor Salazar gave me permission to do so. You are not Max's legal guardian, and so you have no rights in this matter."

A loud knock sounded from the doorway. "Enter!" Headmistress Pteria said.

Alfonso Salazar strode into the room, a magic carpet tucked under his arm. He looked much the same as he had five years ago, but Millie noticed he had more gray hair at his temples. At the same height as Max, Millie could easily see their similarities, the unkempt brown hair and tan skin, though Salazar had brown eyes.

"Max!" he said, going over to his son. "Are you all right?"

Max nodded, not daring to speak.

"You enrolled yourself in school?"

Max nodded again.

"Hmm. And why didn't you ask me?"

In a very small voice, Max said, "I didn't think you'd let me go."

Salazar raised an eyebrow. "Why on earth would you think that? I think school is an excellent idea."

Max goggled at him. "But, but Hepsibat was going on and on about how awful it was and what a disgrace it was that Millie was going and how she'd never, ever allow Cretacia to attend, and you never said anything. I thought you agreed with her."

"Well, that's what you get for assuming," Salazar replied.

"Hepsibat and I don't always see eye to eye on things, but I don't generally argue with her unless I need to." He winked at Hepsibat, who actually blushed. "Now, tell me why you want to come to this school."

"Well, at first, I wanted to come to see Millie," Max said. "I hadn't seen her for so long, and I really missed her." He glared at Bogdana, who turned to glare at Millie again. "I also wanted to get away from Cretacia. She's horrible, Dad, you have no idea! She tortures me!"

Salazar rubbed the stubble on his chin. "I used to think you were exaggerating, that this was just some sibling rivalry that the two of you would work out. However, in light of Cretacia's recent actions, I stand corrected. I'm sorry I didn't believe you."

"But now," Max said, warming up, "I like it here. I've made friends, and I'm learning new things, stuff you haven't taught me. The school has a great library! And a laboratory, and a thaumaturgy teacher, though he doesn't like me much right now, and..."

"All right, all right, breathe already," said Salazar, laughing. "I get the point." He turned to the Headmistress. "I am sorry for the confusion, and I apologize for my son's minor attempt at fraud. But, if you are amenable, I think we can regard this as unusual initiative, rather than criminal intent. I have no objections to Max attending your school." Millie started to see where Max got his flowery speech from.

The dragon blinked. "That is acceptable. If you will just sign..."

"Well, I object!" Bogdana spoke up. "What kind of lesson are you teaching him? That it's acceptable to commit fraud? To lie to everyone?"

Salazar suppressed a smile. "Calm down, Danny. There's no harm here. The lesson I want him to take away from this is that it's generally easier to ask first."

"And you wonder why I haven't visited in five years! You're a bad influence, Alfonso."

"Now, Danny. Let's not air our old arguments in public. School has been good for Max, and from what I've heard, it's obviously been good for Millie. Seeing each other every day is probably good for them both." He sighed. "I wish it had had the same effect on Cretacia."

"Oh, don't you start," Aunt Hepsibat broke in.

"No, I won't," Alfonso said firmly. "We can do that at home. Headmistress, do you have everything you need from my wife?" From the emphasis he placed on *wife*, Salazar sounded unhappy with that arrangement.

"Yes, we are finished for now," replied the Headmistress.

Salazar straightened. "Then we will stop taking up your valuable time, won't we, Hepsibat?"

Aunt Hepsibat looked like she'd eaten a slug, but she nodded.

"And as for you, Max," Salazar said, "get back to class, and I want a full report on everything you've done when you get home."

Max blinked. "Sure, Dad."

"Thank you, Headmistress," said Salazar, taking Aunt Hepsibat by the elbow and steering her out the door. "Have a good day."

The Headmistress turned to Max. "Well, Max, I am disappointed in your methods but pleased with the results. Nonetheless, you will need to return to my office for detention after school today. Understand?"

Max hung his head. "Yes, Headmistress."

"You may go to lunch," said the dragon.

"Thank you, Headmistress." Max winked at Millie as he left.

Headmistress Pteria heaved a large sigh. "Now, Millie, we finally have time to devote to you. Please take a seat."

"Thank you, Headmistress," Millie said, sitting down.

"Let's make this quick," said Bogdana. "I have a trial to prepare for."

"Of course, Councilor," said the Headmistress. "As I explained in my letter, Millie has manifested an unusual degree of talent in the last few days. She has shown aptitude in charms, transformations, and thaumaturgy, with affinities for both spirit magic and kitchen magic."

"Excellent," said Bogdana with satisfaction. "My compliments to you and your staff for helping Millie realize her potential."

"You are quite welcome," Headmistress Pteria told her, drumming her talons on the desk. "However, I have some questions for you. It seems odd to me and to my staff that Millie would have this degree of talent and yet never showed that talent at home. We believe something has been interfering with her magic. Do you have any idea what that could be?"

Bogdana blinked. "Um, well, not really..."

"Mother put a binding on our kitchen," Millie said angrily. "She didn't want me to be a kitchen witch."

"How dare you!" Bogdana protested, rounding on Millie. "Impudent child!"

Headmistress Pteria leaned forward. "Is this true, Councilor?"

"None of your business!" Bogdana spat.

"Ah," the dragon breathed out. "Then it is true. Don't you think that was rather severe?"

Bogdana was turning purple with indignation. "I neither desire nor require your opinion, Pteria. Witches have their own methods and traditions."

Headmistress Pteria shook her head. "I have been reading up on traditional witch education and philosophy. I believe bindings are used as either a last resort to control a young witch not yet capable of managing her ability or as a punishment for misuse of magic. Millie falls into neither of these categories."

Bogdana stood. "I do not have to justify my actions to you."

Headmistress Pteria cocked her head. "No, you don't, but I do need to know about conditions that affect the potential and well-being of my students."

Bogdana glared at the Headmistress. "In that case, I am withdrawing Ludmilla from this miserable institution. I refuse to expose my daughter to such flagrant disrespect!"

Millie felt like she'd been punched. "No!" she wailed. "I don't want to leave!"

Bogdana seized Millie by the arm. "That's my decision. We are leaving. Now." She dragged her out of the Headmistress's office.

"But what about Thea?" Millie cried, glancing back at the little Dodonas in her pot. "I'm supposed to take care of her."

"Not my problem," Bogdana growled.

"Councilor Noctmartis, I beg you to reconsider," Pteria's words echoed down the stairs after them.

Bogdana pulled Millie into the glade. The other students gaped at her over their lunches.

"Mother! Mother, stop! I need to get my lunch cauldron."

"Leave it," Bogdana said. "You won't be needing it anymore." Holding out her broom with one hand, she slung Millie across it with the other, straddled the broom and zoomed off.

"Mother! Slow down! I'm going to throw up!"

Bogdana cackled. "Go right ahead!"

So Millie did.

When they got home, Bogdana dragged her inside and dumped her on the parlor sofa, raising clouds of dust.

"Never again," her mother declared, coughing. "Never again will you humiliate me in public. You never, ever discuss private business with outsiders. Do you have any idea what you've done? If word gets out about the binding, I could be reprimanded by the Coven. I could lose my seat on the Council!"

"You should have thought of that before you did it," Millie pointed out.

"Don't you dare!" Bogdana roared. "Don't you dare blame me for this! After everything I've done for you, all I've sacrificed. You betrayed me!"

"Oh, really? What have you sacrificed, Mother? Just my talent!" Millie jumped up off the sofa. "And what did Aunt Hepsibat mean about my father? She said he's not dead."

Millie's mother hesitated. "That's none of her business," Bogdana snapped.

"It's my business, though," Millie said. "Tell me about my father. You've never even told me his name, just that he's dead and gone. Except I think you're lying. I think he's alive."

Bogdana turned pale, and then flushed a deep, livid green all over. "This is all your father's fault, every last bit. I told you he's dead because he may as well be. You will never, ever see him again."

Max was right. I do have a father. Tears began streaming down Millie's face. "Why, Mother? Why do you keep doing this? I can't see Max, I can't go to school, I can't know my own father. It's wrong! It's wrong, and you know it."

Bogdana looked down at her, grinding her teeth. "It's for your own good," she said finally. "Hate me if you want, but I will protect you. I will make sure you achieve your full potential and rise to lead the Coven. You have a great future, Millie. You just can't see it now." Bogdana raised a hand. "*Lukitse*," she intoned.

Millie felt the ward slam shut around the house. She was trapped again.

"When you are ready to resume your training, I'll be in the workshop," said Bogdana. She turned and stomped away.

Chapter 17

Crepes and Chamomile

That afternoon, Millie heard Petunia whistle at the kitchen gate. She dashed out to find her hopping up and down on the gate and Max pacing anxiously along the Path. Max hurried over.

"I finished my detention during recess so I could come straight over after school. What happened?" he asked.

Millie began to cry. In halting sentences, she told them.

"Muck and muddle!" Petunia cried, clapping her hands to her head. "Your father's alive, and she's been hiding him from you? That's awful! What are you going to do?"

Millie wiped her face with the hem of her apron. "I've thought about that a lot, actually, and I've decided that I'm going to run away."

Petunia gasped. "How? You can't get through the wards."

"No, but I bet Max can." She turned to her brother. "What do you think?"

Max frowned and scratched his head. He placed a hand out, gingerly touching the ward, and closed his eyes to concentrate.

"Even if Max can do this," Petunia prodded, "Millie, where will you go?"

Millie frowned. "I think I'll go to the Logical Realm with Sagara, if she'll let me."

"What?" Petunia screeched. "You still want to help her, after all this?"

Millie nodded. "Think about it. What's the one thing I love to do most?"

"Cook!" Petunia looked thoughtful. "You're going to go to the Logical Realm to be a chef?"

"I think it's the only thing I can do. Mother won't let me do magic the way I want, and she won't let me go to school to learn. If I run away but stay in the Enchanted Forest, she can track me with magic. But there's no magic in the Logical Realm. I can just disappear."

"But you just figured out your magic," Petunia said. "Are you really going to give that up?"

Millie thought about it, hard. "I don't want to give up magic, but I don't think this is any better, when Mother could bind my magic whenever she wants."

Max blew out a long breath and opened his eyes. "I don't think I can do this. There are several wards here now, and they're pretty complex. I can't deactivate them without her knowing."

"Hmm. What do you know about the wards, Millie?" Petunia asked. "Who can go in and out?"

"Only Mother," Millie replied. "She's very protective of her privacy. No one gets in or out except her unless she takes down the ward."

Max's eyes suddenly grew wide. "Then you'll have to be Mother," he said excitedly. "What's one kind of magic you know you can do?"

"Charms?" Millie asked.

"Transformations!" Petunia cried. "Millie, if you can turn Horace into a frog, you can turn yourself into your mother!

Then you can just walk right out."

Millie considered this. "Yes," she said. "I think I can do that. I have all the ingredients. And I know how to make the cure, too. Max, did you manage to make that Remedial English potion today?"

Max grinned. "Naturally." He pulled out two vials. "I made an extra for Sagara, just in case her English isn't as good as she claims. But if you're going with her, maybe you should use it."

"Oh, that's all right," Millie said. "I speak English pretty well."

"What?" Petunia spluttered. "Since when do you speak English?"

Millie shrugged. "As long as I can remember. Mother speaks it, too. My favorite cookbook is in English."

Max raised an eyebrow. "That's just too convenient."

"Oh, come on. She's taught me some Elvish and Dwarvish, too. Is that weird?"

"It's weird that she'd think English was useful," Petunia pointed out. "No one in the Enchanted Forest speaks it."

"Look, right now, it doesn't matter," Millie said firmly. "Max, can you find the location of the portal? Say, tonight?"

Max's eyes widened. "Tonight? You want to go tomorrow?"

"It's the perfect time," Millie told them. "Mother will be distracted by Cretacia's trial tomorrow night. She'll be running all over the Forest, talking with Coven members, councilors, and the Dodonoi representative."

Max nodded. "You're right. My family will be distracted, too. I should have no trouble sneaking into Dad's workroom."

"But we'll need Sagara," Petunia protested. "Should Max fly over to the Sylvan Vale?"

"That might make her grandmother suspicious." Millie blinked. "I have a better idea. Excuse me? Miss Elm? Can you hear me?" she called across the Path.

The elm tree stirred, rustling. Millie could almost hear words in the crackling of the leaves. She had the tree's attention. "My friend Sagara said that trees spread gossip faster than a carpet can fly. Can you do that?" The elm tree rustled and dipped a branch in affirmation. "Oh, good. If you don't mind, could you please send a message to Sagara? She lives in the Arela household." Millie stopped, twisting her hands in her apron. What should she say? "Um, please tell Sagara that she should contact Max right away."

The elm tree bowed, just a bit, and then began furiously rustling to the oak tree next to it, which rustled to the next tree, and the next.

"Well," Max said, "I think that's all we can do. We had better go prepare."

Millie nodded. "I have a lot of work to do. Can either of you scry yet?" Max and Petunia shook their heads.

"Since none of us speaks tree, why don't we meet back here tomorrow after school?" Max suggested. "That will give Millie plenty of time to make her potion, and it'll give us time for last-minute preparations."

Millie nodded. "And it won't make anyone suspicious if you come visit your poor grounded sister after school."

Max grinned. "This should be fun. Come on, Petunia. I'll give you a ride home."

Petunia clapped her hands in excitement. "See you tomorrow, Millie!"

"Tomorrow," Millie echoed sadly, wishing she could go along with them. She'd even ride the magic carpet again. Instead, she turned and trudged back inside.

The following morning, Millie woke up early and hurried down to the kitchen. She found her lunch cauldron sitting in the sink. *Mother must have brought it in*, she thought. She pulled down **Simple Pleasures** and opened it at the orange ribbon: crepes, her mother's favorite breakfast. Millie stoked up the fire, buttered a cast iron griddle, and set it on the stovetop to heat. Then she swiftly whisked together the flour, powdered sugar, baking powder, salt, eggs, milk, water, and vanilla extract. With a wide ladle, she poured batter onto the now steaming griddle and pushed it into a wide, flat circle to cook.

While the crepe cooked, Millie chopped some bacon ends into small bits and tossed them into another skillet to fry. Pausing to flip the first crepe, she scrambled some eggs with fresh tarragon, parsley, ground pepper and salt, then poured them in with the bacon to cook. Millie took the first crepe off the griddle and added a second. Then she grated some nice hard cheese to go with the eggs.

When the scrambled eggs were done, Millie pulled the last crepe off the griddle, adding it to the large stack she'd made. She took these out to the dining table, then returned with the grated cheese, several jams, and a jar of honey. As she set the table, she could hear her mother rattling about upstairs, so Millie put on the tea kettle.

When Bogdana came down to the table, Millie was standing there, head bowed. "I'm sorry, Mother," she said. "I shouldn't have tattled on you."

"Well," her mother said, trying and failing to hide her delight. "Crepes. How nice." She paused, then flicked her fingers over the food. "Hmm, no charms."

Millie shook her head. "No charms. Just breakfast."

Bogdana sat down, took a crepe and placed it on her plate, loaded it first with cheese, then added some still steaming scrambled eggs. She rolled it up and took a bite, closing her eyes in pleasure.

Millie set the teapot down on the table, chamomile and lemon perfuming the air. She sat down across from her mother and had a crepe with cheese and raspberry jam, eggs on the side. She served her mother tea, then returned to the kitchen with her empty plate as her mother started in on her third crepe, blueberry jam and honey.

"I'm glad to see you've improved your attitude," Bogdana said, wiping crumbs from the corners of her mouth. "The trial is tonight. I'll be very busy today, meeting with the other members of the Coven, the Enchanted Forest Council, and the Dodonoi representative, so I expect you to prepare on your own. Will you bake something for tonight?"

"I have something special in mind," Millie said.

"And you'll charm it?"

Millie nodded.

"Excellent," said Bogdana. She licked the plate clean and rose from the table. "I'll be back in time for dinner, and then we had better get to the circle early, so have everything ready."

"Goodbye, Mother," Millie said quietly.

"Farewell, my dear," said Bogdana, heading out the door with her broomstick. "Happy baking."

Horace glided out of the pantry. "You're going to do it? You'll charm the whole Coven?"

"Darkness! Of course not," said Millie. "I'm going to run away from home."

Horace's jaw dropped. He picked it up off the floor and popped it back into place. "Running away? But where will you go? What will you do?"

"Better if you don't know," Millie told him. "I'll try to send a letter once I'm settled."

Horace began to cry, great ghostly tears falling and evaporating into mist. "Oh, Millie. I can't say you're wrong, but I'll miss you. It's going to be dreary here with just grouchy old Bogdana for company. And I'll miss your cooking. Will you bake something for me before you go?"

Millie grinned. "Oh, yes. I intend to make my specialty."

"Really? You mean it?" Horace did a small jingling jig of happiness.

"Promise," Millie told him. "But right now, I have a potion to brew."

I need something of Mother's, Millie thought. She went up to the second floor bathroom with its ancient, creaky pipes and enormous claw-footed tub. Millie checked her mother's broken-toothed comb. It held two crinkled black hairs. *That will do.*

Grimly, Millie went down to her mother's workshop. Her mother had never forbidden Millie to use it unsupervised because Millie had never wanted to use it before. Now she pulled out all the components for a transformation potion. Carefully, she stoked the fire, set the cauldron over it, and mixed the bubbling brew. This time, she threw in her mother's hairs as she called out, *"Muutu sammakoksi."*

Once again, she felt the tingle of her magic, and then the scent of rich chocolate filled the room. Hastily, Millie filled a bottle with the potion and corked it. Then she had an idea. Pulling out a second cauldron, she hung it over the fire and began again.

When she was done, Millie baked her secret weapon. It contained chocolate, of course. Lots and lots of chocolate. She pulled it out of the oven, let it cool, and cut it into ample squares. She set one on a plate for Horace. The rest she placed in a cauldron with a lid, then sealed the lid with wax. And then she dressed in one of her best witch's gowns and waited for school to get out.

Chapter 18
Millie's Secret Weapon

At long last, Millie heard a very soft whistle from outside. She retrieved her sealed cauldron and picked up a canvas satchel she'd packed earlier. On a whim, she stopped and slipped **Simple Pleasures** into the satchel. Millie stepped outside to the kitchen gate.

Max, Petunia, and Sagara stood outside. Sagara was dressed again in the strange blue trousers with a tight-fitting shirt. Millie nearly wilted with relief.

"Max, did you find it?" Millie called.

Max grinned. "Indubitably! It's in the Salivary Swamp."

"So we're going?" Millie said.

Sagara gave her a wry grin. "If you can get out of your yard."

Millie nodded and pulled out a vial with a black ribbon tied around the neck. "Okay. Here goes." Without pausing to let herself get nervous, she pulled off the stopper and drank it all down.

For a moment, she didn't feel any different. And then she felt herself growing taller, bonier. Angrier.

It wasn't fair. It simply wasn't fair, being the youngest daughter of the Baba and having such a minor talent as healing.

She wanted power, real power, the kind her mother had. She wanted to make every one of her four sisters stop flaunting their powers and tormenting her. So what if Hepsibat could build magnificent golems? So what if Ospecia could transform water into steel? Did that give them the right to grind her nose in it? To put mud in her shoes and charm off all her warts and call her a useless healer?

Well, she wasn't going to let that happen to her daughter. Millie would have real power, the kind she herself had never known. Ludmilla would not suffer as she had suffered. Ludmilla...

"Millie! Millie!"

Millie snapped open her eyes and found herself with her hands clenched, looking down at Max calling her from beyond the gate.

"Come on, Millie!" Max hissed at her. "Hurry up!"

A wave of sorrow passed through Millie. Poor Mother. She'd been an apprentice witch once, too. Millie'd had no idea how humiliated Bogdana had felt growing up. But that didn't excuse her mother's actions. Millie shook the feeling off. She unlatched the gate and stepped through. For a moment, she felt the wards probe her, stretch around her. And then she passed them all. She was free.

Quickly, Millie whipped out a bit of orange peel and popped it into her mouth. Instantly, she shrank down and returned to her normal old self.

Petunia flung her arms around Millie's ankle. "You did it!"

"Shh!" warned Max, but he hugged Millie, too.

Sagara watched them, her head cocked to one side. She held out a hand. "Nice work," Sagara said.

Millie took her hand and solemnly shook it. "Thanks." Then she turned to the elm tree. "And thank you, too."

The elm tree brushed her head gently.

Sagara looked surprised. "She says you're welcome."

"Okay," Max said. "Let's get going. We haven't got much time before Mother notices that Millie's gone. Also, I'm coming along. I want to see for myself what Dad's been up to in the Logical Realm."

"I thought you might say that, so I made something extra." Millie turned to Petunia. "I don't think it's fair to leave you behind. If we don't come back, you could be blamed for our disappearance. But I think I know a way for you to join us." She pulled out another potion, this one with a blue ribbon. "This is a simple transformation potion. It will turn you into a human."

Petunia stared at the bottle. "Me? A human? No offense, but I like myself as I am."

"This is just for while we're in the Logical Realm," Millie explained. "When you come back, you can take the antidote and be yourself again." She held up another piece of orange peel.

"But what will I wear?" Petunia spluttered. "I can't go in daffodil petals!"

Millie patted her satchel. "I brought you one of my gowns and a spare pair of clogs."

"I don't know. Can I think about it?"

"Right up until we step through the portal," Sagara said.

Max hopped from foot to foot. "Come on, we should go. Mother could come home anytime."

"Right," Millie said. "Let's go."

He led them to his magic carpet, and they all settled in, Petunia tucked in Millie's apron pocket, the cauldron nestled in the crook of Millie's arm.

Max tapped the carpet with his wand, and they zoomed away, causing several birds to twitter at them angrily.

"Can't we go any faster?" Millie complained.

Max burst out laughing. "I was going slower for you.

Hang on tight." He tapped the carpet again, and they sped forward faster than Millie had ever gone. And she discovered that she was not afraid. Racing over the trees to the portal, Millie laughed out loud with delight.

"You know what?" Sagara yelled in her ear. "I think you're not afraid of heights. I think you're just afraid of not being able to control where you're going."

Maybe, Millie thought. *Maybe she's right.*

They swung out over the glittering pools and noxious odors of the Salivary Swamp. Sagara flung out an arm. "There! That's the portal."

A small round lake lay nestled near the western edge of the swamp. In the middle of the lake, there stood a very small island crowned with two enormous weeping willows. Suddenly, the magic carpet quivered and began to lose altitude, gliding slowly to a stop on the shore of the lake.

"That's a powerful ward," Max said. "I presume this is where we meet the guardian of the portal."

A large, snakelike head rose from the lake before them, its dark scales dripping with slime so green and oozy, Bogdana would have loved it. It studied them with its red, glowing eyes. Millie stifled a little shriek and clutched her cauldron close to her.

"You presume correctly, little wizard," said the head as another emerged. And another, and another. Millie could hear Petunia counting under her breath.

"Nine," the pixie whispered.

Sagara made a disgusted noise. "He's a hydra, Petunia. Of course he has nine heads." Sagara turned bravely back to the hydra's nine heads, though Millie could see she was trembling. "Greetings, o guardian!" Sagara said. "We are on errantry, and we seek passage through the portal."

Another head hissed at her. "You must overcome our

three challenges. Are you prepared?"

"We are," Sagara asserted, with only the slightest tremor in her voice.

"Test of Wit," intoned three of the heads together. "Answer this riddle." A single head cleared its throat and then recited dramatically, "I never was, am always to be. No one ever saw me, nor ever will. And yet I am the confidence of all, to live..."

"Tomorrow," Petunia called out.

The head snapped back. "What? But I didn't even finish."

"Oh, come on," Petunia said. "That's one of the oldest riddles ever. Everyone knows that one."

The head looked seriously annoyed, so Millie said loudly, "I didn't know it." Sagara snorted, but she also looked impressed.

"Fine," said the head, and it slunk away with its two companions, making room for three more heads.

"Test of Wisdom," the heads pronounced, and one continued, "Argus the dragonsmith needs 3 pecks of dragonscales to make a centaur suit of armor. A peck is 120 scales. He already has 67 green scales and 118 purple scales. How many more scales must Argus obtain?"

"Ooh, a math problem," Sagara said happily. "3 pecks is 360 scales. 67 plus 118 equals 185. 360 minus 185 equals 175. So Argus needs 175 more scales."

The head looked annoyed. "Final answer?" it muttered hopefully.

"Yes, that is my final answer," Sagara said firmly.

"Hmmph," said the heads, and they slid away, making room for the final three heads. These were the meanest, nastiest-looking heads yet, with sharp teeth as long as Millie's arm.

"Test of Courage," the final three heads announced together.

"You must defeat us and win your way to the island."

"But we have no weapons!" Max cried out.

"Yes, we do," Millie replied, breaking the wax seal and pulling the lid off her cauldron. "Here you go!" And she grabbed a brownie and hurled it into the nearest head's gaping mouth.

Surprised, the head reared back. "Hey! What? Um, nommmm. This is delicious! Bob, you have to try one."

Another head snaked forward. "Is that chocolate?"

"Triple chocolate brownies, my specialty," Millie told him. "Have one!" And she lobbed another brownie into the air, which the head caught with a snap.

"Marvelous!" it mumbled around the brownie.

"I want one," cried the third head, followed by all six of the others.

"Quick, help me," Millie called to the others. Together, they dug into the cauldron and began heaving brownies into the horrible, gaping maws. Soon, all nine heads were munching contentedly.

"Excellent," they murmured. "Superb. Exquisite. Every adventurer should be so considerate. Really, no one thinks about what we might want. They usually try to shoot us or teleport us or put us to sleep." They paused a moment to swallow. Then, in unison, they proclaimed, "You may pass."

Beneath them, the magic carpet quivered to life.

"You charmed them, didn't you?" Max asked Millie quietly as they seated themselves.

"That was the strongest charm I've ever cast," Millie said. "I thought it might come in handy."

"Enough talking," Petunia growled. "Let's go before they figure it out."

Max twisted a tassel, and they soared over the hydra, across the lake, and right to the base of the two willows.

They were ancient weeping willows, leaning toward each other so that their branches formed a graceful arch, curtained by their leaves. Sagara marched up to them and announced, "This is the place."

"Wait a minute," Max said. "Sagara, I made a spare Remedial English potion." He produced a small vial from his pocket. "Do you want it?"

"What did you use as source material?" Sagara asked, frowning.

Max shrugged. "All those books in English that Dad has in his library. It worked fine when I took it yesterday. How do you think I managed to read Dad's notes?" Max grinned at her, and then he said, in English, "*Live long and prosper.*"

Sagara frowned. "That's not an English greeting I'm familiar with. Usually, people just say *hello* or *hi.*"

"Well, that's what people in Dad's books say."

"It was in English," Millie said slowly. "So I guess it worked."

Sagara shook her head. "I think I'll stick with what English I've learned."

"Well, then, I'll take it," Petunia announced. "After all, if I'm going with you, I should speak the language."

Millie hugged her. "I'm so glad you're coming!"

Sagara rolled her eyes. "Fine, but you should drink it once you're human, and you can't transform until after you've used the pixie dust. Fresh is best, you know. Now, can we get on with this? We haven't got all day." She marched up to the trees.

The willows rustled and sighed. "Authorization?" one asked in a voice like a summer breeze. Millie looked up and found two faces staring down at them. *Dodonoi.* Master Quercius had said there were two on special assignment.

Sagara glanced back at the others, startled. "Um, we are

travelers seeking passage."

"Only travelers with the authorization of the Enchanted Forest Council may pass." They felt a ward go up before them. Sagara looked anguished. "My brother's notes didn't mention this."

Max reached out a hand and tapped the ward. "Hmm... this actually looks like Dad's work. I think I know how he constructed it." He glanced back at the others. "I can take this ward down, but only for about a minute or two. Sagara, Petunia, get ready."

Sagara bowed.

Max turned to the ward. Placing both hands on it, he closed his eyes. Millie felt the ward begin to stretch and twist, trying to stay in place against Max's assault. Sweat broke out on Max's forehead. Suddenly, he cried out, "*Hajoa!*" And the ward snapped like a bubble popping.

Quickly, Petunia stepped forward, took off her cap, and shook her head furiously, sparkling powder flying off her head and into the portal. Sagara stood beside her and chanted in halting High Mystery, "*Tästä valtakunnasta seuraavaan, salli meidän kulkea.*"

The Dodonoi both began to shimmer.

"Pixie dust is dandruff?" Max whispered hoarsely to Millie. "Ew." Millie elbowed him in the ribs.

"You may pass," said the Dodonoi. "Come on!" Sagara said, stepping through.

Petunia's lip trembled. "Quick, give me the potions."

Millie gave her the transformation potion, then held the red witch's gown over her as she drank. A moment later, Petunia filled the dress, her head and arms popping through their holes. Her skin had turned a dark, dark brown, the color of rich chocolate, and her hair had turned a glossy black.

Max handed her the Remedial English potion, which

she chugged. *"Geronimo!"* Petunia cried, and she jumped through the portal.

"Ready?" Max asked Millie.

Millie started to speak, but then they both heard an ear-splitting shriek behind them. They turned and saw someone fighting with the hydra.

"It-it can't be," Max stammered. "She's under ward!"

"It's Cretacia," Millie breathed.

"Out of my way," Cretacia was screaming. "I don't care about your stupid portal. I just want *HER!*" She pointed a bony finger at Millie, then turned and pointed at a head. *"Jäädy!"* The head froze.

"Out of order," grumbled the other heads. "Test of Courage comes last."

"Quick, we have to go!" Millie grabbed Max's hand. "On the count of three. One, two, THREE!"

Chapter 19
Ice Cream in Salem

Together, they took a step forward into the blinding golden light. Millie felt herself dissolving, becoming the light. And then, as though she were a breath held too long, she burst out into ordinary sunlight, surrounded by willows.

Max rubbed his eyes. "It didn't work?"

"I wouldn't say that," said Millie, staring. They were on a small spit of land, surrounded by ocean. Boats chugged by, unlike any Millie had ever seen. They had no sails of any kind. How did they move? "Oh, darkness! What is that smell?" The air smelled horrible: salty and smoky and irritating. Millie coughed to clear her throat, but the smell remained.

"What are those?" Max asked. Millie turned to where he was pointing and saw strange carriages moving without any horse or ox to pull them, trailing a thin stream of smoke behind them. They followed a road covered with a hard, black substance a little like cooled lava. Humans, more humans than Millie had ever seen at one time except at Coven meetings, milled about wearing colorful and surprisingly varied clothing, but here and there, Millie spied someone in familiar black, and she counted three peaked witches' hats. Many humans, she noticed, were wearing the peculiar blue trousers that Sagara wore.

Petunia stared all around her. "This is the weirdest place I've ever seen."

She was still barefoot. Hastily, Millie pulled out the clogs, and Petunia slipped them on. They were a bit big.

"Any sign of Cretacia?" Max asked.

Petunia stomped in a circle, getting used to the clogs. "Cretacia? Why would she be here?"

"She showed up at the portal just before we jumped through," Millie told her.

"Oak and ash! I hope she didn't make it through," Sagara said.

"I hope she did," Petunia declared, raising her fists. "No magic here. I bet she's never been in an honest fight in her life."

Max stopped scanning the park around them. "The ward would be back up by now. If she's not through, she won't be anytime soon."

"Come on," Sagara said, coughing. "Let's find my mother."

"How do we do that?" Max protested.

Sagara shrugged. "I have a map." She pulled out **Welcome to Witch City**.

Millie turned to Sagara. "What do we do?"

"First," Sagara said, "we take a bus. That's a large carriage for transporting many people." She led them to the road and looked for a particular signpost along it. She found one, marked with numbers. "This should work," she said.

An elderly woman sat on a bench near them, a cane leaning against her knee. Her white hair rose in an uneven cloud around her face, thick hairs sprang from her chin, and her spectacles made her brown eyes look enormous. If Millie hadn't known better, she'd have guessed the woman was a witch. Perhaps she thought she was.

She eyed them suspiciously. In English, she said, "What

are you kids doing out of school?"

Awkwardly, Millie said, "We do not school today."

The woman frowned. "You talk funny. Are you legal?"

"We are tourists," Sagara said carefully. "We are visiting Salem."

The woman picked up her cane and prodded Sagara with it. "Then where," *prod*, "are your," *prod*, "parents?" Sagara winced and edged away.

"Our parental units are in proximity to this location," Max replied.

"Ha!" said the woman. "Trying to trick me? You're illegal! Foreigners! I should call the cops!"

"The what?" Millie asked, not familiar with the term.

"Holy cow, she doesn't even know what cops are!" the woman cried. "The police, you little rat." She fumbled in her pocket and produced a slim, gleaming device. She tapped it, and it began to glow with colorful glyphs and letters.

Max backed away. "I thought there was no magic here," he told Sagara in Canto.

"That's technology," she replied. "But it's also powerful. I think that's a communication device, sort of like a scrying bowl. She may be contacting a guardian of this place."

"Oh, darkness," Millie said. She rummaged in her cauldron. In English, she asked the woman, "Would you like brownie?"

The woman shrank away from the lovely pastry. "Get that thing away from me! You're touching it with your filthy hands!"

Max lost his patience. He drew his wand, pointed it at her, and shouted, "*Liikkumatta!*"

The woman shrieked. "Help! Assault!"

Other humans were turning to watch them, and a few began moving toward them.

"What do we do?" Millie whispered.

Sagara glanced at the gathering crowd and the shrieking woman. Desperate, she cried, "Run!" and dashed away down the sidewalk. With no better plan, Max, Millie, and Petunia dashed after her.

The woman did not follow, and her shrieks soon faded behind them. Sagara gave a happy cry and ducked into a doorway.

"Are we safe?" Max asked.

Sagara peered out a window. "I think so. We can bide here a minute and figure out where we need to go. But first, let's get some ice cream."

"Oh!" Millie cried. "I've read about that, but I've never tasted it."

Sagara led them over to a glass case containing tubs filled with strange, creamy substances in a bewildering array of colors and swirls. Sagara pulled a handful of dull green papers from her pocket. "My treat," she said. "Take your pick."

Millie chose boysenberry sorbet, Max chose double chocolate chunk, Petunia chose salted caramel, and Sagara selected cake batter. The attendant scooped each of these into small cone-shaped pastries and handed them over in exchange for some of the paper. Then, licking their cones happily, the four of them headed back out onto the sidewalk.

"This place is amazing," Max said. "I've never seen so many buildings all together. And the carriages! And so many people! I think I saw a dragon flying by, but that can't be right."

"Probably an airplane," Sagara said distractedly, cone in one hand and map in the other. "A flying carriage that takes people great distances. The small ground carriages are called cars."

"That's incredible," Millie said. "I thought it would be terrible here. How can a place survive without magic? But these humans seem to be thriving."

"But there are so few trees," Petunia said sadly. "There were trees where we came through, but not very many. And there were no bushes, no flowers, just a little grass. It wasn't natural, not like a forest."

"They do have forests here," Sagara told her, "but not very many. They cut most of them down. They like having some trees around though, so they make places called parks. That's where we were."

"That's terrible!" said Max. "All those poor trees, all alone. And where do all the people and animals who lived in the forests go?"

Sagara shrugged. "Remember, the only thinking beings in the forests here are humans, and they mostly go to human places like this city. But some of them try to stay in the forests and other wild places. As for the animals, some of them move, but a lot of them die. That's why my brother can come here. If it looks like a species is going to die out, like the poor dodos and river dolphins, he brings them to the Enchanted Forest or other Realms where they'd be comfortable."

"Does that happen a lot?" Millie asked.

"My brother says more and more," Sagara said. "Sometimes they can't always save a species before it disappears."

"How can people live like that?" Max whispered.

"Well, there are advantages, too," Sagara said. "Look around you. You see the buildings and the cars and things. What you don't see is that these people all live much longer, more comfortable lives than a nonmagical human would without technology. And they do things we've never dreamed of. All of the books in your library, Max, and the library at the school, and a thousand libraries like them, they can fit in a single little box, like that one the woman there is talking to. And the best part is, anyone who buys one of those boxes can read those libraries."

"Really?" Max said, amazed. "How is that possible without magic?"

"I don't really understand it yet," Sagara said. "But it has to do with math. My mother knows, and I'm hoping she'll teach me."

"So that's why you're obsessed with arithmancy," Max said.

Sagara nodded. "I want to do the same thing for all the Realms. I want all the knowledge there is to be freely available to everyone."

"I don't know," Petunia said. "Will that change the Realms? What if they all turn into this? It's fascinating and wonderful but also strange and terrible. I wouldn't want the Enchanted Forest to be cut down."

"I'm hoping that we can adapt the best things from this Realm to our own and leave the worst things behind. My mother can explain it better." Sagara looked up from her map and squinted down the street. "All right. We're here, and my mother's office is here, which is actually pretty close. I don't think we need the bus. We go that way."

They walked over the smooth, hard, strangely uniform stone of the city, houses and businesses squeezed tightly together on either side. Petunia darted from window to window, oohing and aahing. They passed many shops selling witches' hats and magic supplies. Some offered herbs and incense, others tarot and palm readings. They passed an obviously fake haunted house and a pirate museum with dummy pirates dangling from the walls. Clothing vendors sold items that said puzzling things like, "Keep Calm and Carry a Wand" and "My other car is a broomstick."

Petunia stared at these for a while, and then she started laughing. "They're jokes! I don't understand all of them, but I'm sure of it. Can we go get a joke book in one of these stores?"

"Um, I don't think I have enough money papers," Sagara told her.

For every shop that was vaguely familiar, there were several others Millie couldn't figure out at all. What was an ATM? What did pharmacy mean? What was a comic book? And there were so many places to eat, with enticing and strange aromas. Many of the foods were completely new to her.

She stopped in front of a store window. There was her Coven dress, all black and artfully tattered. Next to it was the long, wine-colored velvet gown that Bogdana wore frequently. Suddenly, the bottom fell out of Millie's stomach. "My mother has been here," she whispered.

"Hey!" Max said. "I know that sign. It's on the boxes of Thai food my father brings home."

Sagara smirked. "See? I told you."

Millie felt hot and overwhelmed. "Are we nearly there?"

"Just down this way," Sagara said confidently. "I recognize this cobblestone street."

They walked down a road wide enough for cars but apparently intended only for people. At one tall building squashed between several others, next to a shop offering something called "cappuccino," Sagara stopped. "This is it. Look."

The sign on the door read, "Arela Software (upstairs)."

"At last," said Max. "Let's go see your mother."

They trooped up the stairs to a bright, open room where many humans sat in odd, cloth-covered boxes, poking panels of buttons with their fingers. A woman sitting at a desk looked up as they entered. "May I help you?" she asked.

"I am here to see Lillian Arela," Sagara said formally.

"Sagara?" came a shocked voice behind them.

Millie turned around. The woman standing there staring at them might have been an elf once. She was tall and thin and graceful as an elf, but her hair was brown and wildly curly, hiding her ears. And she was dressed like other humans, like Sagara herself in fact, in those snug blue trousers and a pale green shirt that left her arms bare. But Sagara had no doubts. "Mom!" she cried, and flew into the woman's arms.

Lillian hugged her daughter close, laughing. "What a pleasant surprise, dear girl," she said in Canto. "I can't imagine how you managed it. Your grandmother will have absolute fits."

Sagara giggled. "Don't worry, she has no idea I'm here."

Lillian peered over her daughter's head. "And who are your friends?" she asked.

"Oh, sorry," Sagara said. "This is my friend Millie, her brother Max, and my friend Petunia."

Millie curtsied. "Pleased to meet you." Beside her, Max bowed in his wizard robes and said, in clear English, "We come in peace. Take us to your leader."

Petunia nodded. "May the force be with you."

The woman at the desk giggled. "They're adorable, Lillian," she said. "I didn't know your daughter was visiting."

Lillian flashed her an embarrassed smile. "Neither did I, Anna. This is an unexpected surprise."

"You came a long way," Anna said to them. "You're from Portugal, right?"

Millie nodded. "We are here for school trip," she said carefully, the cover story they'd agreed on.

"Why don't you all come in my office?" Lillian said hastily. "Anna, could you hold my calls, please?"

"Sure thing, hon," Anna said.

Max looked puzzled. "What would you hold them in?"

Hastily, Millie grabbed his hand and led him to the office.

Lillian closed the door behind them.

"Blessed Root, Sagara!" Lillian exploded. "That was a

terribly dangerous thing to do. I'm surprised the portal guardian let you pass. And however did you get hold of pixie dust?"

"Befriended a pixie," said Petunia, grinning.

Whatever her mother was expecting, it wasn't that. "Oh," she said shortly. "How is that possible?"

"I transformed her into a human before we came through the portal," Millie said proudly.

Lillian waved that off. "Sagara, no one is supposed to know that I'm here."

"Don't worry, Mom," Sagara said. "I swore them all to secrecy. Formally."

Millie nodded confirmation.

"Thank the stars," Lillian said in relief. "But why are they here?"

"We're just helping a friend," Millie said. "Also, well, I'm sort of running away from home."

Lillian frowned. "I'm really not comfortable with that. Your parents will come looking for you."

"I don't care," Millie said defiantly. "I'm not going back. I want to be a chef."

"A chef?" Lillian looked startled. "Really?"

Petunia nodded vigorously. "Millie is the best cook in the entire Enchanted Forest."

"She can make elfcakes. They're almost as good as yours," Sagara said.

"Wow. I'm impressed," Lillian admitted. "But then why come here?"

Millie pulled **Simple Pleasures** from her satchel. "This is my favorite cookbook. The chef has a restaurant here in Salem. I thought maybe I could study with him."

Lillian flipped through the book and started laughing. "This is my favorite restaurant! I can only afford to go there once a month, but I'd go every day if I could. However did you get this cookbook? And why is the dust cover missing?" She cocked her head, studying Millie's face. "I wonder..."

Lillian tapped at one of those button panels on her desk. The glowing painting above it changed. She turned it to Millie. "Do you recognize this man?"

The painting said, "Savor Salem" across the top. Below it and to the right, there was a picture of a man with thin blond hair, twinkling brown eyes, and a ruddy pink complexion. He looked familiar somehow...

"Millie," Max whispered. "He looks like you."

Petunia whistled. "You're right. He looks just like her."

"I told you my dad said your father wasn't dead!" Max exclaimed. "That's got to be him! It all makes sense! How you speak English, how you got this cookbook. That's your dad."

"I think so, too," Lillian said. "You would have seen his picture on the dust cover if you'd had it. Dean MacRae is an exceptional chef, one of the finest in the country. Of all the humans I've ever known, he's the only one I'd think would have a ghost of a chance of making elfcakes." Lillian sighed. "Oak and ash, I miss elfcakes."

"Dean! Didn't I tell you my dad said his name was Dean?" Max pointed out.

Millie felt like someone had punched her in the stomach. She stared at the man's image. He did seem familiar... "Can we go there?" Millie asked. "Please?"

"Oh, I don't know about that," Lillian said.

"Come on, we *have* to go," Petunia insisted.

"Imagine, Mom," Sagara added. "I at least remember you. And I get to visit you every once in a while. Millie has never met her father."

Lillian gathered Sagara to her. "You know this is not my choice. I never wanted to be separated from you."

"I know, Mom. I understand, I really do," Sagara said. "I just really miss you. Grandmother's all right, but it's just not the same. If it weren't for Millie's elfcakes, I don't know what I'd do."

Lillian looked at Millie, then at her daughter.

"All right," Lillian said. "Let me finish up a couple of things, and I'll take you to the restaurant. It's over at the wharf."

"Oh, thank you," Millie gasped. "Thank you so much."

Lillian gave her a little smile. "I have a soft spot for runaways."

Sagara slid off her mother's lap and stood beside her chair, watching intently as Lillian rapidly danced her fingers over the little buttons marked with English letters. She peered intently at the glowing painting, which Millie realized was something like a magic mirror.

"What do you think she's doing?" Millie whispered to Max.

"Technology magic," Max whispered back. "Want to hear something interesting? Dad has one of those in his laboratory. I've seen him use it, but I couldn't read it before because it was all in English."

After a few minutes, Lillian stopped tapping with a little flourish and sat back. "There. That will keep until tomorrow. Come on, my car's in the basement garage."

They marched out of the little office, and Lillian informed Anna that she was taking the rest of the afternoon off.

"Whatever you say, boss lady," Anna said, winking. "Have a lovely time, all of you."

Millie fairly flew down the stairs after Sagara and her mother. They went down below ground level and through a door into a vast, cavernous, echoing space where dozens of cars lined up. Lillian waved some kind of wand, and a small blue car beeped and flashed its lights. Lillian turned to them. "All right, get in."

Sagara sat in front with her mother, Max, Millie, and Petunia sat in the back seat. Lillian showed them how to fasten their seat belts. Then she pressed a button, and the vehicle began to hum quietly.

"This one's different from the other carriages," Max said. "It's not so loud, and it doesn't smell like smoke."

"It's electric," Lillian said. "I use a device that converts sunlight into energy, and I store that energy in the car. No burning, no smoke."

She drove them out of the garage and into the sunlight, pulling deftly out into the busy street. As they made their way through the city, Sagara consulted her guidebook and called out interesting sights. "Look, the home of Nathaniel Hawthorne, whoever he was. Oh, the place where they hanged people suspected of being witches. Ugh."

"It was all a terrible mistake," Lillian said sadly. "When humans are angry or frightened, they don't think very clearly. Sometimes they do awful things."

"Sounds like most people," said Petunia.

"That way is the House of the Seven Gables," Sagara said.

"We'll have to go there another time," Lillian said. "We're at the restaurant now."

"Really?" Millie squealed. "Where is it?"

Lillian pulled the car to the side of the road and turned it off. "Right there," she said, pointing at a building right at the water's edge. "Everybody out."

The children struggled briefly with their seat belts, then sprang out of the car and onto the sidewalk. Millie ran straight up to the restaurant's door and tugged on it, but it was locked. As the others arrived, Millie began pounding on the door. After a few moments, a woman came to the door, frowning.

"May we come in, please?" Millie asked in her best

English.

The woman shook her head. "No, I'm sorry, we don't open until 5 o'clock."

"Excuse me," said Lillian smoothly. "I'm very sorry to disturb you, but Millie here believes that her father may work here."

"Her father?" asked the woman, glancing again at Millie.

Millie held up the cookbook. "Dean MacRae. I think he is my father."

The woman's mouth formed a round O. "Just a moment," she said and hurried away. A few moments later, they heard a muffled shout, and then a man flung open the door.

As soon as she smelled him, that whiff of musk and herbs and spice, Millie remembered him. He had a bit less of his fine blond hair, and it had gone gray at his temples. His face was flushed, and his eyes were the very same soft brown as Millie's. He was also a bit wider around the middle. Despite that, he seemed smaller somehow. He fell to his knees.

"Daddy?" Millie whispered.

"Yes, my darling dear, oh yes," said Dean MacRae, holding out his arms. "Millie, my Millie, you've found me at last."

And Millie fell right into his arms and hugged him so hard she was sure she would never let go.

Chapter 20

A Bite of Bruschetta

Millie could feel her father's tears hot on her neck. Her own tears were running down her face. She heard Max snuffling behind her, and she turned to him and smiled. "Daddy, this is my brother Max," she said. "And my friend Petunia, my friend Sagara, and her mother, Lillian." Dean looked up. "Good heavens, Max. I never thought I'd get to meet you, laddie, though I've heard a great deal about you." Still hugging Millie close, he stood up and extended a hand to Lillian. "Thank you for bringing my daughter to me, Lillian."

"Don't thank me," she replied. "I think my daughter engineered the whole thing."

Dean huffed a laugh and set Millie down. "Won't you all come in?"

They followed him into the restaurant. It was quite elegant, Millie decided, as her father set her down at a table. Everything was clean and sparkling, the tables covered with crisp white linen, the napkins in little fans protruding from the glasses. They could hear others working in another room nearby, and, oh, the smells! They were wondrous, delightful! Millie had never smelled anything like them. Beside her, she could see Max going nearly cross-eyed with sudden hunger. "That smells..." said Sagara. "That smells... amazing!"

Dean actually blushed. "Well, thank you. Are you hungry? Timmy!" he roared. "Timmy!"

A young man in a white coat and a poofy white hat hurried out of the kitchen. "Yes, chef?"

"Bring us a bruschetta!"

"Right away, chef!" He hurried off.

Dean turned to Millie and hugged her again. She took out a handkerchief and blew her nose, which made him laugh.

"Oh, Millie," her father said. "I am so happy to see you. Not a day goes by that I don't think of you, my wee girl. The last time I saw your mother was when I gave her that cookbook for you. She said you were my daughter for certain, you had such a way in the kitchen. Did you like the book?"

"It's wonderful!" Millie told him, pulling it from her satchel. "I use it almost every day. Horace loves your brownies." She pulled a brownie from her cauldron to demonstrate.

Dean chuckled. "Is that old ghost still banging about your pantry, then?"

Sagara put in, "Millie turned him into a frog."

Millie felt her cheeks turn red. "I turned him back!"

"Like your mother, too, then?" Dean asked. "You certainly have her nose." He nibbled the brownie, and his eyes widened. "This is good. Really good."

"I don't have her nose," she said. "And no, I'm not. My magic is very different than Mother's." And then she told him absolutely everything. The bruschetta arrived, toasted bread piled high with tomatoes, onions, basil, and a sharp cheese. Millie ignored it, telling him about her struggles with magic, and school, and meeting Max, and transforming Horace, and saving Thea from Cretacia, and learning about her mother's binding. Max, Petunia, and Sagara interrrupted frequently when she forgot some detail or got events mixed up. When she finished, he sat back. "So you forgot about me, and she never told you otherwise." He sounded sad. "Well, that explains a lot."

Lillian put down the slice of bruschetta she'd been munching and mumbled, "I think it may be more than that." Millie's father turned to her and held out his hand. "I'm sorry, I've been a poor host. I'm Dean MacRae."

"That I know," said Lillian. "I eat here as often as I can afford to. I've met you twice before, but you certainly can't be expected to remember all your customers. Lillian Arela, once known as Liliea ap Erlaria et Arela."

His eyebrows rose. "Elf?"

She smiled and nodded. "But I live here in Salem now."

"Good gravy," Dean said. "How many others from the Other Side are living here?"

"Not many that I know of," Lillian told him. "Most of us can't live without magic, and those who can generally don't want to. Anyway, I don't think it's entirely Millie's fault. I'm guessing that her mother cast a spell of forgetfulness on her when she was very young."

Dean looked grim. "That makes sense."

"Yeah, I grok that," said Max.

Anger got the best of Millie, and she blurted out, "That wasn't fair. That wasn't right. She should have told me."

Dean put his head in his hands. "She was embarrassed, consorting with an ordinary human. She would never introduce me to anyone, not even her parents. I know she loved me, but she must have been powerfully conflicted. And then, when she was elected to the Council, she just stopped coming." He looked up. "I think I would like to have a word with Bogdana."

"Your wish is granted," said an icy voice behind him.

Millie gasped. Her mother was standing in the entrance of the restaurant.

"Ludmilla, come here," said Bogdana. "We are going home. Now."

Dean stood up and faced her. "Oh, no. I haven't seen my daughter for six years. I am not letting her go that easily."

"Oh, don't start," Bogdana said. "I know it's been a long time. I'm sorry."

Through gritted teeth, he asked, "Did you put a spell on Millie to make her forget me?"

Bogdana turned pale. *Huh*, Millie thought. *Her skin isn't green, and her hair isn't tangled. And she doesn't have many moles or warts. And her nose... her nose is straight. It looks just like mine. And she has dimples.* Millie gasped. *It was all illusion.*

"You have to understand," Bogdana began. "I couldn't have people asking questions. It was time for me to start taking Millie to Coven meetings, and she would have told them about you."

Dean thrust out his chin. "You had no right to take those memories from her."

"It was for her own good," Bogdana said. "She would have missed you so."

"Oh, Mother!" Millie cried. "Yes, I would have missed him, if I'd known. But you know what? That whole time, I was so lonely. I felt like there was a great big hole inside me, and I didn't know why. I only had you, except at Coven meetings, and the other girls are always so mean to me. It was just you and me and Horace until I finally went to school. And all this time, when I was so sad and alone, I WASN'T! I had a father who loved me, and you took that away from me! All because you were worried about what people would think about you."

Bogdana looked down at her daughter, aghast. "I, I never

knew. I'm so sorry, Millie. I had intended to remove the spell when you were old enough. But if I'd known... why didn't you tell me?"

"Would you have listened?" Dean asked quietly.

Bogdana looked at him. "No, probably not. I'd have thought she was just going through a phase and she'd grow out of it." She sighed. "I never intended any of this. I never meant to get involved in any part of the Logical Realm. It just... happened."

Lillian spoke up. "Running from your problems generally just adds new problems to the ones you've run from," she said, hugging Sagara tightly. "Trust me. I have a great deal of experience."

"So do I." Max's father had entered the restaurant. Dean muttered something about getting a better lock.

"Max! Are you all right?" Salazar asked in Canto.

"Affirmative, Dad," Max said calmly, in English. "What are *you* doing here?"

"What am I doing here?" his father exclaimed. "What are you doing here? Do you have any idea how dangerous it is to cross between Realms?" He paused. "When did you learn English?"

Dean chuckled. "From the sound of it, I'd say Max has been reading your science fiction collection."

"Affirmative. And you're one to talk," Max pointed out. "You even dress like a native."

Max's father was dressed comfortably in those blue trousers and a shirt bearing the puzzling words, "Red Sox."

"Hello, Al," Dean said quietly.

Alfonso nodded. "Dean."

Millie looked confused. "Wait, you know each other?"

"We're old friends." Alfonso sighed. "I was going to tell you about this when you were older. Max, I dress like a native because I *am* a native. I grew up here, in the Logical Realm."

"But you speak Canto," Max protested.

"In this part of the Logical Realm, people speak English," Alfonso explained. "In other parts of the Realm, there are other languages, just like in the Enchanted Forest. My parents moved here from a place called Puerto Rico, where they speak Spanish, and Spanish is very similar to Canto. It was easy for me to learn."

"Then how do you know Daddy?" Millie asked.

"I met Dean in college — that's school for adults — and we became friends and lived together as roommates. Then, one day, he brought home this fascinating woman." He nodded at Bogdana.

"Mother?" Max and Millie said together. *Fascinating?* Millie thought.

"I found her in the Salem Woods, where I was hunting wild mushrooms," Dean explained.

"They fell deeply in love, Dean and Danny," Alfonso said. "Eventually, they told me about the Enchanted Forest and the other Realms. I couldn't get it out of my head. I pestered them until they took me through the portal."

"And you discovered you have talent," Lillian said.

Alfonso nodded. "You could have knocked me over with a feather, I was so shocked. But once I'd tasted magic, I couldn't leave it behind. I chose to stay in the Enchanted Forest and learn magic."

Millie looked at her father. "What about you, Daddy? Why didn't you stay?"

"Because," Dean said, "unlike Al, I had no magical talent. And I was just starting my first restaurant here. Danny got pregnant, and you were born." He frowned. "And then things got complicated."

Petunia piped up, "She dumped you. Bogdana went off with Al instead."

Bogdana snarled. "Impudent wretch!"

"It's true, though," Dean said. "I guess I wasn't good enough for her."

"But why, Mother?" Millie asked. "What did he do?"

"It wasn't about Dean," Alfonso said. "It was about me. I made a pretty big splash in the Enchanted Forest. I got elected to the Enchanted Forest Council about the same time Bogdana did."

"But you're not together anymore," Max pointed out. "Now you're with Hepsibat."

Alfonso rubbed the back of his neck. "Yeah, I think that was a bad decision, too. You see, I didn't understand witch culture. For witches, choosing a wizard to be the father of your children isn't about love or family, it's a competition, and apparently I was a prize. But I don't think either one of them ever loved me. Certainly Bogdana never did." He looked at Dean. "Not the way she loved you."

Bogdana grimaced. "Irrelevant. Come, we're going home."

Millie folded her arms and declared, "I'm not going back. I want to stay here with Daddy."

"Out of the question!" Bogdana yelled.

Dean looked startled. "You do?"

"I want to be a chef like you." Millie held up **Simple Pleasures**. "I've made almost everything in here. What's a microwave?"

Bogdana said, "Millie, you have a duty to the Coven. You're a witness in Cretacia's trial. You have to come back."

"Speaking of which," said Alfonso, "is Cretacia here, too? She escaped from her wards sometime this morning. When you kids came through the portal, you set off alarms all over the Enchanted Forest. Bogdana, who had been out searching for Cretacia, beat me to the portal, assuming that she'd been the one to go through it."

"But the portal keeps track of who passes through," Bogdana said. "Imagine my surprise when I found out it allowed a small horde of children through. It told me two human girls, one human boy, and an elf girl. I assumed the human girls were Cretacia and Millie." She glanced at Petunia. "I wasn't expecting a transformed pixie instead."

Alfonso nodded. "I got the same report, but I also detected traces of Cretacia's magical signature. If she didn't take my wards down, she tried very, very hard."

"We saw her," Max admitted. "She was fighting the hydra when we stepped through. But we didn't see her come through after us."

Alfonso looked thoughtful. "So she might have made it through, or she might still be loose in the Enchanted Forest." He rubbed his forehead. "This is a pretty pickle."

Millie folded her arms. "Well, if you can't find her, there can't be a trial. I'm staying here. You'll have to manage without me."

"But Millie, what about school?" Dean asked. "I thought you were enjoying it."

Millie nodded reluctantly. "I did. I do. I'm learning so much, and I like seeing Max every day, and I like being with my friends. But I don't want to live with Mother any more. She put a binding spell on the kitchen so I couldn't do kitchen magic, and she made me forget you. I don't want her to do anything else to me."

Dean frowned at Bogdana. "She's got a point, Danny. I wouldn't trust you either."

"You try raising a child, Dean," Bogdana hissed. "See how well you do."

"I would have, happily, if you'd let me," Dean countered.

"May I make a suggestion?" Lillian spoke up. They all

turned to her, and she cleared her throat. "It's a terrible thing for a daughter to be separated from her mother. I know that all too well. And while I'm not defending Bogdana's actions, I can understand why she did what she did. She was trying to protect herself and Millie.

"But now the cat's out of the bag, as they say here for reasons that still mystify me," Lillian went on. "Dean, Alfonso, and Headmistress Pteria all know that Bogdana has made some bad decisions regarding Millie. And unless Danny plans on casting forgetting spells on all of you, Dean is no longer a secret. If you don't allow Millie to spend time with her father, word will get out."

"Oh, really?" said Bogdana. "And why would I be afraid of any of them? They have no say in how I raise my daughter."

"No, but Baba Luci does," Lillian pointed out. "She's your mother, and she's the head of your Coven. Her job is to make decisions in cases just like this."

"Of course!" said Petunia, "Millie, remember I told you that I think that you should ask Baba Luci for help?"

Bogdana turned white as a ghost at the mention of Baba Luci. "You wouldn't dare," she whispered.

"You're right," Millie said slowly. "This is witches' business, and that's a problem for Baba Luci. She'll know what's best. I want to visit my dad. I'm sure Baba Luci would want that, too. If you want me at the trial, Mother, I'm going to talk to Baba Luci about all of this."

Bogdana covered her eyes with one hand. "Fine. Millie can visit."

"When?" Millie asked eagerly.

"During school break," her mother said. "Right after the next Coven meeting, you get two weeks off. You can come then." She looked at Dean. "Is that acceptable?"

"Two of your weeks is ten days, right?" Dean asked. "I'd

like longer, but I don't want to interrupt her studies. It'll do for now."

Alfonso draped an arm around Max's shoulders. "I think we'll come, too. You should meet your grandparents."

The woman who'd opened the door of the restaurant came up to them. "Excuse me, chef," she said. "I'm sorry to intrude, but we open in ten minutes."

"Ah, yes," he said. "Thank you, Sarah. I'm sorry, everyone, but we'll have to take this elsewhere."

Wistfully, Lillian asked, "Couldn't we stay for dinner?"

A light came into Dean MacRae's eyes. "Oh, yes. Yes, you may. In fact, I insist. Sarah, do we have any early reservations on the corner booth?"

Sarah hurried over to a podium. "Not until 6:30."

"Perfect," he said. "It's reserved now. Come with me, everyone."

That evening, Millie ate the most perfect meal of her life. They started with a salad made with mixed greens, candied pecans, goat cheese, and cranberries. Then there was the soup, lobster bisque, creamy and delicate. The elves, being vegetarians, had a butternut squash soup that Sagara swore was better than elfcakes.

For the main course, Max had a curious stuffed pasta called ravioli. Bogdana chose the rack of lamb. Alfonso selected the seafood platter. Lillian and Sagara had the wild mushroom risotto. Petunia had a sandwich of chopped meat called a burger. And Millie picked the roast duck, which was so tender it melted in her mouth.

They all shared bites, and they spoke very little, except to say "Mmm" and "Yum" and "Ahhhh..." Through all this, Millie's father remained in the kitchen, directing the preparation of the food. At the end of the meal, he sent out a tray with a selection of desserts: dark chocolate mousse cake, crème brûlée, petit fours, and an ice cream sundae complete with hot fudge and whipped cream. The adults had a hot drink called coffee, which all three pronounced blissful. Millie tried a sip but thought it was much too bitter.

When they had all given up eating even another bite, Dean came out and looked Bogdana in the eye.

"So, do you think Millie could learn something from me?" he asked.

Bogdana burped loudly. "Absolutely. I've been a ninny, Millie. This is why I fell in love with your father in the first place. I should have known how important it would be to you. Pteria tells me that kitchen magic is the foundation of all your magical abilities. If being a better cook will help, then I'd be a fool to stand in your way." She sighed. "But we really do have to go back, even if we have to roll all the way there."

He charmed her, Millie thought. *Daddy charmed Mother with food, and he didn't even use any magic.*

"Could you please take Sagara back with you?" Lillian asked. "Her grandmother is probably frantic by now."

"No!" Sagara cried. "Mother, I want to stay here with you!"

"Here we go again," muttered Petunia.

Lillian stroked her cheek. "Too soon, dear heart. But I will give you a message for your grandmother, asking if you can come when Millie comes at school break. A child should know her mother. She cannot deny us that. All right?"

Sagara nodded sadly. "But soon, right?"

"Yes, dear heart. Soon." Lillian pulled a scrap of paper from her purse and began writing quickly.

Bogdana slid out of the end of the booth. "Then it is time we went home."

"One moment," Dean said. "I have something for Millie."

"Another cookbook?" Millie asked hopefully.

"Better," he said. From behind his back, he produced

another white, poofy-looking hat. "This is a chef's hat. It's part of the uniform we wear in the kitchen. Since your hat was ruined, I thought you might like a replacement."

Bogdana opened her mouth to protest, then looked at her daughter's shining eyes and closed it again.

Millie put the chef's hat on. "Thank you, Daddy. It fits perfectly."

"I have a good eye." He winked at her. "Now come give us a hug goodbye."

There was a great deal of hugging all around, swollen bellies and all. Then Alfonso and Bogdana led Millie and her friends out of the restaurant, leaving Lillian to discuss elfcakes with Dean.

The sun was low in the sky when they stepped outside. Alfonso waved at a yellow car, which obligingly stopped for them, and they piled in, Bogdana in the front seat beside the driver with the rest crammed into the back. "Salem Willows Park," she told him.

"So," Alfonso asked in Canto. "What did you think of the Logical Realm?"

"It's... interesting," Millie said.

"The food is better," said Max, "but the air is worse. And it's sort of sad that there are only humans here. I miss the dwarves and centaurs and fairies and pixies."

"Pixies!" cried Millie. "Petunia, your parents will be worried sick."

"Ha. I doubt they even noticed I was gone," Petunia said. "I have to admit, though, I'll be happy to get back to normal. This skin color is nice, but I miss blue. And it's weird being this big for so long. It'll be bad enough growing to your size again in school tomorrow."

The other three children groaned. "School..."

Epilogue

One month later, Millie arrived at the Coven meeting on the back of her mother's broom with her lunch cauldron hung in the crook of one arm. Instantly, the other apprentice witches surrounded her.

"You're wearing a hat!" Greely cried.

"It's the strangest, ugliest hat I've ever seen," Grooly added.

Greely put her hands on her hips. "What sort of witch's hat is that? It's got no brim. It's not pointy. It's not even black. It looks ridiculous."

Millie smiled at them all. "My father gave it to me."

"It can't be a real witch's hat," Grooly announced. Swift as a snake, she grabbed for the hat. Her hand bounced off harmlessly. Then Greely tried, and then another and another of Millie's cousins. Millie stood quite still and let them. Not one of them succeeded in pulling it off her head.

The twins stood back, panting. "Your mother must have done it for you," Greely gasped out. "Everyone knows you can't do magic."

"Oh, really?" said Millie. "Ask Cretacia if that's true."

They all fell silent at the mention of Cretacia.

"She enchanted it herself," boomed a loud voice behind her. Baba Luci had arrived. "She did it in my hut, with her mother and I attending. It may look funny, but it's a real, honest-to-darkness witch's hat."

"It's a chef's hat, too," Millie said proudly. "I wear it when I'm cooking. Would you like some elfcakes?" She pulled the napkin off the top of the cauldron. The smell of fresh-baked cakes wafted out.

Greely stared. "You made elfcakes?"

Grooly drooled. "I thought only elves could do that."

"Try one and see," Millie said.

"No way," said Greely. "What if she enchanted them? What if they turn us into toads?"

Millie smiled. "I thought you said I couldn't do magic," she pointed out.

"Um," said Grooly.

Greely's hand crept forward. "May I have one? Please?"

"Of course," Millie said.

Grooly's hand darted forward and took one. "Hey, you didn't ask!" Greely protested, trying to wrest it from her. Millie hastily handed Greely a cake of her own, then handed another to the next young witch, and the next, and the next.

Baba Luci smiled down at Millie. "A witch who charms witches."

"They're not charmed, Baba," Millie told her. "They're just ordinary elfcakes."

"Even so, you've made an impression, my dear."

Millie shrugged. "I just want to be myself, Baba."

"Exactly," the Baba said. "Now, how are things with your mother?"

Millie sighed. "She's still mad at me, and she stomps around the house all the time. I'm kinda still mad at her, too. But she's eating my food again, and we've started making healing potions together."

"Good," said Baba Luci. "I'm keeping a close eye on her. I knew something was wrong before, and I'm sorry I didn't figure it out sooner. It never occurred to me that Bogdana was clever enough to bind the kitchen instead of you."

Millie shrugged. "Even Babas make mistakes, I guess."

Baba Luci laughed. "Yes, we do. We're human, after all."

Millie handed Baba Luci an elfcake, then asked casually, "Any sign of Cretacia yet?"

"No, none at all," said the Baba, nibbling her cake. "We've searched high and low, all over the Enchanted Forest and using powerful finding enchantments. It is the Council's opinion that Cretacia is no longer in our Realm."

Millie nodded. "That's what Mother thinks, too. So she did get into the Logical Realm."

"Maybe," said Baba Luci. "I expect you to keep a sharp eye out for her while you're visiting your father."

"Of course," Millie agreed.

"But there are other Realms she could have entered far more easily than the Logical Realm," the Baba pointed out. "It would be impossible to search them all. There's only one thing we know for certain: she's going to come after you one day."

"I know," Millie said. "But she can't attack me in the Logical Realm, so I can worry about that when I get back. Right now, I'm more worried about packing for my trip tomorrow. What do I wear to a baseball game?"

"I have no idea," said Baba Luci. "I guess you'll find out."

Dianna Sanchez is the not-so-secret identity of Jenise Aminoff, whose superpower is cooking with small children. She is an MIT alumna, graduate of the 1995 Clarion Workshop and Odyssey Online, active member of SCBWI, and a former editor of New Myths magazine. Aside from 18 years as a technical and science writer, she has taught science in Boston Public Schools, developed curricula for STEM education, and taught Preschool Chef, a cooking class for children ages 3-5. A native New Mexican and Latina geek, she now lives near Cambridge, MA with her husband and two daughters. This is her debut novel.

Acknowledgements

A surprising number of people helped me to create this novel. First and foremost, my daughters, who served as both inspiration and audience: Annie, who bakes cakes without using a recipe, and Nora, who wanted a story with fairies and unicorns. Also, my amazing and enthusiastic husband, Alex, who never once complained about all the time and money I've spent.

I took three classes while writing this novel, and they were all incredibly helpful: Odyssey Online's Powerful Dialogue in Fantastic Fiction with Jeanne Cavelos, Writing MG/YA Novels with Holly Thompson, and Odyssey Online's Getting the Big Picture revision class with Barbara Ashford. Thanks to my teachers and all my classmates. You went above and beyond the call of duty.

I thrust early drafts of **A Witch's Kitchen** at just about everyone I could reach. Three different critique groups saw various versions of the novel, so thanks to The Mechanics (Michael, Chris, and Wayne), the North Shore YA Meetup (Sue and Dirk), and the Pathfinders (Dirk again, Jennifer, Laura, Lauren, and Marti). Thanks to Dana, who exchanged manuscripts with me. Thanks also to all the kids and their parents who read early drafts, including (but not limited to): Aggie, Sarah, and Ransom; Alice, Elizabeth, and Jason; Allanna and Rebecca; Laura, who provided many of Petunia's jokes; Nancy and her sons; Pattie, Tarik, Faiz and Cora; and the entire Upper Elementary at Harborlight-Stoneridge Montessori School.

Thanks to Nina, who helped me with the phrases of High Mystery (Google Translate is not all that reliable when it comes to translating incantations), and to Crystal who introduced us.

Thanks to the amazing people who organize the New England Society of Children's Book Writers and Illustrators spring conference, and to the Book Doctors who run the Pitchapalooza there and were kind enough to see something in my pitch.

Finally, thanks to the marvelous people at Dreaming Robot Press — Corie, Sean, and Nicole — who helped me polish *A Witch's Kitchen* to a publishable state, like perfect royal icing on a cake.

If you enjoyed *A Witch's Kitchen*, please take a moment to review it where you purchased it!

Stop by the Dreaming Robot Press website, let us know what you think, and take a look at the rest of our science fiction and fantasy books.

DreamingRobotPress.com

Or email us at books@dreamingrobotpress.com

Continue reading for a sneak preview of *The Seventh Crow* by Sherry D. Ramsey.

...SEVEN CROWS, A SECRET THAT HAS NEVER BEEN TOLD...

The Seventh Crow

SHERRY D. RAMSEY

CHAPTER ONE

Rosinda trudged home with her head down, her backpack weighted with the homework Mr. Andrews had assigned for the night. Skeletal leaves crunched under her feet along the side of the road. A low croak made her look up, and she saw the crows. They stood scattered in a loose line in the grassy swath beside the road, their glossy black feathers reflecting the late-afternoon sun, each just a wingspan away from the next. Every one had its bright black eyes fixed on her. Rosinda stopped. The words of Aunt Odder's crow-counting rhyme popped into her head. This was one of the many things she had struggled to relearn over the past year. She counted the crows under her breath, chanting the rhyme.

"One crow, sorrow; two crows, joy; three crows, a letter; four crows, a boy," Rosinda said, her eyes resting briefly on each crow as she counted down the line. "Five crows, silver; six crows, gold—" She trailed off, looking around for a seventh crow. The rhyme always seemed to run out after six. Maybe crows didn't like big groups.

Just like me. She turned back to the road.

From a tree just ahead, a black shape dropped like a falling branch. A seventh crow. This one, bigger than the others, swooped on silent feathers to the ground just in front of Rosinda.

"Seven crows, a secret that has never been told," it said in a gravelly voice.

Rosinda froze, the weight of her backpack forgotten. Had that just happened?

Someone's playing a trick. It wouldn't be the first time. She forced her eyes from the crow, looking to both sides and glancing over her shoulder. Someone could have followed her from school, one of the boys, with one of those gadgets you could talk into and play your voice back in all sorts of weird ways. They must have heard her saying the crow rhyme. A chance to tease her. Yes, they must be hiding in the long grass, or behind a tree—

"There's no one else here, if that's what you're thinking," said the crow, hopping closer. "Just you and me. And them," it said, cocking its head toward the other six crows, "but they don't really count, since they won't be joining the conversation." The crow made a sound almost like a chuckle.

Then it's the accident. Rosinda's throat tightened. The head injury had taken away practically all her memories except for the past year, and now she was losing her mind.

The crow seemed to read her expression. It shook its head, black feathers ruffling. "There's nothing wrong with you. This is real, and it's important."

Rosinda swallowed. "What do you want?" she asked. Her voice was a raspy croak, almost like the crow's. The world seemed very tiny, shrunk down to this autumn-splashed stretch of road, herself, and the seventh crow. She hoped she wouldn't faint.

"I have some things to tell you, Rosinda," the crow said.

Rosinda's hands flew up to cover her mouth. The crow knew her name?

"Please try not to be alarmed," the crow said kindly. It cocked its head to the side, studying her. "Do you want to keep walking or sit in the grass over there?"

Rosinda's legs felt wobbly. "I'll sit," she whispered. Almost as if they knew what she'd said, the other six crows hopped off a little distance. Rosinda walked to a nearby tree, sliding her backpack off and hugging it to her chest. She sat on the carpet of multicolored leaves with her back against the rough bark. The crow followed and stood just beyond her feet, regarding her with bright eyes.

"I'm afraid this is not the best news," the crow said. "Your Aunt Oddeline has been kidnapped."

"What?" Rosinda's heart thudded in her chest. Her Aunt Odder was the only family she had here, with her parents in a hospital in Switzerland for the past year. The year since the accident. "How do you know this?"

"I know because of who I am and where I come from," the crow said. "I think she's safe for now, but you're going to have to trust me. My name is Traveller."

"Who would kidnap Aunt Odder?" Rosinda asked, jumping to her feet. The backpack rolled unheeded in the leaves. "I have to call the police!"

The crow lifted a wing. "That won't do any good. The guards of this land—your police—will have no way to find her."

Rosinda's breath caught in her throat as if she'd been running. "Who kidnapped her?"

The crow shook its head again. "I don't know. I have suspicions, but—no."

"Can you help me find her? There must be something I can do!"

"I don't suppose you know where Prince Sovann is?"

Rosinda shook her head impatiently. "I don't even know who that is."

The crow made a sound like a sigh. "Then you'll have

to come with me, Rosinda. You'll have to come home to Ysterad."

For a brief moment something shimmered at the back of Rosinda's brain, the stir of a thought, or a memory, triggered by the name. She struggled to catch it, bring it to the front of her mind, but it was gone as quickly as it had come, leaving her feeling tired and slightly sick. The autumn air pricked her skin, suddenly cold. The hard, hot feeling in her stomach was anger.

"I have to go home," she said.

"Yes," the crow agreed, "we'll need to gather some things."

"No, I mean I'm going home. Alone. Home to my house. Mine and Aunt Odder's. I don't believe any of this. I'm dreaming, or hallucinating, or maybe I have a brain tumor. Maybe this is something else left over from the accident. I don't know and I don't care." Rosinda's breath came hard and fast. She grabbed her backpack and slung it over her shoulder. "Don't follow me," she said, and hurried back to the road. Rosinda felt the crow's gaze on her back but she wouldn't look at him.

She strode along the graveled shoulder, her thoughts in a jumble. There was no sound behind her, no soft flapping of wings overhead. Maybe the crow had taken her seriously and stayed behind. Rosinda had a flash of misgiving. *What if she got home and Aunt Odder wasn't there?*

She pushed the thought aside and kept walking, the riot of red, gold, and orange leaves now garish and too bright. No cars passed. She and Aunt Odder lived in a small house on an out-of-the-way road, and it took her half an hour to walk home from school. Rosinda didn't mind. She was a loner by nature. She hadn't made many friends in the year since she and Aunt Odder had come to Cape Breton. Maybe other kids were wary around her because of her memory loss, the way sometimes she couldn't think of the right word for something, but she didn't think that was all of it. She just didn't fit in.

Rosinda rounded the last corner, and the house came into view, a narrow, two-story cottage at the top of a curving gravel driveway. It looked completely normal, and Rosinda let out a breath she'd barely realized she was holding. *Everything must be fine.* A wisp of grey smoke curled out of the chimney, Aunt Odder's beat-up little hatchback sat in the driveway. The kitchen window framed the silhouette of Filara, Aunt Odder's cat. Rosinda hurried up the driveway.

"Aunt Odder!" she called when she opened the kitchen door. The radio played softly on the counter. Filara jumped down from the windowsill and bounded across the kitchen floor to Rosinda on silent feet, curling around her legs. Rosinda reached down and stroked the animal's silky head absently as she listened for Aunt Odder's welcoming voice.

It didn't come. The house was silent, as if it also held its breath.

Rosinda slung her backpack onto the kitchen table. "Aunt Odder! Where are you?" she called again. The kettle was still plugged in, the teapot standing beside it with the top open, waiting for hot water. She glanced inside. Two teabags lay on the bottom. Rosinda touched the side of the kettle and felt a bare hint of warmth. It must have boiled a while ago and then shut off.

It wasn't like Aunt Odder to boil water and not make tea.

Rosinda went to the tiny sitting room, her throat and chest tight. The computer hummed quietly on the corner desk near the window. The television was off. Rosinda ran up the stairs two at a time. It took only a glance to see that the two bedrooms and the bathroom were empty.

The house was empty. Aunt Odder wasn't here.

Hot tears blurred Rosinda's vision, but she blinked them back. Before she could decide what to do next, a terrible racket erupted downstairs. Rosinda glanced around, grabbed a heavy, wooden-handled umbrella from beside Aunt Odder's door, and raced back down the stairs. *Could this day get any worse?*

She plunged through the kitchen door and skidded to a stop. Filara stood in the middle of the table, her patchwork of calico fur standing straight out. She hissed and spat in obvious fury.

The crow perched on the corner of the counter near the radio, wings spread wide as it screeched at the cat.

Whether it was the sudden reappearance of the crow, or the noise of the creatures, or her growing concern for Aunt Odder, Rosinda felt her worry turn to anger.

"Stop it!" Rosinda shouted, striding into the kitchen. She banged the umbrella down on the table and scooped Filara up. The cat struggled for a moment, then went quiet in her arms.

The crow immediately folded its wings, ruffling its ebony feathers for a moment until they fell elegantly into place. It made a sound that reminded Rosinda of a man clearing his throat. "Ahem. I apologize, Rosinda," it said in a quiet voice. "The cat startled me when—"

"When you broke into my house?" Rosinda snapped. She didn't want to imagine how the crow had done that.

"Well, yes," the crow admitted. "But you've seen by now I was correct. Your aunt is not here."

"That doesn't mean she's been kidnapped," Rosinda started, but her voice trailed away. What did it mean, after all? Aunt Odder was always here when Rosinda came home from school. If she'd been out in the garden, Rosinda would have seen her. And she hadn't finished making her tea.

Rosinda had to accept that the talking crow was not a hallucination. She felt her anger and her energy drain away. Keeping the cat on her lap, she lowered herself into Aunt Odder's creaky wooden rocker.

"What did you say your name was?" Rosinda asked quietly. Her hands trembled slightly as she stroked Filara's fur for reassurance.

"Traveller," the crow answered. "Do you think we can talk now?"

Rosinda nodded. "I think," she said slowly, "you'd better tell me everything."

CPSIA information can be obtained
at www.ICGtesting.com
Printed in the USA
LVOW04s0528170916
504958LV00028B/744/P